MY GUN IS QUICK

By Mickey Spillane

Born Frank Morrison Spillane in Brooklyn, New York City, in 1918, Mickey Spillane started writing while at high school. During the Second World War, he enlisted in the Army Air Corps and became a fighter pilot and instructor. After the war, he moved to South Carolina, having liked the look of it while flying over. He was married three times, the third time to Jane Rogers Johnson, and had four children and two stepchildren. He wrote his first novel, *I, the Jury* (1947), in order to raise the money to buy a house for himself and his first wife, Mary Ann Pearce. The novel sold six and a half million copies in the United States, and introduced Spillane's most famous character, the hardboiled PI Mike Hammer. The many novels that followed became instant bestsellers, until in 1980 the US all-time fiction bestseller list of fifteen titles boasted seven by Mickey Spillane. More than 225 million copies of his books have sold internationally. He was uniformly disliked by critics, owing to the high content of sex and violence in his books. However, he was later praised by American mystery writers Max Alan Collins and William L. DeAndrea, as well as artist Markus Lüpertz. The novelist Ayn Rand, a friend of Spillane's, appreciated the black-and-white morality of his books. Spillane was an active Jehovah's Witness. He died in 2006 from pancreatic cancer.

My Gun is Quick

MICKEY SPILLANE

An Orion paperback

First published in the United States of America in 1950
by Signet
This paperback edition published in 2015
by Orion Books,
an imprint of The Orion Publishing Group Ltd,
Carmelite House, 50 Victoria Embankment,
London EC4Y 0DZ

An Hachette UK company

1 3 5 7 9 10 8 6 4 2

A CIP catalogue record for this book
is available from the British Library.

ISBN 978-1-4091-5865-3

Typeset by Born Group within Book Cloud
Printed and bound by CPI Group (UK) Ltd, Croydon, CRD 4YY

The Orion Publishing Group's policy is to use papers that
are natural, renewable and recyclable products and
made from wood grown in sustainable forests. The logging
and manufacturing processes are expected to conform to
the environmental regulations of the country of origin.

www.orionbooks.co.uk

*To all my friends
past, present, and future*

CHAPTER ONE

When you sit at home comfortably folded up in a chair beside a fire, have you ever thought what goes on outside there? Probably not. You pick up a book and read about things and stuff, getting a vicarious kick from people and events that never happened. You're doing it now, getting ready to fill in a normal life with the details of someone else's experiences. Fun, isn't it? You read about life on the outside, thinking of how maybe you'd like it to happen to you, or at least how you'd like to watch it. Even the old Romans did it, spiced their life with action when they sat in the Colosseum and watched wild animals rip a bunch of humans apart, revelling in the sight of blood and terror. They screamed for joy and slapped each other on the back when murderous claws tore into the live flesh of slaves, and cheered when the kill was made. Oh, it's great to watch, all right. Life through a keyhole. But day after day goes by, and nothing like that ever happens to you, so you think that it's all in books and not in reality at all and that's that. Still good reading, though. Tomorrow night you'll find another book, forgetting what was in the last, and live some more in your imagination. But remember this: there *are* things happening out there. They go on every day and night, making Roman holidays look like school picnics. They go on right under your very nose and you never know about them. Oh, yes, you can find them all right. All you have to do is look for them. But I wouldn't if I were you, because you won't like what you'll find. Then, again, I'm not you, and looking for these things is my job. They aren't nice things to see because they show people up for what they are. There isn't a Colosseum any more, but the city is a bigger bowl and it seats more people. The razor-sharp claws aren't those of wild animals, but man's can be just as sharp and twice

1

as vicious. You have to be quick, and you have to be able, or you become one of the devoured, and if you can kill first, no matter how and no matter who, you can live and return to the comfortable chair and the comfortable fire. But you have to be quick – and able. Or you'll be dead.

At ten minutes after twelve I tied a knot in my case and delivered Herman Gable's lost manuscript to his apartment. To me, it was nothing more than a sheaf of yellow papers covered with barely legible tracings, but to my client it was worth twenty-five hundred bucks. The old fool had wrapped it up with some old newspapers and sent it down the dumbwaiter with the garbage. He sure was happy to get it back. It took three days to run it down and practically snatch the stuff out of the city incinerator; but when I fingered the package of nice, crisp fifties he handed me I figured it was worth going without all that sleep.

I made him out a receipt and took the elevator downstairs to my heap. As far as I was concerned the dough would live a peaceful life until I had a good, long nap. After that, maybe, I'd cut loose a little bit. At that hour of the night traffic was light. I cut across town, then headed north to my own private cave in the massive cliff I called home.

But the first time I hit a red light I fell asleep across the wheel and woke up with a dozen horns blasting in my ears. A couple of cars banged bumpers backing up so they could swing around me, and I was too damned pooped even to swear back at some of the stuff they called me. The hell with 'em. I pulled the jalopy over to the kerb and chilled the engine. Right up the street under the el was an all-night hash joint, and what I needed was a couple of mugs of good java to bring me around.

I don't know how the place got by the health inspectors, because it stunk. There were two bums down at one end of the counter taking their time about finishing a ten-cent bowl of soup; making the most out of the free crackers and catsup in front of them. Half-way down, a drunk concentrated between his plate of eggs and hanging on to the stool to keep from falling off the world. Evidently he was down to his last buck, for all his pockets had been turned inside out to locate the lone bill that was putting a roof on his load.

Until I sat down and looked in the mirror behind the shelves of pie segments, I didn't notice the fluff sitting off to one side at a table. She had red hair that didn't come out of a bottle, and looked pretty enough from where I was sitting.

The counterman came up just then and asked, 'What'll it be?' He had a voice like a frog's.

'Coffee – black.'

The fluff noticed me then. She looked up, smiled, tucked her nail tools in a peeling plastic handbag and hipped it in my direction. When she sat down on the stool next to me she nodded towards the counterman and said. 'Shorty's got a heart of steel, mister. Won't even trust me for a cup of joe until I get a job. Care to finance me to a few vitamins?'

I was too tired to argue the point. 'Make it two, feller.'

He grabbed another cup disgustedly and filled it, then set the two down on the counter, slopping half of it across the wash-worn linoleum top.

'Listen, Red,' he croaked, 'quit using this joint fer an office. First thing I get the cops on my tail. That's all I need.'

'Be good and toddle off, Shorty. All I want from the gentleman is a cup of coffee. He looks much too tired to play any games tonight.'

'Yeah, scram, Shorty,' I put in. He gave me a nasty look, but since I was as ugly as he was and twice as big, he shuffled off to keep count over the cracker bowl in front of the bums. Then I looked at the redhead.

She wasn't very pretty after all. She had been once, but there are those things that happen under the skin and are reflected in the eyes and set of the mouth that take all the beauty out of a woman's face. Yeah, at one time she must have been almost beautiful. That wasn't too long ago, either. Her clothes were last year's old look and a little too tight. They showed a lot of leg and a lot of chest; nice white flesh still firm and young; but her face was old with knowledge that never came out of books. I watched her from the corner of my eye when she lifted her cup of coffee. She had delicate hands, long fingers tipped with deep-toned nails perfectly kept. It was the way she held the cup that annoyed me. Instead of being a thick, cracked mug, she gave it a touch of elegance as she balanced it in front of her lips. I thought she was wearing a wedding band until she put the cup down. Then I saw that it was just a ring with a fleur-de-lis design of blue enamel and diamond chips that had turned sideways slightly.

Red turned suddenly and said, 'Like me?'

I grinned. 'Uh-huh. But, like you said, much too tired to make it matter.'

Her laugh was a tinkle of sound. 'Rest easy, mister, I won't give you a sales talk. There are only certain types interested in what I have to sell.'

'Amateur psychologist?'

'I have to be.'

'And I don't look the type?'

Red's eyes danced. 'Big mugs like you never have to pay, mister. With you it's the woman who pays.'

I pulled out a deck of Luckies and offered her one. When we lit up I said, 'I wish all the babies I met thought that way.'

She blew a stream of smoke towards the ceiling and looked at me as if she were going back a long way. 'They do, mister. Maybe you don't know it, but they do.'

I don't know why I liked the kid. Maybe it was because she had eyes that were hard, but could still cry a little. Maybe it was because she handed me some words that were nice to listen to. Maybe it was because I was tired and my cave was a cold empty place, while here I had a redhead to talk to. Whatever it was, I liked her and she knew it and smiled at me in a way I knew she hadn't smiled in a long time. Like I was her friend.

'What's your name, mister?'

'Mike. Mike Hammer. Native-born son of ye old city, presently at loose ends and dead tired. Free, white and over twenty-one. That do it?'

'Well, what do you know! Here I've been thinking all males were named Smith or Jones. What happened?'

'No wife to report to, kid,' I grinned. 'The tag's my own. What do they call you besides Red?'

'They don't.'

I saw her eyes crinkle a little as she sipped the last of her coffee. Shorty was casting nervous glances between us and the steamed-up window, probably hoping a cop wouldn't pass by and nail a hustler trying to make time. He gave me a pain.

'Want more coffee?'

She shook her head. 'No, that did it fine. If Shorty wasn't so touchy about extending a little credit I wouldn't have to be smiling for my midnight snacks.'

From the way I turned and looked at her, Red knew there was more than casual curiosity back of the remark when I asked, 'I didn't think your line of business could ever be that slow.'

For a brief second she glared into the mirror. 'It isn't.' She was plenty mad about something.

I threw a buck on the counter and Shorty rang it up, then passed the change back. When I pocketed it I said to Red, 'Did you ever stop to think that you're a pretty nice girl? I've met all kinds, but I think you could get along pretty well . . . any way you tried.'

Her smile even brought out a dimple that had been buried a long while ago. She kissed her finger, then touched the finger to my cheek. 'I like you, Mike. There are times when I think I've lost the power to like anyone, but I like you.'

An el went by overhead just then and muffled the sound of the door opening. I felt the guy standing behind us before I saw him in the mirror. He was tall, dark and greasy looking, with a built-in sneer that passed for know-how, and he smelled of cheap hair oil. His suit would have been snappy in Harlem, edged with sharp pleats and creases.

He wasn't speaking to me when he said, 'Hullo, kid!'

The redhead half turned and her lips went tight. 'What do you want?' Her tone was dull, flat. The skin across her cheeks was drawn taut.

5

'Are you kidding?'

'I'm busy. Get lost.'

The guy's hand shot out and grabbed her arm, swinging her around on the stool to face him. 'I don't like them snotty remarks, Red.'

As soon as I slid off the stool Shorty hustled down to our end, his hand reaching for something under the counter. When he saw my face he put it back and stopped short. The guy saw the same thing, but he was wise about it. His lip curled up and he snarled, 'Get the hell out of here before I bust ya one.'

He was going to make a pass at me, but I jammed four big, stiff fingers into his gut right above the navel and he snapped shut like a jack-knife. I opened him up again with an open-handed slap that left a blush across his mouth that was going to stay for a while.

Usually a guy will let it go right there. This one didn't. He could hardly breathe, but he was cursing me with his lips and his hand reached for his armpit in uncontrollable jerks. Red stood with her hand pressed against her mouth, while Shorty was croaking for us to cut it out, but too scared to move.

I let him almost reach it, then I slid my own .45 out where everybody could get a look at it. Just for effect I stuck it up against his forehead and thumbed back the hammer. It made a sharp click in the silence. 'Just touch that rod you got and I'll blow your damn greasy head off. Go ahead, just make one lousy move towards it,' I said.

He moved, all right. He fainted. Red was looking down at him, still too terrified to say anything. Shorty had a twitch in his shoulder. Finally she said, 'You . . . didn't have to do that for me. Please, get out of here before he wakes up. He'll . . . kill you!'

I touched her arm gently. 'Tell me something, Red. Do you really think he could?'

She bit her lip and her eyes searched my face. Something made her shudder violently. 'No. No, I don't think so. But please go. For me.' There was urgent appeal in her voice.

I grinned at her again. She was scared, in trouble, but still my friend. I took out my wallet. 'Do something for me, will you, Red?' I shoved three fifties in her hand. 'Get off this street. Tomorrow you go uptown and buy some decent clothes. Then get a morning paper and hunt up a job. This kind of stuff is murder.'

I don't ever want anybody to look at me the way she did then. A look that belongs in church when you're praying or getting married or something.

The greaseball on the floor was awake now, but he wasn't looking at me. He was looking at my wallet that I held open in my hand. His eyes were glued to the badge that was pinned there, and if I still didn't have my rod dangling by the trigger guard he would have gone for his. I reached down and pulled it out of the shoulder holster, then grabbed his collar and dragged him out the door.

Down on the corner was a police call-box and I used it. In two minutes a squad car pulled up to the kerb and a pair of harness bulls jumped out. I nodded to the driver. 'Hullo, Jake.'

He said, 'Hi ya, Mike. What gives?'

I hoisted the greaseball to his feet. 'Laughing boy tried to pull a gun on me.' I handed over the rod, a short-barrelled .32. 'I don't think he has a licence for it, so you can lock him up on a Sullivan charge. I'll press charges in the morning. You know where to reach me.'

The cop took the gun and prodded the guy into the car. He was still cursing when I walked up to my heap.

It was early morning when I woke up to stay. Those forty-eight hours were what I needed. I took a hot and cold shower to shake the sleep out of my eyes, then stood in front of the mirror and shaved. I certainly was a mess. My eyes were still red and bleary and I felt like I was ploughing my whiskers under instead of shaving them off. At least I felt better. A big plate of bacon and eggs made my stomach behave to the point where I could get dressed and start the rest of the day off with a decent meal.

Jimmy had a steak in the broiler as soon as I entered the door of his snack bar. Luckily, I liked it rare and it was on deck before it was fully warmed through. While I was shovelling it down Jimmy said, 'That dame in your office has been on the phone all day. Maybe you better call her back.'

'What'd she want?'

'Wondered where you were. Guess she thinks you were out with a broad somewhere.'

'Nuts! She's always thinking something.' I finished my dessert and threw a bill down. 'If she calls up again, tell her I'm on my way up to the office, will you?'

'Sure, Mr Hammer, glad to.'

I patted my meal in place, lit up a smoke and hopped into my car. The trip downtown didn't take long, but I was a half-hour finding a parking place. When I finally barged into the office, Velda looked up with those big brown eyes starting to give me hell before she even opened her mouth. When I got a girl to hold down the office I figured I might as well get a good-looking one as a bean head, and I sure skimmed the cream off the top. Only, I didn't figure she'd turn out to be so smart. Good-looking ones seldom are. She's big and she's beautiful, and she's got a brain that can figure angles while mine only figures the curves.

'About time you got in.' She looked me over carefully for lipstick stains or whatever those tip-offs are that spell trouble for a guy. I could tell by the way she let a slow grin play around with her mouth that she decided that my time was on the job and not on the town.

When I shucked out of my coat I tossed most of the package of fifties on her desk. 'Meal money, kiddo. Take expenses out of that and bank the rest. Any callers?'

She tucked the cabbage in a file and locked it. 'A couple. One wanted a divorce set-up and the other wanted himself a bodyguard. Seems like his girlfriend's husband is promising to chill him on sight. I sent both of them over to Ellison's where they'd get proper treatment.'

'I wish you'd quit making-up my mind for me. That body-guard job might have been all right.'

'Uh-uh. I saw a picture of the girlfriend. She's the bosomy kind you go for.'

'Ah, buys! You know how I hate women.'

I squeezed into the reception chair and picked up the paper from the table. I ruffled through it from back to front, and as I was going to lay it down I caught the picture on the front page. It was down there on the corner, bordered by some shots of the heavyweight fights from the night before. It was a picture of the redhead lying cuddled up and against the kerb-stone. She was dead. The caption read, HIT-AND-RUN DRIVER KILLS, ESCAPES.

'The poor kid! Of all the rotten luck!'

'Who's that?' Velda asked me.

I shoved the paper over to her. 'I was with that kid the other night. She was a street-walker and I bought her a coffee in a hash joint. Before I left I gave her some dough to get out of the business, and look what happened to her.'

'Fine company you keep.' Her tone was sarcastic.

I got sore. 'Damn it, she was all right. She wasn't after me. I did her a favour and she was more grateful than most of the trash that call themselves people. The first time in a month of Sundays I've done anything half-way decent and this is the way it winds up.'

'I'm sorry, Mike. I'm really sorry, honest.' It was funny how she could spot it when I was telling the truth. She opened the paper and read the news item, frowning when she finished. 'She wasn't identified. Did you know her name?'

'Hell, no. She was a redhead, so I called her Red. Let's see that.' I went over the item myself. She was found in the street at half-past two. Apparently she had been there for some time before someone had sense enough to call the cop on the beat. A guy who had passed her twice as she lay there told the cop that he thought she was a drunk who had passed out. It was reasonable enough. Over there you find enough of them doing just that. But the curious part was the complete lack of identification on her.

9

When I folded the paper up I said, 'Look, stick around a while; I have a little walking to do.'

'That girl?'

'Yeah. Maybe I can help identify her some way. I don't know. Call Pat and tell him I'm on my way down.'

'O.K., Mike.'

I left the car where it was and took a cab over to the redbrick building where Pat Chambers held down his office. You want to see that guy. He's a Captain of Homicide and all cop, but you couldn't tell it to look at him. He was young and charged with knowledge and the ambition to go with it, the best example of efficiency I could think of. It isn't often that you see cops hobnobbing with private dicks, but Pat had the sense to know that I could touch a lot of places outside the reach of the law, and he could do plenty for me that I couldn't do for myself. What started out as a modest business arrangement turned into a solid friendship.

He met me over in the lab where he was running a ballistics test. 'Hullo, Mike, what brings you around so early?'

'A problem, chum.' I flipped the paper open in front of him and pointed to the picture. 'This. Have you found out about her?'

Pat shook his head. 'No . . . but I will. Come on in the office.' He led me into the cubbyhole off the lab and nodded to a chair. While I fired a cig he called an extension number and was connected. He said. 'This is Chambers. I want to find out if that girl who was killed by a hit-and-run driver last night has been identified.' He listened a little bit, then frowned.

I waited until he hung up, then: 'Anything?'

'Something unusual – dead of a broken neck. One of the boys didn't like the looks of it and they're holding the cause of death until a further exam is made. What have you?'

'Nothing. But I was with her the night before she was found dead.'

'So?'

'So she was a tramp. I bought her a coffee in a hash house and we had a talk.'

'Did she mention her name?'

'Nope, all I got out of her was "Red." It was appropriate enough.'

Pat leaned back in his chair. 'Well, we don't know who she is. She had on all new clothes, a new handbag with six dollars and change in it, and not a scar on her body to identify her, Not a single laundry mark either.'

'I know. I gave her a hundred and fifty bucks to get dressed up and look for a decent job. Evidently she did.'

'Getting big-hearted, aren't you?' He sounded like Velda, and I got mad.

'Damn it, Pat, don't you give me that stuff, too! Can't I play saint for five minutes without everyone getting smart about it? I've seen kids down on their luck before, probably a damn sight more than you have. You think anyone would give them a break? Like hell! They play 'em for all they can get and beat it. I liked the kid; does that make me a jerk? All right, she was a hustler, but she wasn't hustling for me and I did her a favour. Maybe she gets all wrapped up in a new dream and forgets to open her eyes when she's crossing the street, and look what happens. Any time I touch anything it gets killed!'

'Hey, wait up, Mike, don't jump me on it. I know how you feel . . . it's just that you seemed to be stepping out of character.'

'Aw, I'm sorry, Pat. It's kind of got me loused up.'

'At least you've given me something to go on. If she bought all new clothes we can trace them. If we're lucky we can pick up the old stuff and check them for laundry marks.'

He told me to wait for him and took off down the corridor. I sat there for five minutes and fidgeted, and cursed people who let their kids run loose. A hell of a way to die. They just lower you into a hole and cover you up, with nobody around but the worms, and the worms don't cry. But Pat would find out who she was. He'd put a little effort behind the search and a pair of parents would turn up and wring themselves dry with grief. Not that it would do much good but at least I'd feel better.

Pat came back looking sour. I guess I knew what was coming when he said, 'They covered that angle downstairs. The sales clerks in the stores all said the same thing . . . she took her old clothes with her and wore the new ones.'

'Then she must have left them at home.'

'Uh-huh. She wasn't carrying them with her when she was found.'

'Nope, I don't like that, either, Pat. When a girl buys a new outfit, she won't look at the old one, and what she had on when I met her was a year out of date. She probably chucked them somewhere.'

Pat reached into his desk and came up with a notepad: 'I think the best we can do is publish her picture and hope someone steps up with an identification. At the same time we'll get the bureau checking up in the neighbourhood where you met her. Does that suit you?'

'Yeah. Can't do more than that, I guess.'

He flipped the pages over but, before I could tell him where the hash house was, a lab technician in a white smock came in and handed over a report sheet. Pat glanced at it, then his eyes squinted and he looked at me strangely.

I didn't get it, so I stared back. Without a word he handed me the sheet and nodded to dismiss the technician. It was a report on Red. The information was the same that Pat had given me, but down at the bottom was somebody's scrawled notation. It said very clearly that although there was a good chance that death could have been accidental, the chance was just as good that she had been murdered. Her neck had been broken in a manner that could have been caused only by the most freakish accident.

For the first time since I'd known him, Pat took a typical cop's attitude. 'A nice story you gave me, Mike. How much of it am I supposed to believe?' His voice was dripping with sarcasm.

'Go to hell, Pat!' I said it coldly, burning up inside.

I knew damn well what was going on in that official mind. Just because we had tangled tails on a couple of cases before, he thought I was pitching him a fast one. I got it off my chest in a hurry. 'You used to be a nice guy, Pat,' I said. 'There was a time when we did each other favours and no questions asked. Did I ever dummy up a deal on you?'

He started to answer, but I cut him off. 'Yeah, sure, we've crossed once or twice, but you always have the bull on me before we start. That's because you're a cop. I can't withhold information . . . all I can do is protect a client. Since when do you figure me to be putting the snear on you?'

This time Pat grinned. 'O.K., that makes me sorry twice today. Do me another favour and admit I had a half-way decent reason to be suspicious. You're usually in something up to your neck, and you aren't above getting a little free info even from me, and I can't blame you. It's just that I have to look out for my own neck once in a while. You know the pressure that's being put on our department. If we get caught short we have a lot of people to answer to.'

He kept talking, but I wasn't listening to him. My eyes kept drifting back to that report sheet until that one word, MURDERED, kept jumping at me like it was alive. I was seeing Red standing there with the dimples in her cheeks, kissing her finger and smiling a smile that was for me alone. Just a two-bit tramp who could have been a lady, and who was, for a few short minutes, a damn decent friend.

And I had jinxed her.

My guts were a tight little ball under my belt, because Red wasn't the only one I remembered. There was the greaseball with the rod and the dirty sneer. There was the way Red had looked at him with terror in her eyes, and I felt my fingernails bite into my palms, and I started cursing under my breath. It always starts that way, the crazy mad feeling that makes me want to choke the life out of some son of a bitch, and there's nothing to grab but air. I knew damn well what it was then. They could cross all the probable words off in front of murder and let it stand alone.

Pat said, 'Give, Mike.'

'There's nothing to give,' I told him. 'I'm teed off. Things like this give me the pip. I might as well have killed her myself.'

'What makes you think it's murder?' He was watching me closely again.'

I flipped the sheet to his desk. 'I don't know, but she's dead and what difference does it make how she died. When you're

13

dead you're dead and it doesn't matter much to you any more how you got that way.'

'Let's not have any tangents, Mike. What do you know that I don't?'

'What she looked like when she was alive. She was a nice kid.'

'Go on.'

'Nuts! There isn't any place to go. If she was killed accidentally, I feel like hell. If she was murdered . . .'

'Yeah, Mike, I've heard it before . . . if she was killed you're going to go out all by yourself and catch the bastard and rub his nose in the dirt. Maybe so hard that you break his neck, too.'

'Yeah,' I said. Then I said it again.

'Mike.'

'What?'

'Look, if it's a kill it belongs to my department. It probably isn't, but you get me so damn excited I'm getting positive that it is, and I'm getting mad, too, because you have thoughts in that scrambled brain of yours that will make the track nice and muddy if it's another race. Let's not have any more of that, Mike. Once was enough. I didn't mind so much then, but no more of it. We've always played it square, though only God knows why I set myself up to be knocked down. Maybe I'm the jerk. Are you levelling with me on what you know?'

'I'm levelling, Pat.' I wasn't lying. What I had told him was the truth. I just hadn't told him the rest. It's awfully nice to get so goddamn mad at something you want to bust wide open, and it's a lot better to take that goddamn something you're mad at and smash it against the wall and do all the things to it you wanted to do, wishing it could have been done before it was too late.

Pat was playing cop with his notebook again. 'Where did you meet her?' he asked me.

'A joint under the el on Third Avenue. I came off the bridge and ran down Third and stopped at this joint along the way. I don't remember the street because I was too tired to look, but I'll go back and check up again and find it. There's probably a thousand places like it, but I'll find it.'

This isn't a stall, is it?'

'Yeah, it's a stall. Lock me up for interfering with the process of the law. I should have remembered every detail that happened that night.'

'Can it, Mike.'

'I told you I'd find it again, didn't I?'

'Good enough. Meanwhile, we'll pull an autopsy on her and try to locate the old clothes. Remember, when you find the place, let me know. I'll probably find it without you anyway, but you can make it quicker . . . if you want to.'

'Sure,' I said. I was grinning, but nothing was funny. It was a way I could hold my mouth and be polite without letting him know that I felt as if ants were crawling all over me. We shook hands and said civilized 'so longs' when I wanted to curse and swing at something instead.

I don't like to get mad like that. But I couldn't help it. Murder is an ugly word.

When I got downstairs I asked the desk sergeant where I could get in touch with Jake Larue. He gave me his home number and I went into a pay station just off the main corridor and dialled the number. Jake's wife answered, and she had to wake him up to put him on, and his voice wasn't too friendly when he said hullo.

I said, 'This is Mike Hammer, Jake. What happened to that punk I gave you the other night?'

Jake said something indecent. Then, 'That was some deal you handed us, Mike.'

'Why?'

'He had a licence for that gun, that's why. You trying to get me in a jam or something?'

'What are they doing, giving licences away in New York State, now?'

'Nuts! His name is Feeney Last and he's a combination chauffeur and bodyguard for that Berin-Grotin guy out on the Island.'

I whistled through my teeth and hung up. Now they were giving out licences to guys who wanted to kill people. Oh, great! Just fine!

15

CHAPTER TWO

It was a little after four when I got back to the office. Velda was licking envelopes in an unladylike manner and glad of an excuse to stop. She said, 'Pat called me a little while ago.'

'And told you to tell me to behave myself like a good boy, I suppose.'

'Or words to that effect. Who was she, Mike?'

'I didn't find out. I will though.'

'Mike, being as how you're the boss, I hate to say this, but there are a few prosperous clients knocking on the door and you're fooling around where there isn't any cash in sight.'

I threw my hat on the desk. 'Wherever there's murder there's money, chick.'

'Murder?'

'I have that idea in mind.'

It was nice sitting there in the easy chair, stretched out in comfort. Velda let me yawn, then: 'But what are you after, Mike?'

'A name,' I said. 'Just a name for a kid who died without one. Morbid curiosity, isn't it? But I can't send flowers with just "Red" on them. What do you know about a guy called Berin-Grotin, Velda?' I watched a fly run across the ceiling upside down, making it sound casual.

After a moment she told me: 'That must be Arthur Berin-Grotin. He's an old society gent about eighty, supposedly one of the original Four Hundred. At one time he was the biggest sport on the Stem, but he got tangled with old age and became almighty pious trying to make up for all his youthful escapades.'

I remember him then, mostly from stories the old-timers like to pass out when they corner you in a bar for a hatful of free drinks. 'Why would a guy like that need a bodyguard?' I asked her.

Velda dug back into her memory. 'If I remember correctly, his estate out on the Island was robbed several times. An old man would be inclined to be squeamish, and I can't say that I blame him. I'd hire a bodyguard, too. The funny part is that the burglar could have had what he wanted for the asking by simply knocking on the door. Arthur Berin-Grotin is a sucker for hard-up stories . . . besides being one of the city's biggest philanthropists.'

'Lots of money, hey?'

'Umm.'

'Where did you get the dope on him?'

'If you'd read anything but the funnies, you'd know. He's in the news as often as a movie star. Apparently he has a fierce sense of pride, and if he isn't suing somebody for libel, he's disinheriting some distant relative for besmirching the fair name of Berin-Grotin. A month ago he financed a million-dollar cat and dog hospital or something. Oh, wait a minute . . .'

She got up and began ruffling through a heap of newspapers on top of the file. After a brief search she pulled out a roto-gravure section, a few weeks old, and folded it back. 'Here's something about him.'

It was a picture taken in a cemetery. Amid a background of tombstones and monuments was the half-built form of a mausoleum. There were two workers on the scaffolding laying marble slabs in place, and from the looks of it money was being poured into the job. Next to it was the artist's concep-tion of the finished job, a classic Greek-temple arrangement. Arthur Berin-Grotin was playing it safe. He was making sure he'd have a roof over his head after he died.

Velda put the paper back on the pile. 'Is he a client, Mike?'

'Nope. I happened to run across his name and was interested.'

'You're lying.'

'And you're getting fresh with the boss,' I grinned at her. She stuck out her tongue and went back to her desk. I got up and told her to knock off early, then jammed on my hat. There were a few things that I had in mind, but I needed a little time to pass before I could get started.

Downstairs I found a bar and called for a beer. I was on my third when the paper boy came in with the evening edition. I flipped him a dime and spread it on the bar. Pat had done a good job. Her picture was on the front page. Under it was the question, 'Do you know this girl?' Sure, I knew her. Red. I couldn't forget her. I was wondering if anybody else was having trouble forgetting her, too.

I tucked the paper in my pocket and walked down to my car. The taxis and commuters were jamming traffic all the way downtown, and by the time I had crossed over to Third Avenue it was nearly six o'clock. I didn't have a bit of trouble finding that hash house again. There was even a place to park right outside it. I went in and climbed on a stool and laid the paper down in front of me with the picture up. Down at the end Shorty was pushing crackers and soup over to another bum. He hadn't seen me yet.

When he did he went a little white around the nostrils and he couldn't seem to take his eyes off my face. He said, 'Whatta ya want?'

'Eggs. Bacon and eggs . . . over light. And coffee.'

He sort of sidled down the counter and fished in a basket for the eggs. One dropped and splattered all over the floor. Shorty didn't even seem to notice it. The bum was making a slobbering noise with his soup and the bacon on the griddle started to drown him out. Behind the grill was a stainless steel reflector, and twice I caught Shorty looking in it at me. The spatula was big enough to handle a cake, yet he couldn't balance an egg on it. He made each on the third try.

Shorty was suffering badly from the shakes. It didn't help any when he had to push the paper away to set the plate down and saw Red's picture staring at him.

I said, 'One thing about eggs: you can't spoil them with bum cooking. No matter what you do they still taste like eggs.' Shorty just stared at me. 'Yeah, eggs are eggs. Once in a while you get a bad one, though. Makes me mad as hell to get hold of one. Did you ever smash a bad egg wide open? They make a noisy pop and stink like hell. Bad eggs can be poison, too.'

I was half-way done before Shorty said, 'What are you after, mister?'

'You tell me.'

Both of us looked down at the paper at the same time.

'You're a copper, ain't'cha?'

'I carry a badge . . . and a rod.'

'A private snooper, eh?' He was going tough on me.

I laid my fork down and looked at him. I can make pretty nasty faces when I have to. 'Shorty, maybe just for the hell of it I'll take you apart. You may be a rough apple, but I can make your face look like it's been run through a grinder, and the more I think of the idea the more I like it. The name is Mike Hammer, chum . . . you ought to know it down here. I like to play games with wise guys.'

He was white around the nostrils again.

I tapped the picture, then let my finger stay on the question underneath. Shorty knew damn well I wasn't fooling around any more. I was getting mad and he knew it, and he was scared. But just the same he shrugged. 'Hell, I don't know who she is.'

'It wasn't the first time she had been in here. Quit holding out.'

'Ah, she came in for about a week. Sometimes she tried to make pick-ups in here and I threw her out. She was Red to me and everybody else. That's all I knew about her.'

'You got a record, haven't you, Shorty?'

His lips drew back over his teeth. 'You bastard!'

I reached out and grabbed his shirt and held him against the counter. 'When a guy gets out of stir he goes straight some-times. Sometimes he don't. I'm betting that if the cops decided to look around a little bit they could find you had a finger in some crooked pie, and it wouldn't take them a week to put you back up the river.'

'H-honest, Mac, I don't know nothing about the dame. Look, I'd tell you if I did. I ain't no trouble-maker and I don't want no trouble around here! Why don't'cha lemme alone?'

There was a greaseball in here that night. His name is Feeney Last. How often has he been in?'

Shorty licked his thick lips nervously. 'Hell, maybe twice. I dunno. He went for the redhead, that's all. He never even ate in here. Lay off, will ya.'

I dropped the handful of shirt. 'Sure, pal, I'll lay off.' I threw a half buck on the counter and he was glad to grab it and get over to the register away from me. I swung off the stool and stood up. 'If I find out you know any more than you told me, there's going to be a visitor in here looking for you. A guy in a pretty blue uniform. Only when he finds you he's going to have a tough time making any sense out of what you tell him. It's not easy to talk when you've just choked on your own teeth.'

Just before I reached the door he called, 'Hey, Mac.'

I turned around.

'I – I think she had a room some place around the corner. Next block north.'

He didn't wait for an answer. He got real busy swabbing the broken egg off the floor.

Outside I started the car, changed my mind, then walked up Third to the street corner. It would have taken a week to comb the dingy apartments that sprawled along the sidewalks and I wasn't in the mood for any leg work.

On one corner was a run-down candy store whose interior was obscured by flyspecked signs, but for all its dirt it served as a neighbourhood hangout. In front of the paper stand were three young punks in sharp two-tone sports outfits making dirty cracks at the girls passing by. A husky blonde turned and slapped one across the jaw and got a boot in the tail for her trouble. This time she kept on going.

I angled across the street and walked up to the kid holding his jaw, trying to rub out the red blotch. I opened the button on my jacket and reached back for a handkerchief, just enough so the sling on the shoulder holster was visible across my shirt for a second. They knew I was carrying a rod and looked at me as if I were a tin god. The kid even forgot to rub his face any more. Nice place to live.

'There's a cute little redhead who has a room around here, Buster. Know where I can find her?'

The kid got real important with the man-to-man line I was handing him and gave me a wink. 'Yeah, she had a place upstairs in old-lady Porter's joint.' He jerked his head down the street. 'Won't do ya no good to go there. That little bitch got herself killed last night. All the papers got her pitcher on the front page.'

'You don't say! Too bad.'

He edged me with his elbow and slipped me a knowing look. 'She wasn't no good anyway, buddy. Now, if you want a real woman, you go up to Twenty-third Street and . . .'

'Some other day, feller. While I'm here I'll look around this end of town.' I slipped him a fin. 'Go buy a beer for the boys.'

I walked away hoping they'd choke on it.

Martha Porter was oversize female in her late fifties. She wore a size dress that matched her age and still she peeked out in places. What hair wasn't yanked back in a knot straggled across her face and down, the nape of her neck, and she was holding the broom ready to use it as a utensil or a club.

'You looking for a room or a girl?' she said.

I let a ten-spot talk for me. 'I saw the girl. Now I want to see the room.'

She grabbed the bill first. 'What for?'

'Because she copped a wad of dough and some important papers from the last place she worked and I have to find it.'

She gave me an indifferent sneer. 'Oh, one of them skip-tracers. Well, maybe the papers is there, but you won't find no dough. She came here with the clothes on her back and two bucks in her pocket-book. I took the two bucks for room rent. Never got no more from her neither.'

'Where'd she come from?'

'I don't know and I didn't ask. She had the two bucks and that's what the room cost – in advance, when you don't have no bags.'

'Know her name?'

'Why don't you grow up, mister! Why the hell should I ask when it don't mean nothing. Maybe it was Smith. If you want to see the room it's the next floor up in the back. I ain't even been in there since she got killed. Soon as I seen her face in the papers I knew somebody would be around. Them broads give me a pain in the behind.'

The broom went back to being a broom and I went up the stairs. There was only one door on the landing and I went in, then locked it behind me.

I always had the idea that girls were kind of fussy, even if they were living in a cracker barrel. Maybe she was funny at that. It was a sure thing that whoever searched the room wasn't. The bed was torn apart and the stuffing was all over the place. The four drawers of the chest lay upside down on the floor where someone had used them as a ladder to look along the wall moulding just below the ceiling. Even the linoleum had been ripped from the floor, and two spots on the wall where the plaster had been knocked off were poked out to let a hand feel around between the partitions. Oh, it was a beautiful job of searching, all right. A real dilly. They had plenty of time, too. They must have had, because they would have had to be quiet or have the young elephant up here with the broom, and the place wouldn't have looked like that if they had been hurried.

One hell of a mess, but I started to grin. Whatever caused the wreckage certainly wasn't found, because even after they had looked in the obvious places they tore apart everything else, right down to the mouse-hole in the baseboard.

I kicked aside some of the junk on the floor, but there wasn't much to see. Old magazines, a couple of newspapers, some underwear and gadgets that might have been in the drawers. What had once been a coat lay in strips with all the hems ripped out and the lining hanging in shreds. A knife had been used on the collar to split the seams. On top of everything was a film of dust from a spilled powder box, giving the place a cheaply perfumed odour.

23

Then the wind blew some of the mattress stuffing in my face and I walked over to close the window. It faced on a fire-escape and the sash had been forced with some kind of tool. It couldn't have been simpler. On the floor by the sill was a white plastic comb. I picked it up and felt the grease on it. A few dark hairs were tangled around the teeth. I smelled it.

Hair oil. The kind of hair oil a greaseball would use. I wasn't sure, but there were ways of finding out. The hag was still in the corridor sweeping when I went out. I told her somebody had crashed the place before I got there and liked to knock it apart. She gave one unearthly shriek and took the steps two at a time until the building shook.

It was enough for one day. I went home and hit the sack. I didn't sleep too well, because the redhead would smile, kiss her finger and put it on my cheek and wake me up.

At half-past six the alarm went off with a racket that jerked me out of a wild dream and left me standing on the rug shaking like a kitten in a dog kennel. I shut it off and ducked into a cold shower to wash the sleep out of my eyes, then finish off the morning's ceremonies with a close shave that left my face raw. I ate in my shorts, then stacked the dishes in the sink and laid out my clothes.

This had to be a new-suit day. I laid the tweeds on the bed and, for a change, paid a little attention to the things that went with it. By the time I had climbed into everything and ran a brush over my shoes I even began to look dignified. Or at least sharp enough to call on one of the original Four Hundred.

I found Arthur Berin-Grotin's name in the Long Island directory, a town about sixty miles out on the Island that was a chosen spot for lovers, trapshooters and recluses. Buck had my car gassed up and ready for me when I got to the garage, and by the time nine-thirty had rolled around I was tooling the heap along the highway, sniffing the breezes that blew in from the ocean. An hour later I reached a cut-off that sported a sign emblazoned with Old English lettering and an arrow that pointed to Arthur Berin-Grotin's estate on the beach.

Under the wheels the road turned to macadam, then packed crushed gravel, and developed into a long sweep of a drive that took me up to one of the fanciest points this side of Buckingham Palace. The house was a symbol of luxury, but utterly devoid of any of the garishness that goes with new wealth. From its appearance it was ageless, neither young nor old. It could have stood there a hundred years or ten without a change to its dignity. Choice field stone reached up to the second floor, supporting smooth clapboard walls that gleamed in the sun like bleached bones. The windows must have been imported; those on the south side were all stained glass to filter out the fierce light of the sun, while the others were little lead-rimmed squares arranged in patterns that changed from room to room.

I drove up under the arched dome of a portico and killed the engine, wondering whether to wait for a major-domo to open the door for me or do it myself. I decided not to wait.

The bell was the kind you pull – a little brass knob set in the door-frame – and when I gave it a gentle tug I heard the subtle pealing of electric chimes inside. When the door opened I thought it had been done by an electric eye, but it wasn't. The butler was so little and so old that he scarcely reached above the door-knob and didn't seem strong enough to hold it open very long, so I stepped in before the wind blew it shut, and turned on my best smile.

'I'd like to see Mr Berin-Grotin, please.'

'Yes, sir. Your name, please?' His voice crackled like an old hen's.

'Michael Hammer, from New York.'

The old man took my hat and led me to a massive library panelled in dark oak and waved his hand towards a chair. 'Would you care to wait here, sir. I'll inform the master that you have arrived. There are cigars on the table.'

I thanked him and picked out a huge leather-covered chair and sank into it, looking around to see how Society lived. It wasn't bad. I picked up a cigar and bit the end off, then looked for a place to spit it. The only ash tray was a delicate bowl of rich Wedgwood pottery, and I'd be damned if I'd spoil it.

Maybe Society wasn't so good after all. There were footsteps coming down the hall outside so I swallowed the damn thing to get rid of it.

When Arthur Berin-Grotin came into the room I stood up. Whether I wanted to or not, there are some people to whom you cannot help but show respect. He was one of them. He was an old man, all right, but the years had treated him lightly. There was no stoop to his shoulders and his eyes were as bright as an urchin's. I guessed his height to be about six feet, but he might have been shorter. The shock of white hair that crowned his head flowed up to add inches to his stature.

'Mr Berin-Grotin?' I asked.

'Yes, good morning, sir.' He held out his hand and we clasped firmly. 'I'd rather you use only the first half of my name,' he added. 'Hyphenated family names have always annoyed me, and since I am burdened with one myself I find it expedient to shorten it. You are Mr Hammer?'

'That's right.'

'And from New York. It sounds as though one of you is important,' he laughed. Unlike his butler, his voice had a good solid ring. He pulled a chair up to mine and nodded for me to be seated.

'Now,' he said, 'what can I do for you?'

I gave it to him straight. 'I'm a detective, Mr Berin. I'm not on a case exactly, but I'm looking for something. An identity. The other day a girl was killed in the city. She was a redheaded prostitute, and she doesn't have a name.'

'Ah, yes! I saw it in the papers. You have an interest in her?'

'Slightly. I gave her a handout, and the next day she was killed. I'm trying to find out who she was. It's kind of nasty to die and not have anyone know you're dead.'

The old man closed his eyes slightly and looked pained. 'I understand completely, Mr Hammer.' He folded his hands across his lap. 'The same thought has occurred to me, and I dread it. I have outlived my wife and children and I am afraid that when I pass away the only tears to fall on my coffin will be those of strangers.'

'I doubt that, sir.'

He smiled. 'Thank you. Nevertheless, in my vanity I am erecting a monument that will bring my name to the public eye on occasions.'

'I saw the picture of the vault in the papers.'

'Perhaps I seem morbid to you?'

'Not at all.'

'One prepares a house for every other phase of living . . . why not for death. My silly hyphenated name will go to the grave with me, but at least it will remain in sight for many generations to come. A bit of foolishness on my part, yes; I care to think of it as pride. Pride is a name that has led a brilliant existence for countless years. Pride of family. Pride of accomplishment. However, the preparations concerning my death weren't the purpose of your visit. You were speaking of this . . . girl.'

'The redhead. Nobody seems to know her. Just before she was killed your chauffeur tried to pick her up in a joint downtown.'

'My chauffeur?' He seemed amazed.

That's right. Feeney Last, his name is.'

'And how did you know that?'

'He was messing with the redhead and I called him on it. He tried to pull a rod on me and I flattened him. Later I turned him over to the cops in a squad car to haul him in on a Sullivan charge and they found out he had a licence for the gun.'

His bushy white eyebrows drew together in a puzzled frown. 'He . . . would have killed you, do you think?'

'I don't know. I wasn't taking any chances.'

'He was in town that night, I know. I never thought he'd act like that! Had he been drinking?'

'Didn't seem that way to me.'

'At any rate, it's inexcusable. I regret the incident extremely, Mr Hammer. Perhaps it would be better if I discharged him.'

'That's up to you. If you need a tough boy around maybe he's all right. I understand you need protection.'

'That I do. My home has been burgled several times, and

although I don't keep much money on hand, I do have a rather valuable collection of odds and ends that I wouldn't want stolen.'

'Where was he the night the girl was killed?'

The old gent knew what I was thinking and shook his head slowly. 'I'm afraid you can dismiss the thought, Mr Hammer. Feeney was with me all afternoon and all evening. We went to New York that day and I kept several appointments in the afternoon. That night we went to the Albino Club for dinner and from there to a show, then back to the Albino Club for a snack before returning home. Feeney was with me every minute.'

'Your chauffeur?'

'No, as a companion. Here in the country Feeney assumes servant's garb when I make social calls, because others expect it. However, when we go to the city I prefer to have someone to talk to, and Feeney wears mufti, so to speak. I'm afraid I have to tell you that Feeney was in my company every minute of the time.'

'I see.' There was no sense in trying to break an alibi like that. I knew damn well the old boy wasn't lying, and the hardest guy to shake was one whose character was above reproach. I had a nasty taste in my mouth. I was hoping I could tag the greaseball with something.

Mr Berin said, 'I can understand your suspicion. Certainly, though, the fact that Feeney saw the girl before she died was coincidence of a nature to invite it. From the papers I gathered that she was a victim of a hit-and-run driver.'

'That's what the papers said,' I told him. 'Nobody saw it happen, so how could you be sure? She was somebody I liked . . . I hate like hell to see her buried in a potter's field.'

He passed a hand over his face, then looked up slowly. 'Mr Hammer . . . could I help in some' way . . . for instance, could I take care of decent funeral arrangements for her? I . . . would appreciate it if you would allow me to. Somehow I feel as though I should. Here I have everything, while she . . '

I interrupted with a shake of my head. 'I'd rather do it; but thanks anyway. Still, it won't be like having her family take care of her.'

'If you do need assistance of any sort, I wish you would call on me, Mr Hammer.'

'I might have to at that.'

The butler came in then with a tray of brandy. We both took one, toasted each other with a raised glass and downed it. It was damn good brandy. I put the glass on a side table, hating myself because it looked like everything stopped here. Almost, I should say. The greaseball was still in it, because he might possibly know who the redhead was. So I made one last stab at it.

'Where did you get this Last character?'

'He came well recommended to me by a firm who had used his services in the past. I investigated thoroughly and his record is excellent. What connection could he have had with the deceased girl, do you suppose?'

'I don't know. Maybe he was only making use of her services. Where is he now, Mr Berin?'

'He left for the cemetery with the name plate for the tomb early this morning. I instructed him to stay and see that it was properly installed. I doubt if he will be back before late this afternoon.'

There was as much here as I wanted to know. I said, 'Maybe I'll run out and see him there. Where's the cemetery?'

He stood up and together we started walking towards the door. The little old butler appeared from out of nowhere and handed me my hat. Mr Berin said, 'Go back towards the city for ten miles. The cemetery lies west of the village at the first intersection. The gate-keeper will direct you once you reach it.'

I thanked him for his time and we shook hands again. He held the door open for me and I ran down the steps to the car. He was still there when I pulled away and I waved so-long. In the rear-view mirror I saw him wave back.

The gate-keeper was only too happy to show me all the pretty tombstones and the newly dug graves. He took over the right seat of the car like a tour guide on a sightseeing bus and started a spiel that he hardly interrupted by taking a breath.

It was quite a joint, quite a joint. From the names on all the marble it seemed as if only the rich and famous died. Apparently there were three prerequisites necessary before they'd let you rot under their well-tended sod: Fortune, Fame or Position. Nearly everyone had all three. At least very few went to their reward with just one.

It was easy to see that the winding road was leading to a grand climax. In the north-east corner of the grounds was a hillock topped by a miniature Acropolis, and the guide was being very particular to keep my attention diverted the other way so it would come as a complete surprise. He waited until we were at the foot of the hill, then pointed it out with a flourish, speaking with awed respect in his voice.

'This,' he said, 'is to be a great tribute to a great man . . . Mr Arthur Berin-Grotin. Yes, a fitting tribute. Seldom has one done so much to win a place in the hearts of the people.' He was almost in tears.

I just nodded.

'A very sensible man,' he continued. 'Too often those final preparations are hurried and a person's name is lost to posterity. Not so with Mr Berin-Grotin. . . .'

'Mr Berin,' I corrected.

'Ah, you know him then.'

'Somewhat. Do you think it would be O.K. if I looked at the place close up?'

'Oh, certainly.' He opened the door. 'Come, I'll take you there.'

'I'd rather go alone. I may never have another chance to get back, and . . . well, you understand.'

He was sympathetic at once. 'Of course. You go right ahead. I'll walk back. I must see to certain plots at this end, anyway.'

I waited until he was lost among the headstones, then lit a cigarette and walked up the path. The men were working on the far side of the scaffolding and never saw me come up. Or else they were used to sightseers. The place was bigger than it looked. Curved marble columns rose upwards for fifteen feet, overshadowing huge solid-bronze doors that were embellished

30

with hand-crafted Greek designs.

The lintel over the doors was a curved affair held in place with an engraved keystone. Cut in the granite was the three-feather emblem of the royal family, or a good bottle of American whisky. Each plume, the tall centre one and the two outward-curving side plumes, was exact in detail until they could have passed for fossil impressions. There were words under it in Latin. Two of them were Berin-Grotin. Very simple, very digni-fied. The pride of a name; and the public could draw its own conclusions from the grandeur of the structure.

I started to walk around the side, then flattened against a recess in the wall. The greaseball was there, jawing out the workman for something or other. His voice had the same nasty tone that it had had the other night, only this time he had on a brown gaberdine chauffeur's uniform instead of a sharp suit. One of the workmen told him to shut up and he threw a rock at the scaffolding.

Just on a hunch I reached in my pocket and took out the plastic comb, and slid it down the walk so that it stopped right by his feet. He didn't turn around for a minute, but when he did he kicked the comb and sent it skittering back in my direc-tion. Instinctively, his hand went to his breast pocket, then he bent over and picked it up, wiped it on his hand and ran it through his hair, then returned it to his shirt.

I didn't need any more after that. The greaseball was the guy who'd made a mess out of the redhead's room.

He didn't see me until I said, 'Hullo, Feeney.'

Then his lips drew back over his teeth and his ears went flat against the side of his head. 'You dirty son of a bitch,' he snarled.

Both of us saw the same thing at the same time. No guns. Feeney must have liked it that way because the sneer turned into a sardonic smile and he dropped his hand casually into his pocket. Maybe he thought I was dumb or something. I was just as casual when I flicked open the buttons of my nice new jacket and slouched back against the wall.

'What do you want, shamus?'

'You, greaseball.'

'You think I'm easy to take?'

'Sure.'

He kept on grinning.

I said, 'I went up to the redhead's room last night. What were you looking for, Feeney?'

I thought he'd shake apart, he got so mad. There was a crazy light going in his eyes. 'There was a comb on the floor by the window. When you doubled over to get out it dropped out of your pocket. That comb you just picked up.'

He yanked his hand out of his pocket and the partially opened blade of the knife caught on cloth and snapped into place. I had my jacket off one arm and flipped it into his face. For a second it blinded him and the thrust missed my belly by an inch. He jumped back, then came in at me again, but my luck was better. The knife snagged in the jacket and I yanked it out of his hand.

Feeney Last wasn't easy. He ripped out a curse and came into me with both fists before I could get the coat all the way off. I caught a stinger on the cheek and under the chin, then smashed a right into his face that sent him reeling back to bounce off one of the columns. I tore the sleeve half off the jacket shucking it, and rushed him. That time I was a damn fool. He braced against the pillar and lashed out with a kick that lands in my gut and turned me over twice. If I hadn't kept rolling, his heels would have broken my back. Feeney was too anxious; he tried it again. I grabbed his foot and he landed on the stone flooring with a sickening smash.

No more chances. I could hardly breathe, but I had enough strength left to get a wristlock and make him scream with pain. He lay like that, face down and yelling, while I knelt across his back and dragged his hand nearly to his neck. Little veins and tendons stretched in bas-relief under his skin, and the screams died to a choking for air.

'Who was she, Feeney?'

'I dunno!'

The arm went up another fraction: His face was bleeding from pressing it into the stone. 'What were you after, Feeney?

Who was she?'

'Honest to God . . . I dunno. God . . . stop!'

'I will . . . when you talk.' A little more pressure on the arm again. Feeney started talking. I could barely hear him.

'She was a whore I knew from the Coast. I went up there and fell asleep. She stole something from me and I wanted it back.'

'What?'

'Something I had on a guy. He was paying off and she stole it. Pitchers of the guy and a broad in a hotel room.'

'Who was the redhead?'

'I swear it, I dunno! I'd tell you, only I dunno. Oh, God, oh, God!'

For the second time Feeney fainted. I heard footsteps behind me and looked up to see the two workers standing there in coveralls. One had a newly smashed nose and a black eye and he was carrying a stonemason's hammer. I didn't like the way he held it.

'You in on this, chums?'

The guy with a black eye shook his head, 'Just wanted to make sure he got it good. He's a wise guy . . . too quick to use his hands. Always wants to play boss. If we weren't getting plenty for this job we would have chucked it long ago.' The other agreed with a nod.

I stood up and pulled on what remained of my new suit, then picked Feeney up and hoisted him on my shoulder. Just across from my car was a newly opened grave with the canopy up and chairs all set, waiting for a new arrival. I leaned toward and Feeney Last dropped six feet to the bottom of the grave and never moved. I hope they'd find him before they lowered the coffin, or somebody was going to get the hell scared out of him.

The gate-keeper came to the side of my car as I was pulling out to say a friendly word and be complimented on his handi-work. He took one look at me and froze there with his mouth open. I put the car in gear. 'Mighty unfriendly corpses you have in this place,' I said.

CHAPTER THREE

I hit New York in the middle of a rainstorm and drove straight to my apartment to change my clothes and down a bottle of beer. As soon as I finished I grabbed a quick bite in a lunch-eonette and headed back towards the office. The rain was still coming down when I found a parking space two blocks away, so I hopped a cab to save my only remaining suit.

It was after five, but Velda was still there. So was Pat. He looked up with a grin and waved hullo. 'What are you doing here?' I asked.

'Oh, just stopped by to give you some news. Velda makes good company. Too bad you don't appreciate her more.'

'I do, but I don't have a chance to show it.' She wrinkled her nose at me. 'What news?'

'We found the guy that killed the redhead.'

My heart started hammering against my ribs. 'Who?'

'Some young kid. He was drunk, speeding, and beat out the red light. He remembered hitting somebody and knew he was in the wrong, whole hog, and kept on going. His father turned him in to us.'

I had to sit down after that. 'You sure, Pat?'

'As sure as you were that she was killed deliberately.' He laughed, and said, 'I was all hopped up for a while, but it's been turned over to another department and I can relax. Every time I'm on the same trail as you. I get the jumps. You ought to be a city cop, Mike. We could use you.'

'Sure, and I'd go bats trying to stay within all the rules and regulations. Look, what makes you so sure the kid did it?'

'Well, as far as we can determine, it was the only accident along the avenue that night. Then, too, we have his confession. The lab checked the car for fender dents and paint chips on her

35

clothing, but the kid had anticipated that before he confessed and did a good job of spoiling any traces that might have been left. We had a good man on the job and he seems to think that the unusual nature of the accident was caused because she was hit a glancing blow and broke her neck when she struck the edge of the kerb.'

'It would have broken the skin, then.'

'Not necessarily. Her coat collar prevented that. All the indications point that way. The only abrasions were those caused by the fall and roll after she was hit. Her cheek and knees were skinned up, but that was all.'

'What about identification.'

'Nothing yet. The Bureau of Missing Persons is checking on it.'

'Horse manure!'

'Mike,' he said, 'just why are you so damn upset about her name? There are thousands of kids just like her in the city and every day something happens to some of them.'

'Nuts, I told you once. I liked her. Don't ask me why, because I don't know, but I'll be damned if I'm not going to find out. You aren't going to stick her in a hole in the ground with an "X" on a slab over her head!'

'O.K., don't get excited. I don't know what you can do about it when there's a full-staffed bureau working on it.'

'Horse manure to the bureaux, too.'

I jammed the butt in my mouth and Pat waited until I lit it, then he got up and walked over to me. He wasn't laughing any more. His eyes were serious and he laid an arm on my shoulder and said, 'Mike, I kind of know you pretty well. You still got a bug up your tail that says she's been murdered, right?'

'Uh-huh!'

'Got the slightest reason why?'

'No.'

'Well, if you find out, will you let me know about it?'

I blew a stream of smoke at the ceiling and nodded my head. I looked up at him and the old friendship was back. Pat was one of those guys with sense enough to know that other people had hunches besides the cops. And not only hunches. There's a lot of experience and know-how that lies in back of what people call hunches.

'Is she in the morgue now?' I asked him. Pat nodded. 'I want to see her.'

'All right, we'll go down now.'

I looked at Velda, then the clock, and told her to blow. She was putting on her coat when we went out the door. On the way Pat didn't say much. I fought the traffic up to the old brick building and slid out to wait for Pat.

It was cold inside there. Not the kind of cold that comes with fresh air and wintry mornings, but a stale cold that smelt of chemicals and death. It was quiet, too, and it gave me the creeps. Pat asked the attendant for the listing of her personal belongings, and while he ruffled through a desk drawer we waited, not speaking.

There wasn't much. Clothes – but everybody wears clothes. Lipstick, powder and some money; a few trinkets of no account every girl totes in a handbag. I handed the listing back. 'Is that all?'

'All I got, mister,' the attendant yawned. 'Want to see her?'

'If you don't mind.'

The attendant went down the row of file cases, touching them with his finger like a kid does with a stick on a picket fence. When he came to the 'Unidentified' row he cheeked a number with a slip in his hand and unlocked the second case from the bottom. For all he was concerned, Red could have been a stack of correspondence.

Death hadn't changed her, except to erase some of the hardness from her face. There was a bruise on the side of her neck and abrasions from the fall, neither seemingly serious enough to be fatal. But that's the way it is. People go under subway cars and get back on the platform, scared but laughing; others pile a car over a cliff and walk away. She gets clipped lightly and her neck is broken.

'When's the autopsy, Pat?'

'There won't be one now. It hardly seems necessary when we have the driver. It isn't murder any more.'

Pat didn't see me grimace then. I was looking at her hands folded across her chest, thinking of the way she held that cup of coffee. Like a princess. She had had a ring, but there wasn't one now. The hand it had graced was scratched and swollen, and the marks where some bastard had forced the ring off went unnoticed among the others.

No, it wasn't stolen. A thief would have taken the handbag and not the ring while she had lain in the gutter. And girls aren't ones to forget to wear rings, especially when they're dressed up.

Yeah, Pat was wrong. He didn't know it, and I wasn't about to tell him . . . yet. It was murder if ever I saw one. And it wasn't just a guess now.

'Seen enough, Mike?'

'Yep. I've seen everything I want to see.' We went back to the desk and for a second time I checked the listing of her belongings. No ring. I was glad to get out of there and back into fresh air.' We sat in the car a few minutes and I lit up a cigarette.

'What's going to happen to her now, Pat?'

He shrugged. 'Oh, the usual thing. We'll hold the body the regular time while we check information, then release it for burial.'

'You aren't burying her without a name.'

'Be reasonable, Mike. We'll do everything we can to trace her.'

'So will I.' Pat shot me a sidewise look. 'Anyway,' I said, 'whatever happens, don't put her through the disposal system. I'll finance a funeral for her if I have to.'

'Uh-huh. But you're thinking you won't have to again. All right, Mike, do what you want to. It's officially out of my hands now, but damn it, man . . . if I know you, it will be back in my hands again. Don't try to cut my throat, that's all. If you get anything, let me know about it.'

'Of course,' I said, then started up the car and pulled away from the kerb.

The letter was three days late. The address had been taken from the telephone book, which hadn't been revised since I moved to my new apartment. The post office had readdressed it and forwarded it to me. The handwriting was light and feminine, touched with a gracious Spencerian style.

My hand was shaking when I slit it open; it shook even more when I started to read it, because the letter was from the redhead.

Dear Mike,

What a lovely morning, what a beautiful day and I feel so new all over I want to sing my way down the street. I can't begin to tell you 'thank you' because words are so small and my heart is so big that anything I could write would be inadequate. When I met you, Mike, I was tired . . . so tired of doing so many things . . . only one of which had any meaning to me. Now I'm not tired at all and things are clear once more. Some day I may need you again, Mike. Until now there has been no one I could trust and it has been hard. It isn't a friendship I can impose, upon because we're really not friends. It's a trust, and you don't know what it means to me to have someone I can trust.

You've made me very happy.

Your Redhead.

Oh, damn it to hell, anyway. Damn everybody and everything. And damn me especially because I made her happy for half a day and put her in a spot where living was nice and it was hard to die.

I folded the letter up in my fist and threw it at the wall.

A bumper bottle of beer cooled me off and I quit hating myself. When I killed the quart I stuck the empty under the sink and went back and picked up the letter, smoothing it out on the table top. Twice again I read it, going over every word. It wasn't the kind of letter a tramp would write; the script and the phrasing had a touch of eloquence that wasn't used by girls who made the gutter their home. I've seen a lot of bums, and I've fooled around with them from coast to coast, and one thing I know damn well . . . they're a definite type. Some give it away and some sell it, but you could pick out those who would and those who wouldn't. And those who would had gutter dirt reflected in everything they did, said and wrote.

Red had been a decent kid. She had to give up her decency to do something important. Something had a meaning for her . . . and some day she was going to need me again. She needed me more now than she ever did. O.K., I was hers, then.

They don't start walking the streets until midnight, if that's what you're after. But if you're in a hurry there are guys you can see who will steer you straight to a house and pick up their cut later. Usually they're sallow-faced punks with sharp pointed faces and wise eyes that shift nervously, and they keep toying with change in their pockets or a key chain hooked to high-pleated pants as they talk out of the corner of their mouths.

Cobbie Bennett was like that. As long as there are girls who make a business out of it, you'll find guys like Cobbie. The only shadow he cast was by artificial light, and he looked it. I found him in a dirty bar near Canal Street, his one hand cupped around a highball and his other hooked in his belt, in earnest conversation with a couple of kids who couldn't have been more than seventeen. Both of them looked like high-school seniors out to spend a week's allowance.

I didn't wait for them to finish talking. Both kids looked at me once when I nudged in beside them, turned a little white and walked away without a word.

'Hullo, Cobbie,' I said.

The pimp was more like a weasel backed into a corner than a man. 'What do you want?'

'Not what you're selling. By the way, who are you selling these days?'

'Try and find out, banana nose.'

I said O.K. and grabbed a handful of skin around his leg and squeezed. Cobbie dropped his drink and started cursing. When spit drooled out of the corner of his mouth I quit and ordered him another drink. He could hardly find his face with it. 'I could punch holes in you and make you talk if I felt like it, pal,' I grinned.

'Damn it, what'd you do that for?' His eyes were squinted almost shut, chopping me up into little pieces. He rubbed his leg and winced. 'I don't have to draw you pitchers, you know what I'm doing. Same thing I been doing right along. What's it to you?'

'Working for an outfit?'

'No, just me.' His tone was sullen.

'Who was the redhead who was murdered the other night, Cobbie?'

This time his eyes went wide and he twitched the corner of his mouth. 'Who says she was murdered?'

'I do.' The bartender drew a beer and shoved it at me. While I sipped it I watched the pimp. Cobbie was scared. I could see him try to shrink down inside his clothes, making himself as unobtrusive as possible, as though it weren't healthy to be seen with me. That put him in a class with Shorty . . . he had been scared, too.

'The papers said she was hit by a car. You call that murder?'

'I didn't say what killed her. I said she was murdered.'

'So what am I supposed to do?'

'Cobbie . . . you wouldn't want me to get real sore at you, would you?' I waited a second, then, 'Well. . . .?'

He was slow in answering. His eyes sort of crawled up to meet mine and stayed there. Cobbie licked his lips nervously, then he turned and finished his drink with a gulp. When he put the glass down he said, 'You're a dirty son of a bitch, Hammer. If I was one of them hop-heads I'd go get a sniff and a rod and blow your goddam guts out. I don't know who the hell the redhead was except another whore and I don't give a damn either. I worked her a couple of times, but mostly she wasn't home to play ball and I got complaints from the guys, so I dropped her. Maybe it was lucky for me that I did, because right after it I got word that she was hot as hell.'

'Who passed the word?'

'How should I know? The grapevine don't come from one guy. Enough people said it, so I believed it and forgot her. One of the other babes told me she wasn't doing so good. The trade around here ain't like it is uptown. We don't get no swells . . . some kids maybe, like them you loused up for me, but the rest is all the jerks who don't care what they get so long as they get it. They heard the word and laid off, too. She wasn't making a nickel.'

'Keep talking.' He knew what I was after.

Cobbie rapped on the bar for another drink. He wasn't talking very loud now. 'Get off me, will you! I don't know why she was hot. Maybe some punk gun-slinger wanted her for a steady and was getting rough. Maybe she was loaded three ways to Sunday. All I know is she was hot and in this business a word is good enough for me. Why don't'cha ask somebody else?'

'Who? You got this end sewed up pretty tight, Cobbie. Who else is there to ask? I like the way you talk. I like it so much that I might spread it around that you and me have been pretty chummy and you've been yapping your greasy little head off. Why should I ask somebody else when I got you to tell me. Maybe I don't know who to ask.'

His face was white as it could get. He hunched forward to get his drink and almost spilled that one too. '. . . Once she said she worked a house. . . ' He finished the highball and muttered the address as he wiped his mouth.

I didn't bother to thank him; it was favour enough to throw my drink down silently, pick up my change and walk out of there. When I reached the street I crossed over and stood in the recess of a hallway for a few minutes. I stuck a butt between my lips and had just cupped my hands around a match when Cobbie came out, looked up and down the street, jammed his hands in his pockets and started walking north. When he rounded the corner I got in the car and sat there a few minutes, trying to figure just what the hell was going on.

One red-headed prostitute down on her luck. She was killed, her room was searched, and her ring was missing.

One trigger-happy greaseball who searched her room because she stole his blackmail set-up. He said.

One ex-con who ran a hash house the redhead used for a hangout. He was scared.

One pimp who knew she was hot but couldn't say why. Maybe he could, but he was scared, too.

It was a mess no matter how you looked at it, and it was getting messier all the time. That's why I was so sure. Death is like a bad tooth . . . no matter what's wrong with it, you pull it out and it's all over. That's the way death usually is; after that people can talk all they want, they even do things for dead joes that they wouldn't do for the living. Death is nice and clean and antiseptic. It ends all trouble. Someone gathers up your belongings, says a word of praise, and that's it. But the redhead's was a messy death. There was something unclean about it like a wound that has healed over on top, concealing an ugly, festering sore brewing a deadly poison that will kill again.

When the butt burned down to my fingers I started the car and shoved off, threading my way across town to the address Cobbie had given me. New York had its sinkholes, too, and the number of this one placed it smack in the middle of the slime. It was a one-way street of rats' nests, with the river at one end and a saloon on each corner, peopled with men and women that had the flat vacant look of defeat stamped on their faces.

I checked the numbers and found the one I wanted, but all it was was a number, because the house was gone. Unless you can call a flame-gutted skeleton of masonry a house. The doorway yawned open like a leper's mouth and each window has its scar tissue of peeling paint.

The end of the trail. I swore and kicked at the kerb.

A kid about ten looked at me and said, 'Some jerk t'rew a match out the winder inta the garbage coupla weeks ago. Most of the dames got killed.'

These kids knew too much for their age nowadays. I needed a drink bad this time. The joint on the left was closer, so I went in and stood at the bar making tight fists with my hands until the nails cut into my palms. Now this, I kept thinking, now this! Did every corner to this have a blank wall I couldn't hurdle. The bartender didn't ask . . . he shoved a glass and a bottle under my nose and drew a chaser from the beer tap, then made change from my buck. When I had the second he put all the change in the register, then came back and waited.

'One more?'

I shook my head. 'Just beer this time. Where's your phone?'

'Over in the corner.' He jerked his head towards the end of the bar while he pulled the beer. I went down to the booth and dropped a nickel in, then dialled Pat at his home.

This time I had a little luck because he answered. I said, 'This is Mike, chum. Need a favour done. There was a fire in one of the bawdy houses down the street here and I want to know if there has been an investigation made. Can you check it?'

'Guess so, Mike. What's the number?' I gave it to him and grunted when he checked it back to me. 'Hang up while I call and I'll buzz you back. Give me your number there.'

He got that, too, and I hung up. I went down and got my beer, then went back to the seat in the phone booth and sat there sipping the stuff slowly. The minute it rang I snatched it off the hook.

'Mike?'

'Yeah.'

'The fire happened twelve days ago. A complete investigation was made because the place had been condemned for occupancy a month before and nothing had been done about it. The fire started accidentally and the guy who flipped the lit match out the window is still in the hospital recovering. Apparently, he was the only one who got out alive. The flames blocked the front door and the rear was littered with junk so as to be impassable.

'Three girls perished on the roof, two in the rooms and two jumped to their deaths before the firemen could get the nets up. Destruction was complete because the floors caved in completely.'

Pat didn't give me a chance to thank him. Before I could say a word his voice thinned out and had an edge on it. 'Give me what you know, Mike. You aren't there out of curiosity and if you're still thinking in terms of murder I want a trade. And right now, too.'

'O.K., sharp guy,' I laughed. 'I'm still trying to find out who the redhead was. I met a guy who knew where she had worked before she free-lanced and I wound up here.'

This time Pat was the one who laughed. 'Is that all? I could have told you that if you'd called me.' I froze on the phone. 'Her name was Sanford, Nancy Sanford. She used several first names, but seemed to stick to Nancy most of the time, so we picked it as her own.'

My teeth grinding together made more sound than my voice. 'Who said so?'

'We have a lot of men on the Force, Mike. A couple of the patrolmen got on to her.'

'Maybe you know who killed her, too.'

'Sure. The kid did. The lab finally found traces of fender paint on her clothes, and strands of fibres from her dress on the car. It was as simple as that.'

'Was it?'

'Uh-huh. Besides, we have a witness. At least a witness who saw her just a few minutes before she was killed. A janitor was putting out the ashes and saw her staggering up the street, dead drunk. She fell, got up again and staggered some more. Later she was discovered a half-block away in the gutter where she was hit.'

'Did you trace her parents – anybody at all who knew her?'

'No, we couldn't get that far. She did a good job of wiping out all traces of her past.'

'So now she gets the usual treatment . . . pine box and all.'

'What else, Mike? The case is closed except for the kid's trial.'

I snarled into that mouthpiece, 'So help me, Pat, if you lower her coffin before I'm ready, I'll beat the hell out of you, cop or no cop!'

Pat said quietly, 'We're not in a hurry, Mike. Take your time, take your time.'

I sat the receiver back in its cradle gently and stood up, saying her name over and over again. I must have said it too loud, because the willowy brunette at the corner table looked up at me with a quizzical expression in eyes that had seen through too many bottles of liquor. She was a beaut, all right, not part of this section of town at all. She had on a black satin dress with a neckline that plunged down to her belt buckle, and she sat there with her legs crossed, unconscious of what she was giving away for free.'

The heavily rouged lips parted in a smile and she said, 'Nancy . . . always Nancy. Everybody's looking for Nancy. Why don't they pay a little attention to pretty Lola?'

'Who was looking for Nancy?'

'Oh, just everybody.' She tried to lean her chin on her hand, but her elbow kept slipping off the table. 'I think they found her, too, because Nancy isn't around any more. Nancy's dead. Did you know Nancy was dead? I liked Nancy fine, but now she's dead. Won't pretty Lola do, mister? Lola's nice and alive. You'll like Lola lots when you get to know her.'

Hell, I liked Lola already.

CHAPTER FOUR

When I sat down beside the brunette the bartender watched me so hard the three drunks at the rail turned around too. The drunks didn't matter, they couldn't see that far, so I turned on my best nasty look and the bartender went about his business. Just the same he stayed down at the end where he could hear things if they were said too loud.

Lola uncrossed her long, lovely legs and leaned towards me. The big, floppy hat she was wearing wobbled an inch away from my eyes. 'You're a nice guy, mister. What's your name?'

'Mike.'

'Just Mike?'

'It's enough. How would you like to go for a ride and sober up a little.'

'Ummm. You got a nice shiny convertible for Lola to ride in? I love men with convertibles.'

'All right.'

She stood up and I held her arm to keep her straight. Nice, very nice. Deep-dish apple pie in a black satin dress. I steered her towards the door, hardly taking my eyes off her. Tall, and as long as you didn't look too close, as pretty as they come. But close looks were what counted. She had that look around the eyes and a set of the mouth that spelled just one thing. She was for sale cheap.

My heap wasn't what she expected, but it was comfortable and she leaned back against the cushions and let the breeze blow across her face and fluff out her hair. Her eyes closed and I thought she was asleep until she reached up and tugged off the floppy hat. Then she did go to sleep.

I wasn't going anywhere . . . just driving, taking it easy along the main Stem, following anybody that was ahead of me.

Somehow we got to the approach of the Manhattan Bridge and it was easier to go across than to cut out of traffic. This time I was behind a truck that led the way down Flatbush Avenue at a leisurely pace. Evidently he was in no hurry because he didn't bother going through light changes and never jumped the reds. He set such a nice pace that when he parked at Beverley Road for ten minutes I sat behind him and waited until he came back and followed him some more. The first thing I knew we had the lights of the city behind us and were skirting Floyd Bennett Field, and the air was carrying the salty tang of the ocean with it. We crossed the bridge then and he turned left, but I didn't follow. The winding macadam on the right led in the direction of the breezes and I took it to a gate and on into Rockaway Point.

We had been parked for an hour before Lola woke up. The radio was turned low, making music that mingled with the air and the stars and if murder hadn't led me here it could have been pretty nice.

She looked at me sleepily and said, 'Hullo, you.'

'Hi, kid.'

'Where is Lola this time?'

'At the beach.'

'And who with?'

'A guy called Mike . . . that's me. I found you back in the city under a rock. Remember?'

'No, but I'm glad you're with me.' She twisted on her hip, and slouched back, looking at me. No remorse, no bewilderment. Just curiosity.

'What time is it?'

I said, 'After midnight. Want to go home?'

'No.'

'Want to take a walk, then?'

'Yes. Can I take off my shoes and walk in the sand?'

'Take off everything if you want to.'

'Maybe I will when we get down on the beach, Mike.'

'Don't do anything of the kind. I'm too damn susceptible.'

It was pretty good strolling down that narrow lane, jumping the cracks in the sidewalk and making faces at the moon. Lola slipped her hand into mine and it was warm and soft, but holding tight as though I was something worth holding on to. I was remembering what Red said about guys like me never having to pay, and I wondered how true it was.

She took off her shoes like she wanted to and walked in the sand, kicking at mounds with her toes. When we reached the bulkhead we jumped down and walked to the water, and I took off my shoes too. It was cold, but it was nice, too nice to spoil by talking yet, and we waded up the beach, stepping up the wooden jetties and jumping to the other side, until there was nothing left but straight sandy beach, and even the houses were in the background.

'I like it here, Mike,' she said. She let go my hand and picked up a clamshell, looking at it as if it were a rare specimen. I put my arm around her and we stepped out of the water that licked at our feet and walked to the rolling hillocks of the dunes. After we sat down I handed her a cigarette, and in the light of the flame I saw that her face had changed and was at peace with itself.

'Cold?' I asked.

'A little chilly. I haven't much on under the dress.'

I didn't question it; I just gave her my coat, then leaned back on my elbows while she hugged her knees, staring out at the ocean.

When she took a long last drag on the cigarette she turned around and said, 'Why did you bring me out here, Mike?'

'To talk. I need somebody to talk to.'

She leaned back on the sand. 'My mind's unfogging, Mike,' she said. 'Was it about Nancy?'

I nodded.

'She's dead, Mike. I liked her, too.'

'Who killed her?'

There was a long moment of silence while Lola searched my face. 'You're a cop, aren't you?'

'A private dick. And I'm not hired by anybody, either.'

'And you think she was murdered instead of being killed by a hit-and-run driver.'

'Lola, I don't know what to think. Everything's going around in circles right now. Let's say I didn't like the way she died.'

'Mike . . . what if I said I thought she was murdered, too?'

I jumped at that. 'What makes you think so?'

'Oh, I don't know. Lots of things, maybe. If she wasn't murdered, she was killed accidently before she *could* be murdered. Let's say that, Mike.'

I turned on my side and my hand covered hers. The moonlight on the white V of the plunging neckline made it hard to concentrate. Her skin was white and smooth, in sharp contrast to the black satin. The only thing I could think of was the kind of bra she would be wearing under a dress like that. It would have to be an engineering marvel.

'How did you get to know her, Lola?'

Her answer was simple enough. 'We worked together.'

'You?' It didn't seem right.

'Don't I look the type?'

'Maybe . . . if a guy had dough and a convertible and was looking for an interesting side line in life. But not down in that section. What were you doing there?'

'I worked in a house up the street.'

'I thought all the girls were killed in the fire.'

'They were, but I wasn't there at the time. I was . . . in a hospital. I had been there quite a while. I left today.'

She looked at the sand and traced two letters in it – V.D.

'That's why I was in the hospital. That's why I was working down there instead of playing for guys with dough and convertibles. I had that once and lost it. I'm not very smart, am I, Mike?'

'No,' I told her, 'you're not. Anybody can do what you're doing and make a living at it. You never had to go in for that, neither did Nancy. There's no excuse for it. No matter what happens, there's only one way you wind up. No, Lola, there's no excuse for it.'

'Sometimes there is.'

She ran her fingers through my hair, then dropped her hand to cover mine. 'Maybe that's why Nancy and I were so close . . . because there was some excuse for it. I was in love, Mike . . . terribly in love with a guy who was no damn good. I could have had anybody I wanted, but no, I had to fall for a guy who was no damn good at all. We were going to get married when he ran away with a two-bit bum who hung around all the saloons in town. I was pretty disgusted, I guess. If that was all men wanted I figured on playing the game. I played it pretty good, too. After that I had everything, but I never fell for anybody.

'At first I was bitter about it, but living became too easy. I had something men wanted, and they were willing to supply the overhead charges. It got so good that it wasn't worthwhile playing one sucker at a time. Then one day I met a smart girl who introduced me to the right people, and after that the dates were supplied and I made plenty of money, and had a lot of time to spend it in, too.

'I had a name and a phone number, and if they had the dough all they had to do was call. That's why they called us call-girls. The suckers paid plenty, but they got what they wanted and were safe. Then one day I got drunk and slipped up. After that I wasn't safe to be with any more and the suckers complained, and they took away my name and my phone number, so all I had left was to go on the town.

'There's always people looking for left-overs like me. One got me set with an outfit that had a house and a vacancy and I worked there, then they set me down a couple of notches until I wound up in the place where I met Nancy. Most of the girls in the racket just drifted into it, that's why Nancy and I became friends. She had a reason for being there, too. It wasn't the same reason, but it was a reason and it put us above the others.

'One day I got smart. I pulled out of it and went to the hospital. When I was there Nancy was killed, and when I got back to the house it was burned. I came back to get Nancy, but she was gone, and she was the only friend I had left, so I went down to Barney's and got drunk.'

'Where you made a very professional pass at me.'

'I didn't mean to, Mike. I was drunk and I couldn't get out of the habit, I guess. Forgive me?'

When she turned the neckline fell away and I was ready to forgive her for anything. But first there was more I had to find out.

'Nancy . . . what about Nancy . . . did she follow the same route you did? About working her way down the ladder, I mean.'

'It happens to the best of them sooner or later, Mike. Yes, Nancy was a call-girl too, only she had made the grade before me.'

'And did she have to go to the hospital, too?'

A puzzled frown tugged at her forehead. 'No, that was the strange part about it. She was very careful. First she was in the big money, then suddenly she quit it all and dropped out of sight. She was forever running into people that hadn't seen her for a long time, and it frightened her. She stayed in the business as though it were a place to hide.'

'Hiding from what?'

'I never found out. Those were things you didn't ask about.'

'Did she have anything worth hiding?'

'If she did I didn't see it, though she was mighty secretive about her personal belongings. The only expensive thing she had was a camera, an imported affair that she used when she had a job once. You know, taking pictures of couples on the street and handing them a card. They would send the card in with a quarter and get their picture.'

'When was that . . . recently?'

'Oh, no, quite some time ago. I happened to see some of the cards she had left over and asked about them. I think the name was QUICK PIC . . . or something like that.'

I put a cigarette in my mouth and lit it, then gave her a drag from it. 'What's your whole name, Lola?'

'Does it matter?'

'Maybe.'

'Bergan. Lola Bergan, and I come from a little town called Byeville down in Mississippi. It isn't a big town, but it's a nice town, and I still have a family there. My mother and father think I'm a famous New York model and I have a little sister that wants to grow up and be just like me, and if she does I'll beat her brains out.'

There wasn't any answer to that. I said, 'Lola, there's just one thing more. Answer me yes or no fast, and if you lie to me I'll know it. Does the name Feeney Last mean anything to you?'

'No, Mike. Should it?'

'No, perhaps not. It meant something to Red and some other people, but it shouldn't involve you. Maybe I'm on the wrong trolley.'

'Mike . . . did you love Nancy?'

'Naw, she was a friend. I saw her once and spoke to her a few minutes and we got to be buddies. It was one of those things. Then some son of a bitch killed her.'

'I'm sorry, Mike. I wish you could like me like that. Do you think you could?'

She turned again, and this time she was closer. Her head nestled against my shoulder and she moved my hand up her body until I knew that there was no marvel of engineering connected to the bra because there was no bra. And the studded belt she wore was the keynote to the whole ensemble, and when it was unsnapped the whole affair came apart in a whisper of black satin that folded back against the sand until all of her reflected the moonlight from above until I eclipsed the pale brilliance, and there was no sound except that of the waves and our breathing. Then soon even the waves were gone, and there was only the warmth of white skin and little muscles that played under my hand and the fragrance that was her mouth.

The redhead had been right.

At one-fifteen I awoke with the phone shrilling in my ears. I kicked the cover off the bed and shuffled over to the stand, wiping the sleep from my eyes. Then I barked a sharp hullo into the phone.

53

Velda said, 'Where the devil have you been? I've been trying to get you all morning.'

'I was here. Sleeping.'

'What were *you* doing last night?'

'Working. What did ya want?'

'A gentleman came in this morning, a very wealthy gentleman. His name was Arthur Berin-Grotin and he wants to see you. I made an appointment for two-thirty here in the office and I suggest you keep it. In case you didn't know, the bank balance can stand relining.'

'O.K., kid, I'll be there. Was his stooge with him?'

'He came alone. Maybe he had someone waiting, but he didn't come up.'

'Good! Stick around until I show up. Won't be long. 'Bye honey.'

For ten minutes I splashed around in the shower, then made a bit to eat without drying off. A full pot of coffee put me back in shape and I started to get dressed. My suit was a mess, wrinkled from top to bottom, with the pockets and cuffs filled with sand. There were lipstick smears on the collar and shoulders, so it went back into the closet behind the others until I could get it to the tailor's. That left me with the custom-built tweed that was made to be worn over a rod, so I slapped on the shoulder holster and filled it with the .45, then slipped on the jacket. I looked in the mirror and grunted. A character straight out of a B movie. Downstairs I got a shave and a haircut, which left me with just enough time to get to the office a few minutes before the old gent.

Mr Berin-Grotin came in at exactly two-thirty. My switch box buzzed and Velda called in from the waiting-room, 'A gentleman here to see you, Mike.'

I told her to send him in and sat back in my swivel chair, waiting. When he opened the door I got up and walked over with my mitt out. 'Glad to see you again, Mr Berin. Come over and park.'

'Ah, thank you.' He took an overstuffed leather chair by the desk and leaned forward on his cane. In the light from the window I could see a troubled look about his eyes.

'Young man,' he said, 'since you left me I have given more and more thought to the plight of the girl you were so interested in. The one that was found dead.'

'The redhead. Her name was Nancy Sanford.'

His eyebrows went up. 'You discovered that already?'

'Hell, no, the cops got that angle. All I ever found out was some junk that makes no sense.' I leaned back and fired up a smoke, wondering what he wanted. He told me soon enough.

'Did they find her parents . . . anyone who would take care of . . . the body?'

'Nah. There's not much they can do, anyhow. The city is filled with a thousand girls like her. Ten to one she's from out of the state and has been away from home so long nobody gives a damn any more. The only one who's trying to give her back her past is me. Maybe I'll be sorry for it.'

'That is exactly what I came to see you about, Mr Hammer.'

'Mike . . . I hate formalities.'

'Oh, yes . . . Mike. At any rate, when you left I thought and thought about the girl. I made a few judicious calls to friends I have with the newspapers, but they couldn't help in the least. They said the girl was just a . . . a drifter. It seems a shame that things like that must happen. I believe that we're all to blame somehow.

'Your deep concern has transferred itself to me, and I think I may be of some help to you. I am continually giving to charities of some sort . . . but that's a rather abstract sort of giving, don't you think? Here is a chance for me to help someone, albeit a trifle late, and I feel I must.'

'I told you once, I'll take care of the funeral arrangements myself,' I said.

'I realize you intend to . . . but that's not what I mean. What I wish to do is to employ you. If you carry on an investigation you must be financed, and since I am as anxious as you to have her remains properly cared for, I would be deeply grateful if you would let me give you the means of locating her relatives. Will you do it?'

It was a break I hadn't expected. I took my feet off the desk and swung the chair around. 'It's all right with me,' I told him.

'I would have poked around anyway, but this makes it a lot easier.'

He reached in his jacket pocket for his wallet and thumbed it open. 'And what are your rates, Mike?'

'A flat fifty a day. No expense account. The fifty takes care of it all.'

'Have you any idea how long it may take?'

I shrugged my shoulders. 'Who can tell. Sometimes chasing a name is easy, sometimes not.'

'In that case, let me do this . . .' He laid a sheaf of crisp new bills on my desk. The top one was a beautiful fifty. 'Here is one thousand dollars. Not a retainer . . . but payment in full. Please stay with it until you think it has been spent. If you find out about the girl quickly, good. If you don't locate her history in twenty days, then it is probably a hopeless task and not worth your time. Is that a satisfactory arrangement?'

'I'm stealing your money, Mr Berin.'

His face brightened into an easy smile and the trouble lines were gone. 'I don't think so, Mr Hammer. I have become familiar with your record and know how far you are capable of going. With an added incentive of having an interest in the girl yourself, you should make excellent progress. I hope so. It isn't a pleasant thing to see someone go like that . . . no one to know or care. . . .'

'I care.'

'Yes, I know you do, Mike, and I care, too, because yours is a genuine, unselfish interest to restore some touch of decency to her. She couldn't have been all bad. Do whatever you think is necessary, and in the interim, if there is a need for more money you will call on me, won't you?'

'Certainly.'

'The whole affair makes me feel so very small. Here I am preparing for a grand exit from this life, spending thousands that will be a memorial to my name, and this girl dies as if she had never existed. You see, I *know* what aloneness is; I *know* the feeling of having no one to call your own, not even an entombed memory to worship. My wife, as you may know, was an ardent sportswoman. She loved the sea, but she loved it too much. During one of her cruises aboard a yacht that should never have been out of still waters she was washed overboard. My only son was killed in the First World War. His daughter was the dearest thing to my heart, and when she died I knew what it was like to be utterly, completely alone in this world. Like my wife, she loved the sea too dearly, too. It finally took her during a storm off the Bahamas. Perhaps you understand now why I have erected a memorial to myself . . . for there is not even so much as a headstone for the others, except perhaps a cross over my son's grave in France. And that, too, is why I want no one else to share my burden of having nothing left, nothing at all. I am thankful that there are people like you, Mike. My faith in the kindnesses of man was extremely low. I thought that all people cared about was money, now I know I was quite wrong.'

I nodded, blowing a streamer of smoke at the ceiling. 'Money is great, Mr Berin, but sometimes a guy gets pretty damn sore and money doesn't matter any more. A guy can get just plain curious, too . . . and money doesn't matter then either.'

My new client stood up, giving me an old-fashioned bow. 'That takes care of the matter, then?'

'Almost. Where do you want me to send my report?'

'I never gave it a thought. It really doesn't matter, but if you come across anything you might feel is interesting, call or write to me at my home. It's entirely up to you. I'm more interested in results than the procedure.'

'Oh . . . one other thing. Is Feeney Last still with you?'

His eyes twinkled this time and a grin crossed his face. 'Fortunately, no. It seems that he had quite a scare. Quite a scare. He saved me the task of discharging him, by resigning. At present my gardener is serving in his capacity. Good day, Mike.'

I stood up and led him to the door and shook hands there. On the way out he gave Velda a gentlemanly bow and strode out the door. She waited until the door had shut and said, 'He's nice, Mike. I like him.'

'I like him, too, kid. You don't have many around like him anymore.'

'And he's got money, too. We're back in business again, huh?'

'Uh-huh.' I looked at the intercom box. She had the switch up and had overheard the conversation. I frowned at her the way a boss should, but it didn't scare her a bit.

'Just curious, Mike. He was such an interesting guy,' she smiled.

I faked a punch at her jaw and sat on the desk, reaching for the phone. When I got the dial tone I poked out Pat's number and held on until he got on the wire. He gave me a breezy hullo and said, 'What's new, kid?'

'A few things here and there, but nothing that you can call withholding evidence. Look, have you had lunch yet?'

'An hour ago.'

'Well, how about some coffee and Danish. I want to know a few things, if you care to tell me.'

'What kind of things?'

'Stuff the police ought to know and the general public shouldn't. Or would you rather have me find out for myself?'

'Nuts to you! It's better to have you obligated to me. I'll meet you in Mooney's as soon as you can make it. How's that?'

'Fine,' I said, then hung up.

Pat beat me to the beanery by five minutes. He already had a table over in the back and was sipping coffee from an oversize mug the place used as a trademark. I pulled out a chair and sat down, I didn't have time to waste; as soon as the waiter came over with my coffee and pastry I got right down to cases. 'Pat, what's the angle on the call-girl racket in this town?'

The cup stopped half-way to his mouth. 'Now, that's a hell of a question to ask me. If I tell you, it implies that I'm crooked and I'm looking the other way. If I don't, I look stupid for not knowing what goes on.'

I gave him a disgusted grunt, then: 'Pat, there are certain things that are going to happen in every town no matter how strait-laced the citizens are or how tough the cops are. It's like taxes. We got 'em and we can't get rid of 'em. And who likes taxes except the small group of bureaucrats that handle the mazuma?'

'Now you've made me feel better,' he chuckled. 'There isn't too much I can tell you because those outfits are good at keeping things to themselves. We rarely get complaints because their clientele isn't in a position to lay themselves open to criticism by entering a complaint. However, the police are well aware of the existing situation and try to enforce the letter of the law. But remember one thing – politics. There are ways of bogging the police down and it's a hurdle hard to jump.

'Then there's the matter of evidence! The higher-ups don't run houses or keep books where they can be found. It's a matter of merely suggesting to someone just who is available and letting him do the rest. I think the girls come across with a cut of the take or the proper persons aren't steered in their direction. They may get shoved around a little, too. In fact, there have been several deaths over the years that point suspiciously in that direction.'

'That they got shoved too hard, you mean?' I asked.

'Exactly.'

'How did the coroner call them?'

'Suicides, mainly . . . except for Russ Bowen. You know about him . . . he was the guy who ran a chain of houses and tried to buck the combine. We found him shot full of holes a couple of months ago and his houses closed out. We never could get a line on the killing. Even the stoolies clammed up when we mentioned his name. Yes, Russ was murdered, but the others were all called suicides.'

'And you?'

'Murder, Mike. The cases are still open, and some day we're going to nail the goons that are behind them. Not only the hired hands that did the dirty work, but the ones that run the organizations. They're the ones we want . . . the ones that turn decent kids into a life of filth and despair while they sit back and collect the big money. The ones that can kill and get away with it and sit back and laugh while the papers call it suicide!'

His face was a mask of hate. My eyes caught his and held for a long moment. 'Suicide . . . or accident, Pat?' I queried.

'Yes, both. We've had them that looked that way, too, and . . .'

Now the hate was gone and his face was friendly again, but there was something different about the eyes that I had never seen before. 'You're a bastard, Mike. You set me up very pretty.'

'I did?' I tried to play innocent, but it didn't work.

'Cut it and get to the redhead. Nancy, I believe her name was. What are you handing me?'

I took my time about finishing the Danish. After it soaked long enough in the coffee I fished it out and ate it, licking the sugar from my fingers. When I lit a butt I said, 'I'm not handing you a thing, Pat. You just told me something I've been trying to tell you right along. I've always said Red was murdered. Now, what do you think?'

Pat wrapped his fists into hard knots and pressed them into the table. He had a hard time talking through clenched teeth. 'Damn your soul, Mike, we had that case nicely wrapped up. She was killed accidentally beyond a shadow of doubt, and I'm positive of it. I'm so positive of it I'd bet my right arm against a plugged nickel I couldn't be wrong! Maybe people make mistakes, but the sciences of the laboratory don't!'

It was fun watching him beat his head against the wall. His words turned into a torrent of sharp sounds and he leaned against the edge of the table with fire leaping from his eyes.

'I saw the evidence. I checked on the evidence. I'm certain of the evidence as is everyone else concerned with the case. In the beginning you had me dancing on hot coals because I thought that maybe you were right. Then I knew what had happened and I knew you were wrong. Mind you, I didn't say think – I said *knew*! And right now I still *know* you are wrong and I am *right*.'

'But . . .' I protested.

'But you, you bastard, you've got me all crazied up again and I'm thinking I'm wrong even when I know I'm right! Why don't you drop dead!'

It had been a long time since I had seen Pat like that. I grinned at him and blew a wreath of smoke around his head. The draught made a halo of it and I said, 'The smoke it encircled his head like a wreath.'

'What?'

'Excerpt from the "Night Before Christmas." You probably can't go back that far.'

Pat ran his fingers through his hair and shook his head. 'You give me the pip. Maybe I'm nuts. What makes me get all excited about things like this? Ordinarily I'm cool, calm and collected. I run my office with precision and great efficiency, then you come along and I get like a rookie on his first beat with a gang war going on in the back alleys.'

I shoved the deck of Luckies towards him and he stuck one in his mouth. When I thumbed a match and lit him I said very quietly, 'Pat, offices like yours are great things. You take one lousy little clue and make a case out of it and somebody pays society for a misdeed. Sure, you serve justice. You do more good than a million guys working separately, but there's one thing you miss.'

'Tell me what.' He was getting sarcastic again.

'The excitement of the chase, Pat. The thrill of running something down and pumping a slug into it. Right now you are so damn fond of indisputable proof you can't figure an angle any more. Since when can't murder be made to look like an accident?'

'She was hit by the car, Mike. The driver admits he hit somebody but he was too fuzzy to remember who. The lab found traces on the car. They found traces on her. We had witnesses who saw her staggering down the street dead drunk a little while before she got it. The guy that hit her is ordinarily an upstanding citizen with no underworld connections. We checked.'

I nodded. 'Yet now you're beginning to entertain doubts. Right?'

He said something obscene.

'Right is right! Entertain is no word for it. You have me refuting everything I ever learned and I'll wind up being a stupe. Do you know why?'

'Yeah, but tell me again, Pat.'

This time he leaned on the table and practically hissed through his teeth. 'Because right in here' – he tapped the side of his head – 'you're a sharp article. You could be a good crook, but you're a better cop. You get something and hang on to it longer than anybody else and make something of it. You got a brain and the sense to use it and you have something I haven't got which is a feeling for things. Damn it, I'd like to poke you in the ear.'

'Stop hating yourself. You were going to tell me something. Who's behind the racket?'

'I wish I knew. All I know is a few names of the guys we suspect of having a hand in it.'

'They'll do.'

'Oh, no! First let's hear what you have, Remember, please, that I'm the one who should know things. Of all the crazy things that happen; imagine a cop and a private eye chumming up like we do. Give out, Mike, sing me a song.'

It was going to take a while, so I ordered some more coffee for us both, and when it came I started at the beginning and didn't stop until I brought Pat up to date – all but a few of the more intimate details. He didn't bother to jot anything down; his mind was filing away each item for future reference and I could see him laying the facts side by side, trying to make something of them.

When I finished he put a cigarette in his mouth and sat back thinking. When he fully absorbed everything, he said, 'You have a nice accumulation of events, Mike. Now theorize.'

'I can't,' I told him. 'There's no place to start.'

'Start with Red.'

'She was killed. That means she was killed for a reason.'

'The same reason she had for being in the racket?'

62

'Maybe . . . or maybe the reason developed afterwards. What would a girl in her position have that would make it worth while being killed. Blackmail? I've thought of that, but it doesn't fit. Who would take her word in court? Maybe she had proof of someone's misconduct, but I doubt it. That's a tough racket and she wasn't mingling with anybody who counted. If she was playing against small stuff that same small stuff was tough enough to take care of her clean and simple without a lot of dummying. I have that feeling, as you call it, that the reason was a big one. I'm mad at somebody, Pat, and that person is going to answer to me for her death.'

'Find the motive and you find the murderer,' Pat said. 'What about this Feeney Last character?'

'To me he looks like a punk. When he hit the city he went off on a spree and wound up in Red's neighbourhood. He's the kind of a guy that would pull off a blackmail stunt all right. He said Red swiped his pay-off material and as long as she was what she was I wouldn't put it past her. But there's always another angle to that. He would have lost it, or whoever was being blackmailed paid off to see that it was destroyed. If Red was paid enough she might have lifted it from him while he was with her.'

'Could he have killed her?'

'Sure, but not with any fancy trimmings. Feeney's no artist. He likes knives and guns. The only trouble is . . . he doesn't seem to expect to run into any opposition. No, Feeney didn't kill her. If he did, Red would have died quick and messy.'

Pat dragged on the cigarette again. 'What about your client, Mike?'

'Berin-Grotin? Hell, he couldn't have a hangnail without the papers knowing about it. He's from another generation, Pat. Money, position, good manners . . . everything you could expect of a gentleman of the old school. He's fiercely proud of his name; you know . . . constantly alert that nothing should cloud the escutcheon of his family. The old boy's no fool, either. He wanted protection so he hired Feeney, but he was ready to get rid of him as soon as the jerk got himself in trouble. It seemed to me that he was a little leery of Feeney, anyway. I got the impression that he was happy over what had happened up there in the cemetery.'

'Which brings us to Lola. What there?'

'Nothing. She knew Red.'

'Come on, Mike, she wasn't a complete nonentity, was she?'

'You can say that again.' I let out a little laugh. 'Marvellous personality, Pat. A body that'd make your hair stand on end, Lola's another of the decent kids you were speaking about, that went wrong. Only this one wised up in time.'

'O.K., then let's go back a step. You told me the guy in the hash house and that Cobbie Bennett were afraid of something. Think around that.'

'It doesn't think right, Pat. Shotie was a con and he was more than anxious to stay away from murder. Cobbie's in a racket where nothing looks good except dough. Anything could scare him. Both those guys scare too damn easily, that's why I can't attach too much significance to either one. I've thought it over a dozen times and that's how it shapes up.'

Pat grunted, and I could feel his mind working it over, sorting and filing, trying for an answer. When none came he shrugged his shoulders and said, 'The guys I know who may be part of the game are small fry. They run errands and do the legwork. I've made my own guesses before this, but I won't pass them on to you, for if I do you'll go hog wild and get me in a jam. Yourself, too, and like I said, they were only guesses with nothing to back them up.'

'You usually guess pretty good, Pat. I'll take them.'

'Yeah, but you're not going to get them. But I will do this: I'll see if I can make more out of it than guesses. We have ways of finding out, but I don't want to scare off the game.'

'Good deal! Between the two of us we ought to make something of it.'

Pat snubbed the butt out and stared into the ash-tray. 'Now for the sixty-four dollar question, Mike. You got me into this, so what do you expect me to do?'

'You got men at your finger-tips. Let them scout around. Let them rake in the details. Work at it like it was a murder and something will show up. Details are what we need.'

'All right, Mike, my neck is out so far it hurts. I'm going against everything I know by attaching a murder tag to this and I expect some co-operation from you. All the way, understand?'

'You'll get it.'

'And since I'm putting men on it, what *can* I expect from you?'

'Hell,' I said, 'I have a date with Lola tonight. Maybe she's got a girlfriend.'

CHAPTER FIVE

It was nice to get back to Lola. I found her apartment on West Fifty-ninth Street and walked up two flights to 4-C. Even before I could get my finger off the buzzer she had the door open and stood there smiling at me as if I were somebody. She was dressed in black again and there was no plunging neckline. There didn't need to be. It was easy to see that not even calico or homespun could be demure on her.

Her voice was soft as kitten's fur. 'Hullo, Mike. Aren't you coming in?'

'Just try to keep me out.'

I walked into the foyer, then followed her into a tiny living-room that had been dressed up with all the gimcracks women seem to collect when they live alone. The curtains were starched stiff and the paint was fresh enough to have a lingering smell of turpentine. When I slid into an overstuffed chair I said, 'New place?'

She nodded and sat down opposite me and began mixing highballs from a miniature bar set. 'Brand new, Mike. I couldn't stay in . . . the old place. Too many sordid memories. I have a surprise for you.'

'Yeah, what?'

'I'm a model again. Department store work at a modest salary, but I love it. Furthermore, I'm going to stay a model.'

There was a newness about her as well as the apartment. Whatever she had been was forgotten now and the only thing worth looking at was the future.

'Your former – connections, Lola. How about that?'

'No ghosts, Mike. I've put everything behind me. What people I knew will never look for me here and it's a thousand-to-one chance they'll run into me anywhere else. If they do I can pass it off.'

She handed me the drink and we toasted each other silently. I lit up a Luckie and threw the deck to the coffee table and watched her while she tapped one on a finger-nail. As she lit it her eyes came up and caught me watching her.

'Mike,' she said, 'it was nice last night, wasn't it?'

'Wonderful.' It had been – very.

'But tonight you didn't come up . . . just for that, did you?'

I shook my head slowly. 'No. No, it was something else.'

'I'm glad, Mike. What happened was awfully fast for me. I – I like you more than I should. Am I being bold?'

'Not you, Lola. I'm the one who was off on the wrong foot. You got under my skin a little bit and I couldn't help it. You're quite a gal.'

'Thanks, pal,' she grinned at me. 'Now tell me what you came up for. First, I thought you were only fooling about coming to see me and I got kind of worried. Then I thought maybe I was only good for one thing. Now I feel better again.'

I hooked an ottoman with my toe and got it under my feet. When I was comfortable I dragged in on the butt and blew smoke out with the words: 'Nancy was killed, Lola. I have to find out why, then I'll know who. She was in the oldest racket in the world. It's a money racket; it's a political racket. Everything about it is wrong. The only ones who don't give a damn whether school keeps or not are the girls. And why should they? They're as far down as they can go and who cares? So they develop an attitude. Nothing can hurt them, but they can hurt others very easily . . . if they wanted to. I'm thinking of blackmail, Lola. Would Nancy have tried a stunt like that?'

Her hand was shaking so she had to put the glass down. There were tears in her eyes, too, but she managed a rueful smile and brushed them away. 'That was rough, Mike.'

'It wasn't meant for you, kid.'

'I know, I'm just being silly. No, I don't think Nancy would do that. She might have been a – been no good, but she was honourable. I'd swear to that. If she wasn't what she was she could have been a decent woman. As far as I know she had no vices, but, like I told you, she had a reason for doing what she did. Perhaps it was the money. I don't know. It *is* a quick way to get rich if you have no moral scruples.'

'Supposing money was her reason. Any idea why she might have needed it?'

'That I can't tell you. We had no confidences, merely a bond that held us together.'

The circle was getting me dizzy. 'Look, let's go back further. Go back to the call-girl system. Who ran it?'

For the first time her face went white. She looked at me with fear in her eyes and her lips tight against her teeth. 'No, Mike!' Her voice was barely audible. 'Keep away from them, please.'

'What's scaring you, honey?'

It was the way I said it that made her shrink back into her seat, her fingers digging into the arms.

'Don't make me tell you things I don't want to remember!'

'It isn't things you're afraid of, Lola. It's people . . . what people? Why does it scare you to think of them?'

I was leaning forward now, anxious, trying to make something out of every word she spoke. She was hesitant at first, turning her head from side to side as though someone else could be listening.

'Mike . . . they're vicious. They don't care what they do. They . . . wreck lives . . . as easily as they'd spend a dollar. If they knew I ever said anything they'd kill me. Yes, they would. It wouldn't be the first time, either!'

It might have been Pat talking. The fear left her face and anger took its place, but there was still a quiver in her voice.

'Money is all they're after and they get it. Thousands . . . millions . . . who knows. It's dirty money, but it's good to spend. It isn't like the houses . . . it's bigger. One tight little group has it so organized nobody else can move, and if you try to operate alone something happens to you. Mike, I don't want anything to happen to me!'

I got up and sat on the arm of her chair, then ran my fingers through her hair, 'Nothing's going to happen, baby. Keep talking . . . all of it.'

For an answer she buried her face in her hands and sobbed uncontrollably; I could afford to wait. In five minutes she was cried out, but still shaking. There was a haunted look in her eyes that went with the tenseness in her shoulders and her nails had drawn blood from her palms. I lit another butt and handed it to her, watching while she sucked on it gratefully, taking the smoke down deep, seeking a relief of some sort.

Then she turned those haunted eyes on me and said, 'If they find out I told you . . . or anybody, anything at all, they'll kill me, Mike. They can't afford to have people talk. They can't afford to have people even suspect. I'm afraid! And what could you do . . . it's been going on for ever and it will keep going on as long as there are people. I don't want to die for something like that.'

I picked my words carefully because I was getting mad again. 'Kid,' I told her, 'you don't know me very well. You don't, but there are plenty of guys who do. Maybe they're able to scare the hell out of decent citizens, but they'll drop a load when I come around. They know me, see? They know damn well I won't take any crap from them, and if they get tough about it they'll get their guts opened up for them. I got a gun and I've used it before . . . plenty. I got a licence to use it, which they don't have and if somebody gets killed I go to court and explain why. Maybe I catch hell and get kicked out of business, but if *they* pull the trigger they sit in the hot seat. I'm calling the plays in this game, kid. I like to shoot those dirty bastards and I'll do it every chance I get and they know it. That's why they scare easy.

'And don't you worry about anything happening to you. Maybe they'll know where it came from, but they won't do anything about it, because I'm going to pass the word that I want somebody's skin and the first time they get rough they'll catch a slug in the front or back or even in the top of the head. I don't care where I shoot them. I'm not a sportsman. I'd just as soon get them from a dark alley as not, and they know it. I play it their way, only worse, and somebody is going to worry himself into a grave over it.'

70

My hand was resting on her shoulder, and she turned her head and kissed my fingers. 'You're kind of wonderful, even if you do tell me yourself,' she said.

The haunted look in her eyes was gone now.

Lola took another drag on the cigarette and snubbed it out, then reached for the glasses. When they were filled she handed me mine and we touched them briefly and drank deep. She finished hers with one breath in between, then set it back on the table. She was ready to talk now.

'Nobody seems to know who's behind the system, Mike. It may be one person or it may be several. I don't know the details of the pay-off, but I do know how the racket operates. It isn't a haphazard method at all, and you'd probably fall flat on your face if you knew who was involved. Right now there are some girls with an amazing social standing who were, at one time, no better than me. They got out in time. They made the right contacts between "appointments" and married them.

'You see, the real call-system is highly specialized. The girls are of only the highest calibre. They must be beautiful, well educated, with decorum enough to mingle with the best. Their "clients" are the wealthy. Generally an appointment means a weekend at some country estate or a cruise along the coastline on some luxurious yacht. Of course, there are other appointments less fancy, but equally as lucrative, as when somebody wants to entertain a business associate. Apparently tactics like that pay off to the extent that the money involved means nothing.

'A girl is carefully investigated before she is approached to take part in the racket. It starts when she is seen around town too often with too many men. In the course of her travels she meets other girls already in the racket who seem to have everything they want without having to do much to earn it. These acquaintances ripen into easy friendships and a few hints are passed and the girl begins to take the attitude of why should she do the same things for free when she can get paid for it.

71

'So she mentions the fact and introductions are made to the right people. She is set up in a nice apartment, given an advance and listed in the book as a certain type. When a party wants that type he calls, or makes the arrangement with an in-between, and you're off on your date. Whatever gifts the girl gets she is allowed to keep and some of them make out pretty well. The money that is paid for her services is passed in advance and the girl gets a cut from that, deposited to her account in a bank.

'Oh, it's all very nice and easy, a beautiful deal. There aren't any ties on the girl either. If she happens to run across someone she cares for, she's free to quit the racket and get married, and she can expect a juicy bonus for the time in service. That's one reason why there's no kick-back. The girls never talk because they can't have anyone know of their associations, and the system won't force them to stay because there's nothing more dangerous than a hysterical woman.

'But there are times when one of the girls becomes dangerous. She can develop a conscience, or take to drink and find herself with a loose tongue, or get greedy and want more money on the threat of exposure. Then the system takes care of itself. The girl simply disappears, or has an accident. If we hear of it, it's a lesson to us to do one thing or another . . . keep quiet or get out . . . and keep quiet then, too.

'I learned my lesson well. When I got careless and became a disease carrier I lost my place in the system. Oh, they didn't mention the fact . . . one of the other girls did. I suddenly had an expensive apartment on my hands and no income, so I cashed in what I had and moved on down the ladder. I was too ashamed to go to a doctor and I didn't know what else I could do, so I started drinking. I met some more people again. Those people didn't care what I had. They got me a room in a house and I was in business again. It took me a long time to get smart, but I did, and I went to the hospital. After I came out the house was gone, Nancy was dead and you were there.'

She slumped back in the chair and closed her eyes as though she were exhausted. I said, 'Now some names, Lola.'

Her eyes were mere slits, her voice practically a whisper. 'Murray Candid; He owns some night clubs, but he's always at the Zero Zero Club. He is the contact man I met. He made all the arrangements, but he isn't the top man. The town is worked, in sections and he covers the part I worked. He's dangerous, Mike.'

'So am I.'

'What are you going to do now?'

'I don't know, kid. You can't go in and accuse a guy without proof, even if you know you're right. The law's on his side then. I need proof . . . what could I use to stick him?'

'There are books, Mike . . . if you could find them. They'd love to do without books because they'd be almost clean then, but they can't because they can't trust each other.'

'Would this Candid guy have them?'

'I doubt it. He'd keep temporary records, but the big boy has the important data.'

I stood up and finished my drink. 'O.K., Lola, you did fine,' I said. 'It's something to work on . . . a place to start. You don't have to worry because I won't bring you into it. Sit tight around here and I'll call you from time to time. There are still things you probably know that I don't, but I can't tell what they are yet.'

Lola came up from her seat slowly and slid her arms around my waist. She laid her head on my shoulder and nuzzled her face into my neck. 'Be careful, Mike, please be careful.'

I tilted her chin up and grinned at her. 'I'm always careful, sugar. Don't worry about me.'

'I can't help it. Maybe I ought to have my head examined, but I'm crazy about you.'

She stopped me before I could speak by putting her finger on my lips. 'Not a word, Mike. Let me do the liking. I'm no good and I know it. I'm not going to mess into your life a bit so you can let me go on liking you if I please. No obligations,

Mr Hammer, I'll just sit on the side lines and throw kisses your way, and wherever you are you'll always know that where I am is a girl you'll always have to yourself. You're a nice guy, you big lug. If I had the sense to lead a normal life you'd never get away from me.'

This time I shut her up. Her body was a warm thing in my hands and I pressed her close to me, feeling tremors of excitement run across her back. Her lips were full and ripe, and whatever she had been was cleansed and there was no past for a brief instant. When I kissed her, her mouth was like a flame that fluttered from a feeble glow into a fiery torch.

I had to shove her away roughly before everything else was forgotten. We stood there, two feet apart, and my voice didn't want to come. When it did I said, 'Save yourself for me, Lola, just me.'

'Just you, Mike,' she repeated.

She was still there in the middle of the room, tall and beautiful, her breasts alternately rising and falling with a craving neither of us could afford, when I went out the door.

The Zero Zero Club was a cellar joint off Sixth Avenue that buried itself among the maze of other night spots with nothing more than two noughts done in red neon to proclaim its location. But it was doing a lively business. It had atmosphere; plenty of it . . . that's why they called it the Zero Zero. Both visibility and ceiling were wiped out with cigar smoke.

Down the stairs a cauliflower-eared gent played doorman with a nod, a grunt and an open palm. I gave him a quarter so he wouldn't remember me as a piker. The clock on the wall read eleven-fifteen and the place was packed. It wasn't a cheap crowd because half of them were in evening clothes. Unlike most joints, there was no tinsel or chromium. The bar was an old solid mahogany job set along one wall, and the tables were grouped around a dance floor that actually had room for dancing. The orchestra was set into a niche that could double as a stage for the floor show if necessary.

The faces around me weren't those of New Yorkers – at least those of the men. Most could be spotted as out-of-towners looking for a good time. You could tell those who had their wives along. They sat at the bar and tables sipping drinks, with one eye on the wife and the other on the stray babes, wondering why they had been talked into taking the little woman along.

Yeah, the atmosphere was great, what you could see of it. The Zero Zero Club took you right back to the saloons of a western mining camp, and the patrons loved it. Scattered throughout the crowd were half a dozen hostesses that saw to it that everyone had a good time. I got a table back in one corner that was partially screened by a group of potted plants, and waited. When the waiter came over I ordered a highball, got it and waited some more.

Five minutes later a vat-dyed blonde hostess saw me there and undulated over to my table.

She gave me a big smile from too-red lips and said, 'Having fun?'

'Not so much.'

I leaned over and pulled out a chair for her. She looked around once and sat down with a sigh, using me as a breather between courses. I signalled the waiter and he brought her a Manhattan without asking. She said, 'It isn't tea, friend. You're paying for good whisky.'

'Why tell me?'

'The farmers out there have read too much about hostesses drinking cold tea. They always want to taste it. So we don't drink at all, or have a small cola.'

There wasn't much sense fooling around with chitchat here. I finished my drink, called for another, and while I waited I asked, 'Where's Murray?'

The blonde squinted her eyes at me a moment, checked her watch and shook her head. 'Beats me. He hardly ever gets here before midnight. You a friend of his?'

'Not exactly. I wanted to see him about something.'

'Maybe Bucky can help you. He's the manager when Murray's away.'

'No, he couldn't help me. You remember Nancy Sanford, don't you?'

She set her glass down easily and made little rings on the table with the wet bottom. She was looking at me curiously. 'Yes, I remember her. She's dead, you know.'

'I know. I want to find out where she lived.'

'Why?'

'Look, honey. I'm an insurance investigator. We have reason to believe that Nancy Sanford was actually somebody else. She was using a phoney name. Oh, we know all about her, all right. But if she was this somebody else, we have a policy on her we'd like to clear up. The beneficiaries stand to collect five thousand dollars.'

'But why come here?'

'Because we heard she used to work here.'

There was a sad look in the blonde's eyes this time, 'She was working in a house . . .'

'It burned down,' I interrupted.

'Then she moved over to an apartment, I think. I don't know where, but . . .'

'We checked there. That's where she lived before she died. Where was she before either one?'

'I don't know. I lost track of her after she checked out of here. Once in a while someone would mention seeing her, but I never did. I'm afraid I can't help you at all. Perhaps Murray could tell you.'

'I'll ask him,' I said. 'Incidentally, there's a reward that goes with finding the place. Five hundred bucks.'

Her face brightened at that. 'I don't get it, Mac. Five bills to find out where she lived and not who she was. What's the angle?'

'We want the place because there's someone in the neighbourhood who can positively identify her. We're having trouble now with people putting in phoney claims for the money, and we don't want to lead them to anybody before we get there first, see?'

'In other words, keep all this under my hat until I find out. If I can find out.'

'You got it.'

'I'll buy it. Stop back again soon and see if I learned anything. I'll ask around.' She finished her drink and turned on her 'having fun?' smile, waved to me and went back to the rest of the party. The kid wanted money, all right. She'd keep it under her hat and ask around. It wasn't exactly what I had come for, but it might give me a lead some time.

Five drinks and an hour and a half later Murray Candid came in. I had never seen him before, but when the waiters found something to do in a hurry and the farmers smarted chucking hullos over, looking for a smile of recognition that might impress the girlfriend, I knew the boss had come in.

Murray Candid wasn't the type to be in the racket at all. He was small and pudgy, with red cheeks, a few chins and a face that had honesty written all over it. He looked like somebody's favourite uncle. Maybe he *was* the one to be in the racket at that. The two guys that trailed him in made like they were friends of the family, but goon was the only word that fitted them. They both were young, immaculately dressed in perfectly tailored tuxedos. They flashed smiles around, shook hands with people they knew; but the way they kept their eyes going and the boss under their wing meant they were paid watch-dogs. And they were real toughies, too. Young, strong, smart with a reckless look that said they liked their job. I bet neither one of them smoked nor drank.

The band came on then, with a baby spot focused on the dance floor, and as the house lights were dimming out I saw the trio turn into an alcove over in the far corner. They were heading for the place I wanted to see – Murray Candid's office. I waited through the dance team and sat out a strip act, then paid my check and picked my way through the haze to the alcove and took the corridor that opened from it.

There were two doors at the far end. One was glass-panelled and barred, with EXIT written across it. The other was steel, enamelled to resemble wood, and there was no door-knob. Murray's office. I touched the button in the sill and if a bell rang somewhere I didn't hear it, but in a few seconds the door opened and one of the boys gave me a curt nod.

'He's in. Your name, please?'

'Martin. Howard Martin from Des Moines.'

He reached his hand to the wall and pulled down a house phone. While he called inside I felt the door. It was about three inches thick and the interior lining was of some resilient sound-proofing material. Nice place.

The guy hung up and stepped aside. 'Mr Candid will see you.' His voice had a peculiar sound: toneless, the ability to speak without accentuating any syllable. Behind me the door closed with a soft click and we were in an anteroom that had but one decoration – another door. This time he opened it and I stepped inside at once.

I was half-way across the room before I heard a cough and looked to see another door about to close. The place was lousy with doors, but not a sign of a window.

Murray Candid was half-hidden by a huge oak desk that occupied most of the wall. Behind his head were framed pictures of his floor-show stars and studio photos of dozens of celebrities, all autographed. There was a couch, a few easy chairs and a small radio and bar combination. That was all, except for the other goon that was stretched out on the couch.

'Mr Candid?'

He rose with a smile and stretched out his hand. I took it, expecting a moist, soft clasp. It wasn't. 'Mr Martin from, ah, Des Moines, is that correct?'

I said it was.

'Sit down, sir. Now, what can I do for you?'

The goon on the couch hardly turned his head to look at me, but he rasped, 'He's got a gun, Murray.'

He didn't catch me with my pants down at all. 'Natch, brother,' I agreed, 'I'm a cop. Des Moines police.' Just the same, it annoyed the hell out of me. The coat was cut to fit over the rod and you weren't supposed to notice it. These guys were pros a long time.

Murray gave me a big smile. 'You officers probably don't feel dressed unless you're armed. Now, tell me, what can I do for you?'

I sat back and lit a cigarette, taking my time. When I flicked the match into a wastebasket I was ready to pop it. 'I want a few women for a party. We're having a convention in town next month and we want things set up for a good time.'

If there was supposed to be a reaction it was a flop: Murray drew his brow into a puzzled frown and tapped his fingers on the desk. 'I don't quite understand. You said . . . girls?'

'Uh-huh.'

'But how can I . . .?'

I let him have a grin that was half-leer. 'Look, Mr Candid, I'm a cop. The boys come back home from a big time in the city and tell us all about it; they said you were the one to see about getting some girls.'

Murray's face seemed genuinely amazed. 'Me? I admit I cater to the tourist crowd, but I can't see the connection. How could I supply you with girls. I'm certainly not a – a – '

'I'm just doing like the boys said, Mr Candid. They told me to come to you.'

He smiled again. 'Well, I'm afraid they were mistaken, Mr Martin. I'm sorry I can't help you.' He stood up, indicating that the conversation was over. Only this time he didn't offer to shake hands. I told him so-long and put on my hat, letting the goon open the doors for me.

The boy gave me a polite nod when I went out and let the door hiss shut behind me. I didn't know what to think, so I went to the bar and ordered a drink. When I had it in my hand, cold and wet, I watched the bubbles fizz to the top and break.

Cold and wet. That was me all over. There wasn't a floor or wall safe in the office, nothing, for that matter, where my nice Mr Candid could hide any books if he kept any. But at least it was an elimination, supposing there *were* some books. If they weren't here they were somewhere else. Good enough . . . it was an angle worth playing.

When I finished the drink I got my hat and got clear of the joint. The air above ground wasn't very clean, but it smelled like a million bucks after the fog in the Zero Zero. Directly across the street was the Clam Hut, a tiny place that specialized in sea food and had a bar where a guy could keep one eye on his beer and the other on the street. I went in and ordered a dozen of the things and a brew and started the wait.

I had it figured for a long one, but it wasn't. Before I had half the clams down Murray Candid came out of his place alone and started walking west. His pace was more businesslike than leisurely, a cocky strut that took him up the street at a good clip. I stayed on the other side and maybe fifty feet behind him. Twice he stopped to gas with some character and I made like I was interested in a menu pasted on the window of a joint. Not that I was worried about being seen . . . there were too many people making the rounds for me to be singled out.

By the time we had walked half-way across town and cut up a few streets I figured where Murray was heading. There was a parking lot down the street on my side and he jay-walked across, angling towards it, and I had to grin. Even if he *did* spot me I had the best excuse in the world. My heap was parked in the same lot, too.

I let him go in, then trailed him by twenty feet. The attendant took my ticket and handed me my car keys, trying to keep his eyes open long enough to take his tip.

My car was down in the corner and I hugged the shadows going to it. There was no sound except that of my feet in the gravel. Somewhere a door should be slamming or a car starting, but there was nothing. There was just the jungle noise of the city hanging in the air, and the stillness you would find when the tiger crouches ready to spring.

Then I heard it, a weak cry from between a row of cars. I froze, then heard it again and in a second I was pounding towards the spot.

And I ran up a dark alley of chrome and metal into the butt end of a gun that sent me flat on my face with a yell choked off in my throat. There was no time to move, no room to move before I was being smashed across the head and shoulders. Feet were ploughing into my ribs with terrible force and the gun butt came down again and again.

I heard the sounds that got past my lips, low sounds of pain that bubbled and came out in jerks. I tried to reach up to grab something, anything at all, then a hard toe lashed out and into my cheek and my head slammed against metal and I couldn't move any more at all.

It was almost nice lying there. No pain now. Just pressures and the feeling of tearing flesh. There was no sight, no feeling. Somewhere a monotonous-sounding voice said, 'Enough this time.'

Then another voice argued a little quietly that it wasn't enough at all, but the first voice won and the pounding ceased, then even the hearing stopped. I lay there, knowing that I was asleep, yet awake, dreaming a real dream but not caring at all, enjoying a consciousness that was almost like being dead.

CHAPTER SIX

It was the first slanting rays of the sun that wakened me. They streaked across the rooftops and were reflected from the rows of plate-glass windows in the cars, bringing a warmth that took away the blessed numbness and replaced it with a thousand sharp pains.

My face was in the gravel, my hands stretched out in front of me, the fingers curled into stiff talons that took excruciating effort to straighten. By the time I had dragged myself out from under the car the sweat that bathed my face brought down rivulets of dried blood, mixing with the flesh as cuts reopened under the strain.

I sat there, swaying to the beat of thunder in my head, trying to bring my eyes into focus. Perception returned slowly, increasing proportionately with the ache that started all over and ended nowhere. I could think now, and I could remember, but remembering brought a curse that split my swollen lips again so I just sat there and thought.

The weight that was dragging me down was my gun. It was still there under my arm. A hell of a note. I never had a chance to get to it. What a damn fool I was, running into a trap like that! A plain, stupid jerk who deserved to get his head knocked off.

Somehow my watch survived with nothing more than a scratched crystal, and the hands were standing at 6.15 a.m.; I had been there the whole night. Only then did it occur to me that the cars parked there were all-nighters. Those boys had picked their spot well, damn well!

I tried to get up, but my feet didn't move well enough yet, so I slumped back to the gravel and leaned against the car gasping for breath. It hurt like hell to move even so much as an inch. My clothes were a mess, torn by their feet and the gun. One whole side of my face had been scraped raw and I couldn't touch the back of my head without wincing. My chest was on fire from the pounding my ribs had taken. I couldn't tell if any were broken . . . they felt as if there wasn't a whole one left.

I don't know how long I sat there sifting the gravel through my fingers and thinking. It might have been a minute, maybe an hour. I had a little pile of stones built up at my side, then I picked them off the pile and flicked them at the chrome wheel hub of the car opposite me. They made ping sounds when they hit.

Then one of them didn't make a ping sound and I reached out and picked it up to try again. But it wasn't a stone. It was a ring. A ring with a peculiar fleur-de-lis design, scratched and battered where it had been ground into the gravel and trampled on.

Suddenly I wasn't tired any more. I was on my feet and my lips were split into a wide-mouthed grin because the ring I was holding was the redhead's ring and somebody was going to die when they tried to get it away from me. They were going to die slower and harder than any son of a bitch had ever died before, and when they died I'd laugh my goddamn head off!

My car was where I had left it, against the back wall. I opened the door and climbed in, easing myself into a comfortable position where it wouldn't hurt so much to drive. I jerked it out of the slot and turned around, then when I went past the gate I threw two bucks into the window to pay for the overtime. The guy took the dough and never even looked up.

I thought I could make it home. I was wrong. Long before I had reached the Stem the knifing pains in my side started again and my legs could barely work the pedals. Somehow, I worked the heap across town without killing anybody, and cut up Fifty-sixth Street. There was a parking space outside Lola's place and I swung into it and killed the motor. When a couple of early risers got past me I squirmed out of the seat, slammed the door and clawed my way into the building.

The steps were torture. I was wishing I could die by the time I got to the door and punched the bell. Lola opened the door and her eyes went wide as saucers.

'My God, Mike, what happened?' She grabbed my arm and steered me inside where I could slide down on the couch. 'Mike . . . are you all right?'

I swallowed hard and nodded. 'Yeah. It's O.K. now.'

'I'll call a doctor!'

'No.'

'But, Mike . . .'

'I said no, damn it! Just let me rest up. I'll be all right.' The words came out hard.

She came over and unlaced my shoes, then lifted my feet on to the cushions. Except for her worried expression she was at her loveliest best, with another black dress that looked painted on. 'Going somewhere, kid?'

'To work, Mike. I won't now.'

'The hell you won't,' I said. 'Right now, that's more important than me. Just let me stay here until I feel better. I'm in one piece as far as I can tell and it isn't the first time I've been this way either. Go on, beat it.'

'I still have an hour yet.' Her hands went to my tie and unloosened it and took it off. She got me out of the wreck of my jacket and shirt without doing me much damage and I looked at her with surprise. 'You got a professional touch, honey,' I told her.

'Patriotism. I was a nurse's aid during the war. I'm going to clean you up.'

She lit a cigarette and stuck it between my lips, then went out to the kitchen and I heard water splashing in a pan. When she came back she carried a bowl of steaming water and an armful of towels.

My muscles were beginning to stiffen up and I couldn't take the butt out of my mouth until she did it for me. When I had a couple of deep drags she snubbed it out, then took a pair of scissors and cut through my undershirt. I was afraid to look, but I had to. There were welts along my side that were turning a deep purple. There were spots where the flesh was bruised and torn and still oozing blood. She pressed above the ribs, searching for breaks, and even that gentle pressure made me tighten up. But when she got done we both knew there were no sharp edges sticking out and I wasn't quite ready for a cast or casket yet.

The water was hot and bit deep, but it was soothing, too. She wiped my face clean and touched the cuts with a germicide, then patted it dry. I just lay there with my eyes closed and let her rub my shoulders, my arms, then my chest, grimacing when she hit a soft spot. I was almost asleep again when I felt her fingers open my belt, then my eyes opened half-way.

I said, 'Hey . . . nix . . .' but it was an effort to speak and she wouldn't stop. It hurt too much to move and there wasn't a damn thing I could do but let her undress me, so I closed my eyes again until even my socks were on the pile in the chair and her fingers were magic little feathers that were brushing the dirt and the pain away in a lather of hot, soapy water being massaged in with a touch that was almost a caress.

It was wonderful. It was so good that I fell asleep at the best part and when I woke up it was almost four o'clock in the afternoon and Lola was gone. There was a sheet over me and nothing else. At the table by my elbow was a pitcher of water with nearly melted ice cubes, a fresh deck of Luckies and a note.

When I reached out and plucked it from the ash-tray I wasn't hurting so bad. It said: 'Mike, Dear, Stay right where you are until I get home. All but your unmentionables went in the trash can anyway, so don't expect to run off on me. I took your keys and I will pick up clothes for you from your apartment. Your gun is under the sofa, but please don't shoot it off or the super will put me out. Be good. Love, Lola.'

The clothes! Hell, she couldn't have thrown them away . . . that ring was in the pocket! I tossed back the sheet and pushed myself up and began to ache again. I should have stayed there. My wallet, change and the ring were in a neat little huddle on the table behind the water pitcher.

But at least I was in a position to reach for the phone without an extra effort. I dialled the operator, asked for information, then gave her my client's name and address. The butler took the call, then put me on an extension to Mr Berin-Grotin.

His voice was cheery and alive; mine sort of crackled. 'Mike Hammer, Mr Berin.'

'Oh! Good evening, Mike. How are you?'

'Not what you'd call good. I just had the crap beat out of me.'

'What – what was that?'

'I fell for a sucker trap and got taken but good. My own fault . . . should have known better.'

'What happened?' I heard him swallow hard. Violence wasn't up his alley.

'I was steered to a guy named Murray Candid. I didn't get what I was looking for, so I followed him to a parking lot and got jumped. One of the punks thought he was being kind when he let me go on living, but I'm beginning to doubt his kindness. I'd be better off dead.'

He exploded with, 'My goodness, Mike . . . perhaps you had better not . . . I mean . . .'

If I put a laugh in my voice I was faking it. 'No dice, Mr Berin. They hurt me, but they didn't scare me. The next time I'll be on my toes. In one way I'm glad it happened.'

'Glad? I'm afraid I don't enjoy your viewpoint, Mike. This sort of thing is so . . . so uncivilized! I just don't understand . . . '

'One of the bastards was the guy who killed the redhead, Mr Berin.'

'Actually? Then you have *made* progress! But . . . how do you know?'

'He dropped the ring that he took from Red's finger before he killed her. I have it now.'

There was eagerness in his voice this time. 'Did you see him, Mike? Will you be able to identify him?'

I hated to give the bad news. 'The answer is no to both. It was darker than dark and all I saw was stars.'

'That *was* too bad. Mike . . . what do you intend doing now?'

'Take it easy for a while, I guess.' I was beginning to get tired. I said, 'Look, I'll call you back again later. I want to think about this a little while, O.K.?'

'Certainly, Mike. But please . . . this time be more careful. If anything should happen to you I would feel directly responsible.'

After I told him to quit worrying, I hung up and flopped back on the couch again, this time with the phone in my hand so I could do my talking on my back. I dialled Pat at his office, was told he had left, then picked him up at home. He was glad to hear from me and kept quiet while I went through the story for him. I gave him everything except the news of the ring.

Even at that he guessed at it. 'There's more to it than that, isn't there?'

'What makes you think so, Pat?' I asked him.

'You sound too damn satisfied for a guy who was cleaned.'

'I'm satisfied because I think I'm getting into something now.'

'Who were the guys . . . Candid's boys?'

'Could be, Pat, but I'm not sure. Maybe they had it figured out and got there ahead of us, but maybe that wasn't it at all. I have another idea.'

'Go on.'

'When I went in his office someone was just leaving . . . someone who saw me. I was following Murray and the other was following me. When he knew where Murray was going he scooted ahead in a cab with some boys and waited.'

Pat added, 'Then why didn't Murray horn in when things started to pop?'

'Because he's in a position . . . I think . . . where he has to keep his nose clean and strictly out of anybody else's business. If he knew what was going to happen he didn't care. Of course, that's figuring that he had nothing to do with it in the first place.'

'Could be,' Pat agreed. 'If we were working on more than a vague theory we could move in and find out for sure. Listen . . . you're getting more help with this than you expected.'

He made me curious. 'Yeah?'

'Uh-huh. The kid who ran into her with the car was insured. The company is positive of the cause of death and wants to pay off. Right now they're tracking down the next of kin.'

'Did you tell them anything, Pat?'

'Not a thing. They looked for themselves, got the official police report and that's that. I didn't want to make a fool of myself by telling them I let a jerky private eye talk me into murder. Those boys are pretty sharp, too. And something else. I've had tracers out on your pal.'

'Pal! . . . who?'

'Feeney Last.'

I was tingling all over and I damn near dropped the phone. Even the mention of the greaseball's name set me off.

Pat said, 'He's got a good rep . . . as far as we can tell. Not even an arrest. We found two cities on the West Coast where he was known. In both cases he was employed by businesses who needed strong-arm boys. Feeney's a trouble kid, but good. The local cops informed me that the lesser punks in town were scared stiff of him because, somehow, they got the notion he was a gun-slinger from the old school and would go out of his way to find something to shoot at. Right out of a grade-B western. Feeney played it smart by carrying a licence for the gun and the only time he was ever finger-printed was for the application.'

'But nothing you can hang on him, eh?'

'That's right, Mike.'

'What happened to the licence he had for the job with Berin-Grotin?'

'He even thought of that. It was returned in the mail. The lad isn't taking any chances.'

'So now he sticks to a chiv.'

'What?'

'You don't need a licence for a knife, chum, and Feeney likes cold steel.'

My back was aching and I was getting too tired to talk any more so I told Pat I'd call him later and hung up. I put the phone on the table and rolled into a more comfortable position, then lay there a while trying to think. The redhead's ring was in my hand and her face was in my mind, but now all the hard lines were gone and it was a pretty face that could smile with relief and anxiety.

The ring was large enough to fit my little finger. I slipped it on.

At half-past four I heard a key slide into the lock and I came out of my half-sleep with a gun in my hand and the safety kicked off. Across the knuckles was a thin red line of blood where I had caught on a nail under the sofa going for it.

But it was only Lola.

My expression scared the hell out of her and she dropped the package she was carrying. 'Mike!'

'Sorry, kid. I'm jumpy.' I dropped the rod on the table.

'I . . . brought your clothes.' She picked up the package and came over to me. When she sat down on the edge of the sofa I pulled her head down and kissed her ripe lips.

She smiled, running her fingers across my forehead. 'Feel all right?'

'Fine, honey. That sleep was just what I needed. I'll be sore for a few days, but nothing like somebody else is going to be. It's been a long time since I was jumped like that, but maybe it did me good. I'll keep my eyes open the next time and sink a slug into somebody's gut before I run up a blind alley.'

'Please don't talk like that, Mike.' A little worried frown tugged at the corners of her eyes.

'You're a beautiful girl.'

She laughed, a throaty laugh of pleasure. Then she stood up quickly, grabbed the sheet and flicked it off. 'You're beautiful, too,' she grinned devilishly.

I let out a yell and got my toga back and she only laughed again. When she started for the kitchen I opened the package and took out my clothes. I was knotting my tie when she called that soup was on. I walked into the kitchen and she said, 'I like you better the other way.'

'Quit being so fresh and feed me.'

I sat down at the table while she pulled pork chops from the pan and filled my plate. It wasn't the kind of a meal you'd expect a city girl to cook . . . there was just too much of it. I thought that maybe the whole works was for me until Lola piled it on her plate, too.

She caught my expression and nodded towards the stove. 'That's how I grew so big. Eat up and you'll get the same way.'

I was too hungry to talk at the table until I was finished. She topped it with some pie, gave me seconds while she finished her own, then took a cigarette I offered her.

'Good?' she asked.

'The best. Makes me feel almost new.'

She dragged on the cigarette hungrily. 'Where away, Mike?'

'I'm not sure. First I want to find out why I was worked over. Then I want to find out who did it.'

'I told you Candid was dangerous.'

'That fat monkey isn't dangerous, honey. It's his dough. That's dangerous. It hires people to get things done he can't do himself.'

'I still wouldn't trust him too far. I've heard stories about Murray that weren't nice to hear. You looked for the books, didn't you?'

'No,' I told her. 'He wouldn't keep them in sight. I looked for a place he could stash 'em, but there wasn't even a sign of a safe in the joint. No, that trip was just reconnoitring. Those boys aren't dummies by a long shot. *If* they have any books – and I still think it's a big "if" – they're some place that will take a lot of heavy digging to root out.'

I leaned back in the chair and pulled on the butt. It still hurt to sit up straight, but I was getting over it fast. 'Supposing I do get something on Candid . . . where does it get me? It's a killer I want, not a lot of sensational stuff for the papers.'

This time I was talking to myself rather than to Lola, trying to get things straight in my mind. So far it was just a jumble of facts that could all be important, but it was like going up an endless ladder. Each rung led to the next one with the top nowhere in sight.

'So the redhead was killed. She was killed for a reason. She had a ring on while she was alive, but it wasn't there when she was dead. It was a beautiful kill, too . . . how the hell it happened I don't know, but I'll find out. The killer has a perfect cover-up and it's listed as accidental death. If she was pushed somebody would have seen her get it, or even in his damn drunken stupor the kid who ran her down would have remembered it. But no . . . he thought he did it all alone and took off from there. He remembered enough to cover it up so he would have remembered if she were pushed. But what dame is going to take her ring off? Women aren't like that! And one of those jokers who jumped me had it, so it makes it a legitimate kill and not an accidental one.

'Bats! If it wasn't murder, nobody would give a damn any more, but why did she have to get it? What made her so all-fired important that she had to die? So Feeney Last had his blackmail junk lifted . . . yet you say she wouldn't buy that kind of stuff. She was hot, according to another guy, and nobody would go near her. Feeney's a tough character and has the bull on guys to the extent that they won't talk. But what are they afraid of? Getting beat up, maybe? Or getting shot? Hell's bells, nobody can go around shooting people up in this town. Sure, it's a rough place to be in trouble, but pull a rod and see how far you get! Maybe you can scare somebody for a while, but after a bit the scare wears off and you got to prove you're not kidding. So who would be the guy that could do it and get away with it? Just one – a jerk who thinks he's got enough protection to carry him through.'

For the first time Lola interrupted. 'Is that Feeney Last?'

'Maybe. He's supposed to be a gunman. But he's still no dummy. He proved that by turning in his gun licence when he lost his job with Berin.'

She agreed with a slight nod. 'You think, then, that he might have killed Nancy?'

'That, sugar, is something I'd give a lot to know,' I answered. 'It's a screwy affair, but there's something pretty big at the bottom of it. For somebody to be wiped out, the cause has to be a heavy one. There's too many ways of doing business without being eligible for the chair – unless the risk is worth it.'

'And Nancy was a good risk?'

'What do you think, Lola?'

'You might be right. At least you have her death to prove you're right, but poor Nancy . . . I still can't see why she could be so important . . . to have to die. I told you she had a secretive side . . . but still, if she weren't what she was, Nancy could have been a decent kid. By that I mean she had all the aspects of quality. She was a gentle, kind, considerate . . . oh, you know what I mean.'

'But she seemed to be in the business for a reason. Correct?'

'That's right.'

'You don't think she was getting back at a man . . . doing it to spite a former lover or something?'

'Of course not! She had more sense than that!'

'All right, I was just asking.'

She leaned on the table and looked at me, long and hard. Her voice was husky again. 'Mike . . . just what kind of people are they that kill?'

'Dirty people, kid,' I said. 'They have minds that don't care any more. They put something else above the price of human life and kill to get it, then kill to keep it. But no matter what it is it's never worth the price they have to pay for it.'

'You've killed people, Mike.'

I felt my lips pulling back. 'Yeah, and I'm going to kill some more, Lola. I hate the lice that run the streets without even being scratched. I'm the guy with the spray gun and they hate me, too, but even if I am a private op I can get away with it better than they can. I can work the bastards up to the point where they make a try at me and I can shoot in self-defence and be cleared in a court of law. The cops can't go that far, but they'd like to, don't forget it. People are always running down the police, but they're all right guys that are tied down by a mass of red tape and they have to go through channels. Sure, there are bum cops, too – not many of them. They get disgusted maybe, because things happen that they have to let happen, yet any one of them boils over inside when he sees mugs get away with stuff that would hang a decent citizen.'

Her eyes were looking past me now with an eager, intense look. 'What can I do to help?' she whispered.

'Think, Lola. Think over every conversation you ever had with Nancy. Think of the things she might have said or implied. See if you can pick out just one thing that may be important. Then tell me.'

'I will, Mike, I will. But how will I know if it's important?'

I reached over and laid my hand on hers. 'Look, kid . . . I hate to bring it up, but you were in a money racket. It was a no-good racket, but it brought in the dough. Anything that might have interfered with that income to certain people could be a cause of death, even if it was something they just suspected. When you think of anything that *could* be that something, you're getting warm.'

'I think I understand, Mike.'

'Good girl!' I stood up and stuffed my butts back into my pocket. 'You know where to call me. Don't go out of your way for anything unless it's mighty important, I don't want you to get on anybody's list.'

Lola pushed her chair back and came to me. Together we walked towards the door. 'Why?' she asked. 'Do I mean that much to you, Mike?'

She was lovelier than ever, tall and graceful, with a hidden depth to her eyes as she looked at me. I could feel the firm roundness of her pressing against my body and I folded my arms around her. 'You mean more than you think to me, Lola. Anybody can be wrong. Not everybody can be right again. You're one in a million.'

Her eyes swirled in a film of tears then, and her face was soft as she touched her cheek to mine. 'Please don't, darling. I've got so far to go before I'll ever be right for anyone. Just be nice to me . . . but don't be too nice. I – I don't think I could stand it.'

There was no answering her with words. I reached for her mouth and felt the fire in her lips that ran like a fuse down her body until she curved inward against me with a fierce undulation, and I knew my hands were hurting her and she didn't care.

It was hard to push her away; it was hard for her to let go. I shoved my hat on my head and squeezed her hand without saying anything, but we both knew of the promise it held and I went out of there walking as if there had been no last night at all and my body wasn't stiff and sore nor my face battered and swollen.

CHAPTER SEVEN

There was a parking ticket under the windshield wiper of the car staring me in the face. I pulled it off, read it over and stuck it in the glove compartment. Another few hours to be wasted in a police court. I sat there a minute, my hands on the wheel, trying to line things up in order. Hell, there was no order. I was like the chairman of a meeting trying to rap for quiet with a rubber gavel, when the whole assembly was on its feet shouting to be heard.

Red's ring was there on my finger, a tiny circlet of gold that had slipped around until it looked like a wedding band. I straightened it, held it out in the dimming light to look at it better, wishing the thing could speak. All right, maybe it could – maybe. I jammed the car in gear, pulled up to Ninth Avenue and turned south.

By the time I reached the downtown section most of the smaller shops had closed. I cruised the avenue slowly, looking for a jewellery shop run by an old friend of mine. I found it by luck, because the front had been done over and the lights were out and he was getting ready to go home.

When I banged on the door he twitched the shade aside, recognized me with a big grin and unlocked the door. I said, 'Hullo, Nat. Got time for a few words?'

He was all smiles; a small pudgy man who took prosperity in the same alpaca coat and shiny pants as he did the leaner years. His hand was firm around mine as he waved me in. 'Mike,' he laughed, 'for you I have plenty of time. Come in the back. We talk about old times?'

I put my arm around his shoulders. 'About times now, Nat. I need some help.'

'Sure, sure! Here, sit down.' He pulled out a chair and I slid into it while he opened a bottle of wine and poured a drink for us both.

We toasted each other, then spilled it down. Good wine. He filled the glasses again, then leaned back and folded his hands across his stomach.

'Now, Mike, what is it that I can do for you? Something not so exciting like the last when you made me be bait to trap those chiselling crooks, I hope.'

I grinned and shook my head as I pulled off the redhead's ring and handed it to him. Automatically, his fingers dipped into his vest pocket and came up with a jeweller's glass that he screwed into his eye.

I let him turn it over several times, look at it carefully, then told him, 'That's the job, Nat. Can that ring be traced?'

He was silent for several minutes as he examined every detail of the band, then the glass dropped into his palm and he shook his head. 'Antique. If it has a peculiar history maybe . . .'

'No history.'

'That is too bad, Mike. It is very important that you should know?'

'Very.'

'What I should say, I don't know. I have seen many rings of this type before, so I am quite certain I am right. However, I am just one man . . .'

'You're good enough for me, Nat. What about it?'

'It is a woman's ring. Never inscribed as far as I can see, but maybe an inscription has been worn off. Notice the colour of the gold, see? The composition of the metal is not what is used today to harden gold. I would say that this ring is perhaps three hundred years old. Maybe more, even. It is more durable than most rings, otherwise the pattern would have been worn off completely. However, it is not as pretty as the gold nowadays. No, I am sorry, Mike, but I cannot help you.'

'The pattern, Nat; know anybody who could trace that?'

'If you found the company that made it . . .' he shrugged, 'their records might go back. But see . . . three hundred years means it was made in the Old Country. What with the war and the Nazis. . . .' He shrugged again, hopelessly this time. I nodded agreement and he went on, 'In those days there were no big companies, anyway. It was a father-and-son business. For a ring like this it was a special order and that is all.'

I took the ring back and slipped it on my finger again. 'Well, Nat, it was a good try just the same. At least I cut down a lot of unnecessary footwork.'

His pudgy face warped into a quizzical frown. 'Do not the police have methods to bring out inscriptions that have been worn off, Mike?'

'Yeah, they can do it, but suppose I do find a set of initials. Those would belong to the original owner, and since it's a woman's ring, and no doubt passed down through the family, how often would the name have changed? No, the inscription wouldn't do much good, even if I did find the original owner. It was just an idea I had.' If it hadn't been an antique it might have solved the problem. All it did was set me up in the other alley wondering where the hell I was.

I stood up to leave and stuck my hand out. Nat looked disappointed. 'So soon you must go, Mike? You could come home with me and maybe meet the wife. It has been a year since the last time.'

'Not tonight, Nat. I'll stop back some other time. Say hullo to Flo for me, and the kids.'

'I'll do that. Them kids, they be pretty mad I don't bring you home.'

I left him standing there in the doorway and climbed back in the car. Red's ring was winking at me, and I could see it on her finger again as she graced a battered old coffee cup.

Damn it! . . . I had the key and I couldn't find the lock! Why the devil would a killer take this thing off her finger? What good was it to him if it couldn't be traced? And who was the goon that carried it around with him until he lost it? Hell's bells, it couldn't be a red herring across the path or it never would have turned up again!

My mind was talking back to me then. One part of me drove the car away from the kerb and stopped for red lights. The other part was asking just why I got beat up at all? Yeah, why did I? And why was it planned so nicely? Oh, it was planned quick, but very, very nice! I wasn't important enough to kill, but I did warrant a first-class going-over. A warning?

Sure! What else?

Murray and his boys didn't know me from Adam, but they spotted a phoney in my story and figured me as a wise guy, or somebody with an angle, so it was a warning to steer clear. And one of the goons who had done this warning had killed the redhead or was tied up with it some way.

I was uptown without knowing it. I had crossed over and was following a path I had taken once before, and when I slowed down outside the parking lot I knew what I was after.

I made a U-turn and parked at the kerb across the street, then walked to the corner, waited for the light to change and strolled to the other side. I couldn't be sure if the attendant was the same one who was on the other night; at least this one was awake.

He opened the window when I rapped on it and I said, 'Anybody lose anything in here recently, bud?'

The guy shook his head. 'Just a guy what lost his car keys. Why, find something?'

'Yes, but there's no money involved. A little trinket a dame might like to have back. Just thought I'd ask.'

'Check the ads in the papers. If she wants it bad enough maybe she'll advertise. Got it with you?'

'Naw. Left it home.'

He said, 'Oh!' shut the window and went back to his chair. I started to walk away, but before I reached the building that bordered the lot a car turned in and its lights cut a swath down the rows. I saw a pair of legs jump back from the glare and duck in among the cars.

I stopped flat.

The legs had gone up the same row I had run into last night.

My heart started doing a little dance and the other part of me was saying go to it, that's why you came here in the first place. Maybe you got your hands on something, only don't botch it up this time. Take it easy and keep your eyes open and a gun in your fist.

The car turned its lights out and a door slammed. Feet started walking back towards the gate, and a fat guy in a Homburg said something to the man in the booth, laughed and angled across the street. I waited a second, then put my hands on the fence and hopped over.

This time I didn't take any chances. I stayed between the cars and the wall, keeping my head down and my footsteps soft. Twice the gravel crunched under my shoes and I stopped dead, listening. Two rows up I heard a soft shuffling sound and a shoe kick metal.

I reached inside my coat and loosened the gun in the holster.

The guy was too busy to hear me. He was down on one knee sifting the gravel through his fingers, his back towards me. I stood up from the crouch I was in and waited as he inched his way back.

Another car turned into the lot and he froze, holding his position until it had parked and the driver had left the lot, then he went back to his sifting. I could have reached out and touched him then.

I said, 'Lost something?'

He tried to get up so fast he fell flat on his face. He made it on the second try and came up swinging, only this time I was ready. I smashed one into his mouth and the guy slammed against the car, but that didn't stop him. I saw his left looping out and got under it and came into him with a sharp one-two that doubled him over. I didn't try to play it clean. I brought my knee up and smashed his nose to a pulp and when he screamed he choked on his own blood.

I bent over and yanked him up and held him against the car, then used my fist on his face until his hands fell away and he was out with his eyes wide open.

When I let go he folded up and sat in the gravel staring into the dark.

I lit a match and cupped it near his face, or what was left of it. Then I swore under my breath. I had never seen the guy in my life before. He was young, and he might have been handsome, and the clothes he wore weren't the ready-made type. I swore again, patted his sides to see if he had a rod, and he didn't. Then I lifted his wallet. It was hand-tooled morocco, stuffed with dough, a few cards and a driver's licence issued to one Walter Welburg. Out of curiosity I tapped his pockets and there weren't any keys in them. Maybe the guy *was* looking for that.

Damn! I blew the match out, went down past the cars and hopped over the fence feeling like a dummy.

I left the car where it was and headed across town on the same walk that had taken me into the trap, only this time I wasn't tailing anybody. The street was getting lousy with taxis, and the evening crowd was just beginning to show its face. Already the dives had their doors open like gaping mouths swallowing the suckers, and the noise of a dozen bands reached the sidewalk. Ahead of me the Zero Zero Club was a winking eye of invitation, and the flunky was opening taxi doors, picking himself a hatful of quarters. He didn't see me duck in, so he lost a two-bit tip.

The hat-check girl gave me a bored smile and a ticket, then when she saw the marks on the side of my face she grinned, 'What's the matter . . . she say no and you didn't believe her?'

I grinned right back. 'I was fighting her off, kid.'

She leaned over on the counter and propped her chin in her hands, giving me a full view of what went on down the neckline of her blouse. It was plenty. 'I don't blame her for fighting for it, feller,' she said. 'I'd fight, too.'

'You wouldn't have to.'

I blew her a kiss and she made like she caught it and stuffed it down her neckline. Her eyes got dark and sensuous and she said, 'You have to come back for your hat. Maybe I'll trade you . . . even.'

A couple in evening clothes came in and she turned to them while I went inside. Most of the tables around the dance floor were filled, and a baby spot played over a torch singer who was making more music with her hips than her throat. Neither Murray nor his boys were anywhere around so I found a table in the back and ordered a highball and watched the show.

The waiter brought the drink and before I sipped it half-way through a hand went through my hair and I looked up to see my blonde hostess smiling at me. I started to rise but she pushed me back and pulled the other chair out and sat down.

'I've been looking for you,' she said.

She leaned over and took a cigarette from my pack and tapped it on the table. When I lit it for her she blew a stream of smoke into the air. 'You spoke of five hundred bucks the last time. . . .'

'Go on.'

'Maybe I can deliver.'

'Yeah?'

'But not for five hundred bucks.'

'Holding me up?'

'Could be.'

'What have you got? Five hundred can get me a lot of things.'

The torch singer was coming to the end of the number and the blonde took another drag on the butt, then rubbed it out in the ash-tray. 'Look, get out of here before the lights go on. I'll be through here at one o'clock and you can pick me up on the corner. We can go up to my place and I'll tell you about it.'

'O.K.'

'And you better bring more than five hundred.'

'I'll see what I can do,' I told her.

She smiled at me and laid her hand over mine. 'You know, you seem like a pretty nice joe, mister. See you at one.'

I didn't wait for the lights to go on. I threw the rest of the drink down, waved the waiter over and paid him, then went out to the foyer. The kid at the hat window gave me a mock scowl. 'You're too eager. I don't get off for hours yet.'

I threw a half in the cup while she retrieved my hat, and when she handed it to me she took that stance that showed

103

me where she put the kiss I threw her. And she didn't mind my looking.

I took out a bill, folded it lengthwise and poked it down there out of sight. 'If the boss doesn't find it you can keep it.'

'He'd never think of looking there,' she grinned devilishly. She stood up and there was no trace of the green at all, 'But you can have it back if you want to chase it.'

This time I pushed my hat on my head and started for the door. Hell, I was no Indian giver. But maybe the Indians had something if they played games like that.

My watch said I had a long while to wait, so I cut over two blocks and found a bar that had a few empty stools. I ordered a beer and a sandwich twice, then started in to enjoy a mild evening, but I kept drifting back to the blonde. Something was going to cost me and I hoped it was worth it. Five hundred bucks, just half my fee. It took me two hours to make up my mind, then I went to the phone booth in the back, dropped in a nickel and asked for long-distance.

The operator came on and I gave her my client's number. The gnome squeaked out a hullo, told me Mr Berin had retired for the night, but when I insisted I wanted to speak to him, put the phone down and shuffled off muttering to himself. I had just finished putting in another handful of dimes when Mr Berin gave me a sleepy 'Good evening.'

'This is Mike, Mr Berin. Sorry I had to disturb you, but something important has come up.'

'It did? Is it something I should know?'

'Well, yes. It concerns money.'

He chuckled, the tiredness out of his voice. 'Then I'm glad to be of use to you, Mike. What is it?'

'I may have a line on the redhead. For a dodge I offered a dame five bills. . . .'

'What was that?'

'Five hundred bucks . . . if she did some successful snooping. Apparently she did. But now she wants more. Shall I go for it or do I try to get it out of her some other way?'

'But . . . what is it? Did she . . .?'

'She wouldn't talk. Wants me to meet her later.'

'I see.' He thought a moment. Then, 'What do you think, Mike?'

'It's your show, Mr Berin, but I'd say look it over and if it's worth anything, buy it.'

'Then you think it's worth something?'

'I'd take that chance. The dame's a hostess in the Zero Zero and she knew Nancy. At least she knew her quite a while ago and it looks as if that's where the bones lie buried.'

'Then do it, Mike. The sum is trivial enough . . . at least to me. You, er, look it over, and do what you think is best.'

'O.K., but she wants the dough right away.'

'Very well. You write her a cheque, then call me, and I'll wire that amount to your bank so it will be there in the morning to cover it.'

'Right. I'll buzz you later. Take it easy.'

I stuck the phone back in its cradle and went back to the bar. At twelve-thirty I gathered up my change, whistled at a cab outside and had him drive me over to where I left my heap.

It was five minutes past one when I cruised past the corner and saw the blonde coming towards the kerb. I rolled the window down and yelled for her to hop in. She recognized me, opened the door and slid on to the seat.

'Nice timing. Where to?' I pulled away from the kerb and got into the line of traffic going uptown.

'Straight ahead. I have a place on Eighty-ninth.'

She had a beat-up overnight bag between her feet and I indicated it with a nod. 'That the stuff?'

'Uh-huh.' The blonde opened her purse and pulled out a lipstick. There wasn't much light, but she seemed to be getting it on straight. When I stopped for a red I took a good look at her. Not a bad number at all. The curves looked real and in some spots too good to be true.

She turned her head and looked straight into my eyes, then let a little grin play with the corners of her mouth. 'Curious?'

'About the bag?'

'About me?'

'I'm always curious about blondes.'

She waited to see what I was going to do then, but the light turned green and I rolled with the traffic. At Eighty-ninth I turned over until she told me to stop, then pulled into the kerb and killed the engine. When I opened the door for her I picked up the bag and let her step out.

'You wouldn't think of running off with that, would you?' She hooked her arm in mine.

'I thought of it, then I got curious.'

'About the bag?'

'About you.' Her hand squeezed mine and we walked to the apartment. At the door she fished out a key, opened it, then led me upstairs two flights to a front apartment and flicked on the light.

It was an old high-ceilinged affair done over in a welter of curves and angles the designers call modern. Each wall was a different colour of pastel with tasteful but inexpensive pictures in odd groupings. The furniture looked awkward, but it was comfortable enough.

When I threw my hat over a lamp the blonde said, 'Shouldn't we introduce ourselves? I'm Ann Minor.' She shrugged out of her coat, looking at me peculiarly.

'Mike Hammer, Ann. I'm not an insurance investigator. I'm a private cop.'

'I know. I was wondering if you were going to tell me.' Her laugh was one of relief.

'Who told you that?'

'Me. I knew damn well I had seen you or your picture somewhere before. It didn't come to me until tonight, though.'

'Oh!'

'It was your picture.'

'Was that why you shooed me out of the joint so fast?'

'Yes.'

'Murray isn't fond of cops, not even private ones.'

'What has a legitimate businessman got to be afraid of?'

'Say that again and leave out one word.'

I didn't. I sat there on the arm of a chair and watched her. She hung her coat in a closet, took my hat from the lamp and put it on the shelf and closed the door. Then she turned around fast and walked over to me.

'I'm no kid,' she said. 'I don't think I ever was a kid. You weren't in the club looking for a good time and I knew it. When you mentioned Nancy I had a pretty good idea what you were after, and I get the wim-wams when I think about getting mixed up in anything. Tell me something, how good are you?'

I had a .45 out and pointed at her stomach almost before she finished the sentence. When she had a good look at it I slid it back in the leather and waited. Her eyes were wider than before.

'I hate Murray. There are other guys I hate too, but he's the only one I can point to and say I'm sure I hate. Him and his butt boys.'

'What have *you* got against him?'

'Don't play coy, Mike. He's a rat. I don't like what he does to people. You know what he is or you wouldn't be here now.'

'What did he do to you?'

'He didn't do anything to me. But I saw what he did to other kids. He pays my salary and that's all, but I have to stand by and watch what happens in that place. He's a smooth talker, but he always gets what he wants.'

My fingers were itching to get to the bag on the floor and she knew it. Ann smiled again, reading my mind, then she tapped the wallet in my inside pocket. 'Bring the money?'

'As much as I could get.'

'How much?'

'That depends on what's in it. What are you going to do with the stake?'

'Take a long trip, maybe. Anything to get away from this town. I'm sick of it.'

I walked over and picked up the bag. It wasn't very heavy. There were paint splotches across the top and long scuffed streaks down the side. Maybe here was the answer. Maybe this was the reason the redhead was killed. I ran my hand across the top, tried the catch, but it was locked. 'Yours?' I asked her.

'Nancy's, Mike. I came across it this morning. We have a small prop-room behind the bandstand that's full of junk. I was hunting for some stuff for the dressing-room when I came across it. There was a bus tag on the handle with Nancy's name on it and I knew it was hers.'

'How did it get in there?'

'A long time ago Murray remodelled the place. Probably Nancy was off at the time and when they cleaned out they tossed all the odds and ends in the prop-room. I imagine she figured she lost it.'

Ann went outside and came back with a bottle and two glasses. We both had a drink in silence, then she filled the glasses again and settled into the corner of a sofa and watched me. The way she sat there reminded me of a cat, completely at ease, yet hiding the tension of a coiled spring. Her dress was loose at the shoulders, tapering into a slim waist that was a mass of invitation. She sipped her drink, then drew her legs up under her, letting me see that not even the sheerest nylon could enhance the firm roundness of her thighs. When she breathed, her breasts fought the folds of her dress and I waited to see the battle won.

'Aren't you going to open it?' Her voice was taunting.

'I need an ice pick . . . a chisel – something.' It wasn't easy to speak.

She put her drink on the end table and uncoiled from the couch. She passed too close and I reached out and stopped her, but I didn't have to make the effort because she was in my arms, her mouth burning on mine, pulling herself so close that I could feel every part of her rubbing against me deliciously. I tangled my fingers in her hair and pulled her head back to kiss her neck and shoulders, and she moaned softly, her body a live, passionate thing that quivered under my hands.

When I let her go her eyes were smouldering embers ready to flame; then she gave me that quick smile that showed her teeth white and even, and she drew her tongue deliberately over full, ripe lips that wanted to be kissed some more, until they glistened wetly and made me want to reach out and stop her again.

Before I could, she went out through an archway and I heard her rummage around in a drawer, pawing through cutlery until she found what she wanted. The drawer closed, but she didn't come right back. When she did the dress was gone and she had on a clinging satin robe and nothing else, and she passed in front of the lamp to be sure I knew it.

'Like it?' she asked me.

'On you, yes.'

'And on someone else?'

'I'd still like it.'

She handed me one of those patented gadgets that was supposed to solve every household mechanical difficulty, even to a stuck window. I took it while she fished in my pocket for a cigarette and fired it from a table-lighter. She blew the smoke in my face and said, 'Can't that wait?'

I kissed the tip of her nose. 'No, honey, it can't.'

When I turned around and stuck the edge of the gadget under the clasp of the lock she walked away from me. I pried at the metal until the tool bent in my hand, then reversed it and used the other end. This time I was in luck. The hasp made a sharp snapping sound and flew open. The outside snaps were corroded where the plating hadn't peeled off, but they opened easily enough; but before I could open the bag the light snapped off and there was only the dim glow from the table-lamp at the other end of the room.

Ann whispered, 'Mike?'

I looked around to bark something at her, but nothing would come out because Ann had thrown the robe over the back of the couch and stood there in the centre of the room, a living statue in high-heeled shoes smoking a cigarette that reflected orange-coloured lights from her eyes. She stood with her feet spread apart and her hand on her hip, daring me with every muscle in her body.

She stood there until I grabbed her and squeezed so hard she breathed into my mouth, then she bit me on the neck and slid out of my hands to the couch. I had to follow her.

My hand shook when I reached for a cigarette. Ann grinned up at me, and her voice was soft, almost musical. 'I was wondering if I could be important to anybody anymore.'

I kissed her again. 'You can be important anytime. You happy now that you steered me right off the track?'

'Yes.'

She didn't say a word when I stood up and went back to the table, but her eyes followed me every second. I dragged on the cigarette again, but it caught in my chest and I put it out. This time I laid the case down and flipped open the lid.

I whistled softly under my breath. The bag was crammed full of baby clothes, every one brand-new. I fingered them slowly, the tiny sweaters, boots, caps, other things I had no name for. At the bottom of the bag were two soft cotton blankets, neatly folded, waiting to be used.

A dozen thoughts were going through my head, but only one made any sense. The redhead was a mother. Somebody was the father. A wonderful, beautiful set-up for blackmail and murder if ever I saw one. Only Nancy wasn't that kind of a girl. Then there was one other thing. All the clothes were new. Some of them showed where price tags had been glued on. What about that?

I ran my hand through the pockets of the lining. The ones on the side brought up an assortment of safety pins, a lipstick and a small mirror. The lid pocket held a folder of snapshots. I opened them out and looked at them, seeing a Nancy different from the one I had known. Here was a young girl, sixteen perhaps, on the beach with a boy. Then another with a different boy. Several had been taken on an outing or a picnic, but Nancy seemed to show no special preference for any one fellow.

She was different then, with the freshness of a newly opened flower. There were no harsh lines in her face, no wise look about the eyes. She was new then, new and lively. Her mouth

110

and eyes seemed to smile at me, as if knowing that some day these pictures would be here in front of me. There were only two that showed her hands clearly, but in each one I saw the same thing. She was wearing her ring.

I looked over the backgrounds carefully, hoping to spot some landmark, but there was none. They showed only stretches of water or sand. When I flipped them over there were no marks indicating date or the outfit that developed them. Nothing. Now my blind alley had a wall at the end. A nice high wall that I couldn't get over without a ladder.

I heard Ann speak to me then. She asked, 'Does it help you?'

An idea was beginning to jell and I nodded. I pulled out my cheque-book and wrote in it, then laid the slip on the table. I made up my mind as to the value, but just the same I queried, 'What are you asking for it?'

When she didn't answer I turned around and looked at her, still lying there naked and smiling. Finally she said, 'Nothing. You've paid for it already.'

I snapped the bag shut and went over to the closet for my hat, then opened the door. The redhead had been right all along the line; but Mr Berin still owed me five hundred bucks, to be deposited in the morning. Ann would get that trip she wanted.

I winked at her and she winked back, then the door clicked shut behind me.

CHAPTER EIGHT

I didn't get to sleep that night. Instead, I laid the contents of the bag out in front of me and sat there smoking one cigarette after another, trying to figure out what it meant. Baby clothes. Some pictures. A battered overnight bag. All of them the redhead's. How long ago? Where? Why?

There was beer in the refrigerator and I finished off bottle after bottle, sipping it slowly, thinking, letting my mind wander back and forth over the facts I had. They were mighty little when you tried to put them all together.

The sun came up over the window-sill chasing the night out, and I remembered to call Mr Berin. He answered the phone himself and this time the sleep was in my voice. 'Mike again.'

'Good morning! You're up early.'

'I haven't been to bed yet.'

'You'll pay for lack of self-discipline in later years, young man.'

'Maybe,' I said tonelessly, 'but tonight you pay. I left my friend a cheque for five hundred bucks.'

'Fine, Mike. I'll take care of it at once. Did you learn anything from your – shall I say, source?'

'Not a damn thing, but I will, I will.'

'Then I can consider the money well spent. But please be careful. I don't want you running into any more trouble.'

'Trouble's an occupational hazard in this racket, Mr Berin. I can usually take care of it one way or another. But what I got here won't mean trouble for me. I haven't got the angle lined up yet, but I can see it coming.'

'Good! You've got my curiosity aroused now. Is it a secret or can you . . .?'

'No secret. I have an overnight bag that had been packed with baby clothes. That and a folder of pictures.'

113

'Baby clothes?'

'They were the redhead's – or her baby's.'

He mulled over it a moment and admitted that it presented quite a puzzle, quite a puzzle. I agreed with him.

'What do you intend to do now?' he asked me.

'I don't know. I'm too sleepy to do much, that's for sure.'

'Then go to bed by all means. Keep in touch with me whenever you think I can be of use.'

I said all right and hung up. My eyes were burning holes in my head and too much beer had me stumbling over things. I took a last drag on the butt and clinched it, then lay back on the couch and let the sleep come, wonderful, blessed sleep that pulled a curtain over all the ugly things and left you with nothing but a nebulous dream that had no meaning or importance.

There was a bell. It kept ringing insistently and I tried to brush it away like a fly and it wouldn't leave. Finally I opened my eyes and came back to the present with the telephone going off behind my head. I squirmed around and picked it up, wanting to throw it against the wall.

Velda said hullo twice, and when I didn't answer right away, 'Mike . . . is that you? Mike, answer me!'

'It's me, sugar. What do you want?'

She was mad, but there was relief in her voice. 'Where the devil have you been? I've been calling every saloon in town all morning.'

'I've been right here.'

'I called there four times.'

'I've been asleep.'

'Oh, out all night again. Who was she?'

'Green eyes, blue hair, purple skin. What do you want, or aren't I the boss any more?'

'Pat called early this morning. Something to do with Feeney Last. He wants you to call him back when you can.'

'Well, why didn't you say so!' I sat up quickly, my hand over the cut-off bar. 'See you later, Velda. I'll buzz him right away.'

I held the bar down, let it up and dialled police head-quarters. The guy at the desk said yes, Captain Chambers had been in, but he wasn't now. No, he couldn't say where he was. Official business, and did I want to leave a message. I wanted to swear, but I couldn't very well so I told him never mind and hung up.

It was five minutes to twelve and the day was half-shot. I gathered up the baby clothes and folded them back into the bag, stuffing the photos in the same top pocket, then I went in and took a shower.

Right in the middle of it the phone rang again and I had to wade back into the living-room. It was Pat, but I didn't lace into him for dragging me out of the tub because I was too anxious to get the news.

He chuckled when I answered and said, 'What kind of hours do you keep, pal?'

'If you knew you'd want to change jobs with me. Velda said you have something on Feeney. What gives?'

He got right down to cases. 'When I put out feelers on him they all came back negative. This morning I had one in the mail from the Coast, a return feeler from an upstate sheriff. It seems like Feeney Last answers the description of a guy who is wanted for murder. The only catch is that the guy who could identify him is dead and they have to go from the poop he gave them.'

'That's something.' I thought it over, knowing that a mug like Feeney wouldn't be hard to describe. A greaseball. 'What are you going to do about it?'

'I wrote for the finer details. If it fits we'll put out a call for him. I had copies made of his picture on the gun licence and forwarded them to the sheriff to see if Feeney could be identified there.'

'At least it's handy to have, Pat. He can always be held for suspicion if we need him . . . and if we can find him.'

'O.K., then, I just thought I'd let you know. I have a death on my hands and I have to do the report.'

'Anybody we know?' I asked.'

'Not unless you hang around the tourist traps. She was a hostess at the Zero Zero Club.'

My hand tightened around the receiver. 'What did she look like, Pat?'

'Bleached blonde about thirty. Nice looking, but a little on the hard side. The coroner calls it suicide. There was a farewell note in her handbag along with complete identification.'

I didn't need to know her name. There might have been a dozen bleached blondes in the Zero Zero, but I was willing to bet anything I had I knew who this one was. I said, 'Suicide, Pat?'

He must have liked the flatness of my words. He came back with, 'Suicide beyond doubt, Mike. Don't try to steer this one into murder!'

'Was her name Ann Minor?'

'Yes . . . you . . . how did . . .?'

'Is the body in the morgue?'

'That's right.'

'Then meet me there in twenty minutes, hear?'

It took me forty-five minutes to get there and Pat was pacing up and down outside the place. When he saw my face his eyes screwed up and he shook his head disgustedly. 'I hope they don't try to keep you here,' he said. 'I've seen better-looking corpses than you.'

He went inside, over to the slab where the body was laid out. Pat pulled back the sheet and waited. 'Know her?'

I nodded.

'Anything to do with the Sanford case?'

I nodded again.

'Damn you, Mike. One day the coroner is going to beat your head off. He's positive she was a suicide.'

I took the corner of the sheet from his hand and covered her face up again. 'She was murdered, too, Pat.'

'O.K., pal, let's go some place and talk about it. Maybe over lunch.'

'I'm not hungry.' I was thinking of how she looked last night. She had wanted to be important to someone. To me. She was important to someone else, too.

Pat tugged at my sleeve. 'Well, I'm hungry and murder won't spoil my dinner any. I want to know how a pretty suicide like this can be murder.'

There was a spaghetti joint a few blocks away so we walked over to it. Pat ordered a big lunch and I had a bottle of red wine for myself. After the stuff was served I started the ball rolling with, 'What's your side of it, Pat?'

'Her name is Ann Minor . . . which you seemed to know. She worked for Murray Candid as a hostess four years. Before that a dancing career in lesser clubs, and before that a tour with a carnival as a stripper. Home life, nil. She had a furnished apartment uptown and the super said she was a pretty decent sort.

'The last few months she's been a little down in the dumps, according to her co-workers, but nothing to indicate positively a suicide. The farewell note said she was just tired of it all, life was a bore and she was getting no place, thus the Dutch act. The handwriting checked with the signature on other documents.'

'Baloney!'

'No baloney, Mike. The experts checked it.'

'Then they'd better check it again.'

Pat let his eyes drop when he saw the set of my mouth. 'I'll see that they do.' He went back to his spaghetti, forked in a mouthful, then reviewed the case. 'We reconstruct it this way. Just before dawn she walked down the pier that's being dismantled off Riverside Drive, removed her hat, shoes, jacket . . . laid them down on the planks with her bag on top, and jumped in.

'Apparently she couldn't swim. However, even if she could, she would have drowned because her dress was caught on some bolts below the surface and held her there. About eight-thirty this morning some kids came along to do some fishing and they spotted her stuff first, then her. One of the kids called a cop who called the emergency squad. They didn't bother to work on her.'

'How long had she been dead?'

'Roughly, about four to five and a half hours.'

I poured another glass of the wine out and spilled it down. 'I was with her until two forty-five last night,' I said.

Pat's eyes blazed and he stabbed his fork into the pile of spaghetti. It could have been good, but he wasn't tasting it. 'Go on,' he answered.

'She found an overnight bag that belonged to Nancy. She gave it to me, because before that I had asked her to poke around a little for some history on the redhead. The bag was full of baby clothes, all unused. We went up to her apartment.'

He nodded. 'Was she frightened . . . or remorseful?'

'When I left her she was a pretty happy girl. She was no suicide.'

'Damn it, Mike! I . . .'

'When is the autopsy due?'

'Today . . . right now! You got me dancing again! I wouldn't be surprised to find her full of arsenic, either!' He threw his fork down and pushed away from the table and went over to a wall phone. When he came back he grunted, 'Two hours and there'll be an official report. The coroner's pulling the autopsy now.'

'I bet he won't change the verdict.'

'Why?'

'Because somebody is pretty damn smart.'

'Or dumb: Maybe it's you that's dumb, Mike.'

I lit a cigarette and grinned at him, thinking of something somebody told me once about persons that drown. 'I'm not so dumb, kid. Maybe we'll give the coroner a shock. I liked that blonde.'

'You think this is mixed up with Nancy, don't you?'

'Yup.'

'Positive?'

'Yup.'

'Then get me proof, Mike. I can't move without it.'

'I will.'

'Yeah, when?'

'When we get our hands on someone who knows enough to talk.'

Pat agreed with a flicker of his eyebrows. 'I can see us making him talk.'

'You don't have to,' I reminded him. 'When that party gets to you he'll be so happy to talk he'll spill his guts. You don't have to do a thing.'

'You're going to squeeze it out him, I betcha?'

'Damn right, friend.'

'You know what you're bucking, of course.'

'Yeah, I know. Guys that are paying heavy for protection. Guys who can take care of themselves if that protection doesn't go through. Money boys with private armies maybe.'

'We're on touchy ground,' Pat grated.

'I know it. We're going to run into a lot of dirt unless I miss my guess. There will be people involved who will raise hell. That's where I have the edge, Pat. They can make you smell their stink. Me, I can tell 'em to blow it. They can't take my job away and they can't scare me because I can make more trouble than they can shake a stick at.'

'You're telling me!'

Pat went back to his spaghetti while I finished the bottle of wine and I could almost hear the gears clicking in his head. When he finished he put down his napkin, but before he could enjoy a smoke the proprietor called him to the phone. He kicked his chair back and walked away.

Five minutes later he came back wearing a grin. 'Your murder theory is getting kicked around. The men rechecked on the note. There is absolutely no doubt that the Minor girl wrote it. We had confirmation from several sources. Not a trace of forgery. You can't break it, Mike.'

I scowled at the empty glass in my hand. At least I was smart enough to know that the police labs mean what they say when a positive statement is issued.

Pat was watching me. 'This takes it right out of my department, you know.'

'There's still the autopsy.'

'Want to go watch it?'

I shook my head. 'No, I'll take a walk. I want to think. Supposing I call you back later. I'd like to know what's on the report.'

'O.K.' Pat checked his watch. 'Give me a ring in a couple of hours. I'll be at the office.'

'One other thing . . .'

Pat grinned. 'I was wondering when you were going to ask it.'

He was a sharp one, all right. 'I haven't got the time, nor the facilities for a lot of leg-work right now. How about having your wire service check the hospitals for me. See if they ever had a Nancy Sanford as a maternity case. Get the name of the man, family or anything else, will you?'

'I would have done it anyway, Mike. I'll get it off right away.'

'Thanks.'

I took the cheque and paid it, then said so-long to Pat outside the door. For a while I strolled up the street, my hands in my pockets, whistling an aimless tune. It was a nice day, a lovely day . . . a hell of a day for murder.

Suicide? Not on your life! They worked it so sweet you couldn't call it murder – yet. Well, maybe you couldn't, but I could. I was willing to bet my shirt that the blonde had asked the wrong questions in the wrong places. Somebody had to shut her up. It fitted, very nicely. She was trying to earn that five hundred. She got too much for her money.

When I made a complete circle around the block I ambled over to the car and got in. For a change, the streets were half empty, and I breezed uptown without having to stop for a red light. When I got to Ninety-sixth Street I turned towards the river, found a place to park and got out.

A breeze was blowing up from the water, carrying with it the partially purified atmosphere of a city at work. It was cool and refreshing, but there was still something unclean about it. The river was grey in colour, not the rich blue it should have been, and the foam that followed the wake of the ships passing by was too thick – almost like blood. In close to shore it changed to a dirty brown trying to wash the filth up on the banks. It was pretty if you only stopped to look at it, but when you looked too close, and thought enough, it made you sick.

(*She removed her hat, shoes, jacket . . . laid them down on the planks with her bag on top, and jumped in.*) That would be a woman's way of going it . . . a woman who had given suicide a lot of thought. Not a sudden decision, the kind that took a jump and tried to change her mind in mid-air. A suicide like this would be thought out, all affairs put in order to make it easy for those who did the cleaning up – if it was a suicide. Neat, like it had been planned for a long, long time.

My feet had carried me down to the grass that bordered the water, taking me over towards a pier that was partially ripped up. They had a watchman on it now in a brand-new shack. I was conscious of a face curling into a nasty smile. It was still there when the watchman came out, a short fat guy with a beer bottle in his hand. He must have picked me for another cop because he gave me the nod and let me walk down the runway to the end without bothering to ask questions.

I could hear the music going off in my head. It was always like that when I began to get ideas and get excited. I was getting a crazy, wild idea that might prove a point and bring Pat into it after all, then the crap would really fly. Heads would roll. They'd set up the guillotine in Times Square and the people could cheer like at a circus, then slink back and get ready to start the same thing all over again.

There was an empty peanut-butter jar with dead worms in it on top of the piling. I shook the things out and wiped the jar clean with a handkerchief until it shone, then threw the handkerchief away, too. I climbed down the supports and filled the jar nearly full before I worked my way back, then screwed the lid back on and went back to the street.

Instead of calling Pat I drove straight to his office. He shook hands and invited me down the hall, where he picked up a report sheet then took me back to his cubicle. He handed me the form. 'There it is, Mike. She died by suffocation. Drowning. We called the time right, too. No doubt about it now.'

I didn't bother to read the report. Instead I tossed it back on his desk. 'The coroner around; Pat?'

'He's downstairs, if he hasn't left already.'

'Call and find out.'

He was about to ask a question, but thought better of it and reached for the phone. After a minute he said. 'He's still there.'

'Tell him to wait.'

'It better be good. He's pretty cranky. Besides, he's with the D.A.'

'It's good.'

Pat told the operator to hold him, his eyes never leaving mine. When he hung up he leaned forward over his desk. 'What is it this time?'

I laid the jar on his desk. 'Have him analyse that.'

He picked up the jar and scrutinized it, shaking it to bring the sediment to the top, frowning into the murky ooze inside the jar. When he saw I wasn't going to explain it he got up abruptly and went out the door and I heard the elevator take him downstairs.

I went through half a deck of Luckies before I heard the elevator stop again. His feet were coming towards the office fast and hard and I knew he was mad.

He was. He slammed the jar on the desk and swung around with anger written across his face. 'What kind of a steer did you call that? He analysed all right . . . he told me it was nothing but water filled with every kind of mess there was. Then he wanted to know the whys and wherefores. I looked like a damn fool. What was I going to say, that a private cop is using the police for a work-bench to figure out a crazy scheme? I didn't know what I expected to find in there, but I thought it would be better than that!'

'Why didn't you ask the coroner if it was the same stuff he found in her lungs? Not her stomach, mind you, but her lungs. When you drown you suffocate because that little valve in your throat tightens up the air passage to keep anything from running into your lungs. It doesn't take much to suffocate a person – just enough water to make that little valve jam. There's water in the stomach, but very little in the lungs. Go ahead, ask him.'

Pat's eyes were ready to pop. His teeth bared in an animal-like grin and he said, 'You brainy bastard, you!'

He picked up the phone and called downstairs. The conversation didn't take more than a minute, but there was a lot of excited talk going on. He put the phone back and slid into his chair. 'They're double-checking now, I think you called it.'

'I told you that before.'

'Don't go too fast, Mike. We have to wait for the report. Now tell it your own way.'

'Simple, Pat. Ann Minor was drowned, most likely in her own place. Then she was tossed into the river.'

'That means carrying the body out of the house without being seen, you know.'

'What of it? Who's on the street at that hour? Hell, getting her out isn't the hard job. Dumping her wouldn't be a hard job either.'

'There's only one catch: the suicide note.'

'I got ideas on that, too.'

Pat dropped his head in his hand. 'You know I'm pretty smart. I've been tied up in police work as long as you have. I love it, I'm good at it. But you come up with the ideas. Do you think I'm getting too set in my ways any more? Am I reverting to type or something? What the hell is wrong with me, Mike?'

The only thing I could do was chuckle at him. 'You aren't slowing up, kid. You just forget . . . sometimes a smart crook knows as much as a smart cop. You ought to start thinking like one of *them* sometimes. It helps.'

'Nuts!'

'We have two murders now. They both looked like something else. We haven't proved the first one, but this second shows you the kind of people you're up against. They aren't amateurs by a long shot.'

Pat looked up. 'You were talking about an idea you had . . .'

'No dice. Get your own. This one's a little cock-eyed even for you. If it's what I'm thinking it's just another piece in the puzzle. Maybe it's even from a different puzzle.'

The phone rang again and Pat answered it. His face stayed blank until he finished the conversation. He wasn't too happy. 'My department has it now. The water in her lungs was clear. Traces of soap. She was drowned in a bathtub, probably. Not a sign of contamination.'

'Then cheer up.'

'Yeah, I'll break out in smiles. They're patting me on the back downstairs, but they want to know how I got wise. What the hell will I tell them?'

I pushed the chair back and stood up. 'Tell 'em you made it all up out of your own two little heads.'

When I left, Pat said damn, soft like, 'but he was grinning now.

And I was grinning because I wanted the police in on this thing. Where I was going was too much trouble for one person. Much too much – even for me. The cops has the boys and the guns. They had the brains, too. Pretty soon now those heads were going to roll.

I had my supper in the Automat before I went home. I loaded up a tray with everything they had and picked a table where I was alone and able to think. When I finished I felt better and kept thinking, over a cigarette. All the assorted pieces of the puzzle were clear in my mind, but I couldn't get them together. But at least they were clear and if I couldn't see the picture on the puzzle I knew one thing . . . there would *be* one thing when I got it together. I looked at Nancy's ring again and said, 'Soon, Red . . . very soon now.'

In an hour the day had lost its brightness and a light rain rolled in with the dusk. I turned up my collar and stayed close to the buildings until I reached my car. Traffic was heavier how, but I got on an express street that was running freely and headed home. By the time I made my apartment the rain was coming down hard with no signs of letting up. I drove into the garage, and ran for it. Just the same, I got soaked before I reached the canopy over the gates.

When I tried to get my key in the lock it jammed. I tried again and it jammed again. Then I saw scratches on the brass. The lock had been jimmied. I hauled out my rod with one hand and kicked at the door. It flew open and I charged in there like a jerk wide open to get myself killed, only there was nobody else in there with me.

The lights were on in every room and the place was turned upside down. Nothing was where it belonged. The cushions in the chairs and couch were ripped apart and the breeze was blowing the stuffing through the air like a field of ragweed.

Drawers were emptied and discarded in the middle of the floor. All my clothes were out of the closet and heaped in a pile, the pockets turned inside out. They didn't even overlook the refrigerator. Bottles, cans and cold cuts were drawing flies and dirt on the table and under the sink.

I grabbed the phone and dialled the house number downstairs and waited for the doorman to answer. When he came on I had to fight to keep my voice down. 'This is Mike Hammer in 9-D. Was anybody here looking for me?'

The guy replied in the negative.

'Was anybody hanging around the place today. Anybody who doesn't belong here?'

Another negative. He asked me if there was any trouble.

I said, 'No, but there damn soon will be. Somebody's ruined my joint.'

He got excited at that, but I told him to keep quiet. I didn't feel like answering questions or scaring the neighbours. I went into the bedroom and started to yank the covers from the heap in the corner. The overnight case was there under the layers of wool, the top gaping open and the baby clothes scattered around it. Some of them hadn't even been unfolded. Both side pockets and the top pocket had been ripped completely off and the lining opened so a hand could search underneath.

And the folder of pictures was gone.

I took an inventory of everything in the house, a search that cost me two hours, but the only thing missing was the pictures. Just to be sure I looked again. I needn't have bothered. Fifty-four bucks and a wrist watch lay on top of the dresser untouched, but an old set of films was gone.

They didn't mean anything to me, but they did to somebody else. That's why Ann died. I sat on the wreckage of a chair with a butt dangling from my lips, tallying things up. A lock lay on the floor, smashed from a heel. A cigarette box was forced open, broken. A socket fixture on the wall had been pried loose, leaving the wire ends hanging out like broken fingers.

I looked around me more carefully this time, noticing the pattern of the search. They took the pictures, but they were looking for something else, a something small enough to hide in almost anything. The inkwell had been emptied on the desk, and I remembered the salt and pepper shaker that had been dumped in the kitchen.

Sure, it was simple enough. I lifted my hand and grinned at the ring. 'They'll be back, kid,' I told it. 'They didn't get you that time, so they'll be back. And we'll be waiting for them.'

I could relax now. It was going to cost me, but I could relax. The pattern was taking shape. Nancy was the figurehead. The ring was Nancy. And they wanted her pictures back. What for, I couldn't say. They were old and they didn't show anything, but they were important, too. The baby clothes didn't mean anything to them, but the ring and the pictures did.

My eyes were staring into the distance and I was seeing Nancy's letter to me. Some day she might need me again . . . she was doing many things . . . only one of which had any meaning to her . . . ours was a trust.

Words. Now I had a lot of words. Some of them were tugging at my brain trying to claw their way into the clear. What was it? What the hell was it I was trying to remember? It was shrieking out to be heard and my mind was deaf. I was listening but I couldn't hear it. Damn it, what was there? What was I trying to remember! Somebody said something. It didn't mean a thing then, yet it sank in and stayed there until now. Who said it? What was it?

I shook my head to clear it, hoping to bring it back. The shrill clamour of the phone snapped me out of the fog and I got up and answered it. Pat's voice said hullo with a tone that had a snap to it.

'What's up, Pat?'

'I just want to tell you we went over the thing again. It works out. The coroner and the D.A. are calling it murder. Now they want an answer to the suicide note. It was authentic as hell. What was the idea you had? . . . I'm up the creek without a paddle.'

I answered him listlessly. 'Go ask some questions of her friends. See if she ever talked about committing suicide. There's a chance she did at one time and wrote the note. Somebody could have talked her out of it, then kept the note for future use.'

'You think of everything, don't you?'

'I wish I did, Pat.'

'It isn't going to be as easy as that. I put the whole question to the D.A. and it stood him on his ear. He thought the idea was preposterous.'

'What do you think?'

'I think we got a snake by the tail.'

'That's the only safe way to pick up a snake.'

'I hope you're right. You still playing ball, Mike?'

'All the way, kid. You'll hear from me when I have something. Like now. Somebody broke into my apartment and wrecked it. They were looking for Nancy's ring. They didn't get it, but they did take those snapshots I got from the blonde.'

'Hell!' Pat exploded. 'What made you keep them? You know better than that!'

'Sure, I'll close the barn door after the horse is stolen. I wouldn't have known they were important if they hadn't been lifted. I'm not worried about them. They wanted the ring, why, I don't know. It's impossible to trace the thing, but they wanted it.'

Pat was silent, then he said, 'I've got news for you, too. I got an answer from a hospital in Chicago. We were lucky to get it back so quickly.'

I squeezed the receiver. 'Yeah?'

'Nancy Sanford had a baby there four years ago. She was an unwed mother. She refused to divulge the name of the father and she was put in a charity ward sponsored by a group that takes care of those affairs. It was a stillbirth. Nobody knows where she went after that.'

My hand was shaking and my voice was almost a whisper when I thanked him for the information. Before I could hang up he said, 'That ring . . . better drop it off with me, Mike.'

I laughed harshly. 'Like hell! Nancy is still a suicide on your books. When you call it murder you can have it.'

Pat was arguing about it when I interrupted.

'What are you going to do about the blonde? . . . and Murray?'

'He was just picked up at his club. On his way over now. Listen, about the ring, I want . . .'

I said thanks and cradled the receiver. Murray was about to be questioned. That meant a couple of hours at least, unless he had a good lawyer and good connections. It was enough time.

CHAPTER NINE

Murray Candid had two listings: one at the club and the other in a fancy residential section of Brooklyn. I didn't like either one of them. I tried the one in Brooklyn, and a butler with an English accent answered and told me Mr Candid was out and wasn't expected back until the club had closed for the night, and could I leave a message. I told him never mind, and hung up.

A butler yet! Probably golden candelabra and rare Ming vases, too!

I held my hand over the dial, and on second thought punched Lola's number out. She recognized my voice and smiled over the phone. 'Hullo, darling. Where are you?'

'Home.'

'Am I going to see you?'

She made me feel nice and warm with just a few words. 'In a little while maybe. Right now I'm up to my ears in something. I thought you might be able to help.'

'Of course, Mike. What . . .?'

'Did you know Ann Minor? She worked for Murray.'

'Certainly: I've known her for years. Why?'

'She's dead.'

'No!'

'Yes. She was murdered and I know why. It had to do with Nancy, only the cops are in on this one.'

'Oh, Mike . . . what makes these things happen? Ann wasn't one – one of us. She never did anything wrong. Why, she used to take care of the kids in the racket . . . try to help them. Oh, Mike . . . why? Why?'

'When I know that I'll know who killed her, honey. But that's not the point. Do you know where Murray might have a private hangout? Not his place in Brooklyn, but some place where he could do some trick entertaining or contact business associates?'

'Y-yes. He used to have a place in the Village. It won't be the same one I knew because he changed his spots regularly. He didn't like to stay in one place too long, but he favoured the Village. I . . . was up there once . . . a party. It wasn't nice, Mike; I'd rather not speak about it.'

'You don't have to. Where was the place?'

She gave me the location and I scribbled it down. 'You'd have to ask around to see where he is now. I could find it, I guess, but . . .'

'You sit pat. I'll find it myself. I don't want you sticking your neck out.'

'All right, Mike. Please don't get hurt . . . please.'

I grinned. Not many people worried about me, and it was a nice feeling. 'I'll be real careful, sugar. In fact, I'll call you back later so you'll know everything is all right. O.K.?'

'If you don't I'll never forgive you. I'll be waiting for you.'

I put the phone back easy and patted it.

The evening was well on its way when I finished dressing. I had on the made-to-order suit with space built in for my armoury, looking like something out of the prohibition era. I found my raincoat under the rest of the other stuff and climbed into it, stuffing a pack of butts in each pocket.

When I took one last look around the mess I went out the door and down to the garage for my car. It was raining harder than before, slanting down against the sidewalk, driving people into the welcome shelter of the buildings. Cars were going past, their windshield wipers moving like agitated bugs, the drivers crouched forward over the wheels, peering ahead intently.

I backed out of the garage, turned around and cut over to Broadway, following the main stem downtown. The Village should have been crammed with tourists and regulars, but the kerbs were empty, and even the taxis were backed up behind their hack stands. Once in a-while someone would make a dash for another saloon or run to the subway kiosk with a newspaper

130

over his head, but if life was to be found in the Village this night, it would be found under a roof somewhere.

Down the corner from the address Lola had given me was a joint called Monica's. The red neon sign was a blur through the rain, and when I cruised past I could see a bar with a handful of people on stools huddled over their drinks. It was as good a place to start as any.

I parked the car and pulled up my coat collar, then ducked put and stepped over puddles, my head bulling a path through the downpour. Before I got to the joint my legs were soaked and my feet squished in my shoes.

The heads at the bar came up and round like a chorus line, looking at me. Three belonged to guys trapped there on their way some place else. They went back to their drinks. Two were dames more interested in each other than men and they went back to low, sensual looks and leg holding. The other two were all smiles that exchanged nasty glances as if they were going to fight over the new arrival. Monica's catered to a well-assorted clientele.

Behind the bar was a big, beefy guy with a scar on his chin and one ear cauliflowered to look like a dumpling. If his name was Monica I'd eat my hat. He came down the bar and asked me what it would be. I said whisky and his top lip curled up into a grin.

'Annoder normal.' His voice was a croak. 'The place's gettin' reformed.'

The two patsies made a *moue* at him and looked insulted.

He put the bottle, on the bar in front of me. 'Even th' dames is screwy. Odder place I woiked they kicked hell outa each other to get a guy. Here th' dames don't think of nuttin' but dames.'

'Yeah, there's nothing like a dame,' I said.

'Inside's a coupla loose ones, bub. Go see if ya like 'em.'

He gave me an outsized wink and I picked up my glass, threw a buck on the bar and walked inside. The two babes were there like he said, only they were already taken. Two women in man-tailored suits were showing them a better time than I could have done.

So I sat down by myself at a table next to a piano and watched them. One of the boys from the bar came in and sat a drink in front of me, smirking a little as he pulled out the chair.

He said, 'The bartender's too fresh, don't you think?'

I grunted at him and gulped the drink. These guys give me the pip.

'You're new around here, aren't you?'

'Yeah.'

'From uptown?'

'Yeah.'

'Oh!' Then he frowned. 'You . . . have a date already?'

The guy was asking for a punch in the mouth and he was just about to get it when I changed my mind and muttered, 'I'm gonna see a guy named Murray Candid. He told me where he lived, then I forgot.'

'Murray? He's a *dear* friend of mine. But he moved again only a week ago. Georgie told me he has a place over the grocery store two blocks south. How long have you known him? Why, only last week I . . . say, you're not leaving yet . . . we haven't . . .'

I didn't bother to look back. If the punk tried to follow me I'd wrap him around a pole. The bartender looked at me and chirped that the make-up crowd could spoil the business, and I agreed.

But the guy gave me the steer I wanted. I was lucky. Maybe I should have patted his behind to make him feel good.

I came down the street slowly, made a U-turn and came back. There were no lights on in the store and the shades in the apartment above were drawn and dark. A few cars were parked along one side and I wedged in between them, waiting there a minute until a couple of pedestrians lost themselves in the rain.

It was hard to keep from running. I crossed over, walked towards the store, then stepped into the doorway as if to light a butt, but more to look around. There wasn't anything to see, so I stepped back into the gloom of the hallway and tried the door, feeling it give under my hand. I dragged on the butt and looked at the mailboxes. One said 'Byle' the name on the store. The other was for the top floor and was blank.

That would be it.

My eyes took a few minutes to become accustomed to the darkness, then I saw the stairs, worn and rickety, covered with sections of old carpet. I stayed on the wall side, trying to keep them from creaking, but even as careful as I was they groaned ominously, waiting to groan again when I lifted my foot.

The first-floor landing was a narrow box flanked by a door and a railing with 'Byle' lettered on it in white paint. They should have used green to go with the name. I held on to the rail, using it for a guide, and felt my way to the next flight. These stairs were new. They didn't make a sound. When I reached the door my hand went out for the knob and I stiffened, my ears chasing an elusive sound.

Somebody was inside, somebody moving softly but fast.

I had the knob in my hand, turning it slowly without sound until the catch was drawn completely back. The hinges were well oiled and the door inched open soundlessly, bit by bit until I could see inside. There were no lights on and the shuffling sounds were coming from another room.

When the door was opened half-way I unpacked the .45 and stood there with it in my hand waiting to see what would happen. Something hit the floor and shattered and somebody whispered to somebody else to be quiet for the love of God. That made two of them.

Then the other one said, 'Goddamn it, I cut my hand!'

A chair was pushed back and the glass that was lying on the floor went skittering into the wall.

The first voice said, 'Didn't I tell you to be quiet?'

'Shut the hell up! You don't tell me anything.'

There was the tearing sound of cloth, then it came again. The voice whispered, 'I can't bandage this. I'm going inside.'

He came in my direction, picking his way ground the furniture. I was pressed back against the wall, hanging on to the rod. His hand felt the opening into the foyer and for a second he just stood there, black silhouetted against a deeper black, then his hand brushed my coat and he opened his mouth to yell.

I smashed the barrel of the gun across his forehead with a sickening dull sound and his knees went out from under him. He fell right in my arms, limp and heavy, his head lolling to one side, and I heard the blood drip on to the floor. It would have been all right if I could have laid him down, but his body rolled in my hands and a gun fell out of a holster and banged along the woodwork.

Inside there was a complete silence. Nothing, not even the sound of his breathing. I moved my feet around and swore under my breath, muttering like a guy who had just bumped into a wall.

In a voice barely audible the guy called out, 'Ray . . . was that you, Ray?'

I had to answer. 'Yeah, it was me.'

'Come back here, Ray.'

I threw off my hat, shrugged my coat to the floor. The other guy was about my size and maybe I could get away with it.

Just in time I smartened up and dropped to my hands and knees and went around the corner. The guy was standing there pointing a gun where my belly would have been.

My pal's name wasn't Ray and I answered to it.

He saw me at the same time and a tongue of flame licked out in my direction with a noise that was almost a 'plop,' but I was rolling before he pulled the trigger and slug thudded into the wall.

Somehow I got my feet under me and squeezed the .45 into a roar that shook the room. I wasn't waiting for any return fire. I saw that shadow of a chair and dived for it, hearing the other guy going for cover only a few feet away.

From where I was, the darkness made it impossible to tell whether or not I was exposed, and I lay there, forcing myself to breathe silently when I wanted to pant like a dog. The other guy wasn't so good at it. He gasped, then moved quickly, afraid that he might have been heard. I let him sweat. I knew where he was now, but I didn't fire. He moved again, deliberately, wondering if his first blast had caught me. My leg began to tighten up in a cramp, and there was a tremor in my arm from leaning on it. I wasn't going to be able to hold the tableau much longer.

The guy was getting up his nerve, but carefully. I fixed my eyes a little to one side of where I thought he'd show and waited, scanning the area, not focusing my gaze on any one spot. I tried to remember what they taught us in phase training. It worked in the jungle. Damn it, it *had* to work now . . .'

I saw his head then. Barely enough light came through the curtained windows to give the background a deeper shade, and against it his face was just a spot of motion. He was creeping right into the line of my rod.

My fingers were starting to squeeze when the boy in the hallway came back to life. His feet slammed the wall and his nails scratched the floor. He must have lain there a second, remembered where he was and what had happened, and then he let out a choked-off curse and scrambled to the door.

It pulled the stop on the tension. The guy behind the chair jerked, his breath coming out in a long wheeze and he sprang out of his crouch into a chair that tipped over on me just as the .45 went off.

He screamed, tripped and fell, then got up and hit the wall before he made the door. I fought the chair and the gun went off into an empty room because I heard the other guy falling down a flight of stairs. By the time I was on my feet an engine roared outside and a car ripped into gear and was gone up the street.

There was no use chasing them. I lit a match, found the light switch and turned it on. It only took one look to see what they had been doing. Along one side of the wall was a bookcase with half the books lying on the floor. Some had closed shut, but at least fifty of them were lying there opened and discarded.

I stuck the gun back under my arm and picked up where they left off, yanking the books down and flipping through them. With the light on I made better time, and was half-way across the next to last shelf when one book opened and another fell out of the well that had been cut into the pages.

Somebody was yelling on the street and a door slammed in the apartment below me. I shoved the book under my belt at the small of my back, ran out to the corridor long enough to grab my hat and coat and made a mad dash down the stairs. When I came to the landing the door started to open but banged shut and a bolt clicked into a hasp.

The open front door was a welcome invitation, even with the rain still coming down outside. I took that last flight two at a time, hit the bottom running and felt my head explode into a whirlwind of spinning lights and crazy sounds as something crashed into the side of my neck.

My body wasn't a part of me at all. It collapsed in a limp head and my head cracked the floor, but there was no pain, just a numbness that was lit by another light, a brighter red this time, and there was a pressure on my chest, and in that final moment of recollection I knew that I had walked into a trap and somebody had pumped a bullet into me point-blank.

How long I lay there I couldn't tell. There are times when the body has recuperative powers beyond belief. A sound penetrated, a high wailing sound of a siren, and I climbed to my feet, grasping at the banister for support. Unconsciously I got my coat and hat back in my hands, staggered towards the door and came out. There was a crowd down the street pointing in my direction, but if they saw me they didn't show it. I was glad of the rain and the night then, the shadows that wrapped themselves around me as I lurched across the street looking for my car.

When I found it I half fell across the seat, dragging the door shut behind me. My chest felt crushed and my skull was a throbbing thing that sent tongues of fire lacing down my body. All sensation had been torn loose from my neck, and although I felt nothing there, it hurt to breathe, and hurt even worse to make a sound.

I heard the police car screech to a stop, heard the pounding of feet, the shouts, the excited murmur of a crowd that expanded every minute. I couldn't stay on the seat any longer. The hell with them! The hell with everything! I let my eyes close and my arms relaxed without warning, and I dropped forward on the floor boards, gasping into a puddle of dirt.

I was cold, colder than I had ever been before. I was wet and shivering and I didn't want to raise my head because the Japs were only twenty yards away waiting for me. Some place back of the lines a chow wagon had been rolled up and I could smell hot coffee and stew, hearing the guys line up for chow. I wanted to call for them to come and get me, lay down an artillery barrage so I could get the hell out of the fox hole, but if I yelled the Japs would spot my position and lob a grenade in on top of me. Just to make it worse it started raining harder.

Fighting to get my eyes open was a job in itself. The rain was coming in the open window and I was drenched. I could smell the coffee again, coming from some window. With my hands propped under me I pushed myself back to the seat and got behind the wheel.

The crowd was gone, the police were gone and the street was normal again. Just rain, black squares of windows, a drunk that weaved up the sidewalk. I knew how he felt. My mind was unfogging, bringing with it the throb in my head and chest. I put my hand inside my jacket, felt the tear in the cloth half fearfully, then eased the .45 out. A slug had smashed into the top of the slide mechanism tearing it loose, embedding itself in the blued metal, looking like some nasty amoeba cast in lead. My chest hurt like hell from the impact, but the skin wasn't even broken.

And some place somebody was thinking I was a dead duck.

I reached in back of my belt, feeling for the book. It was still there. I couldn't see what it was so I tossed it in the glove compartment until later.

It was another ten minutes before I felt right enough to drive or strong enough to hold the wheel. I kicked over the motor and turned on my lights.

Right away I got it. The redhead's ring didn't wink back at me in the frosty gleam of the dashboard light. It was gone.

On my little finger was a long pink scratch where it had been yanked off in a hurry. They came back sooner than I expected.

Things were looking up. If they looked higher they'd see the pretty angels.

CHAPTER TEN

Time wasn't important to Lola. She said she'd wait and she did. Hers was the only light in the apartment building, and I saw her shadow pass the drawn curtains twice, then recede back into the room. I didn't forget that other parking ticket; this time I found a spot that wasn't on an express street and pulled to the kerb.

I had to take it easy walking back, wishing the sidewalks were carpeted to ease the shock of my heels pounding the concrete. Every step jarred the balloon of pain that was my head, and when I lit a butt to try to forget it the smoke sent cramps into my lungs that caught and held like a thousand knives digging into my rib-case.

The stairs looked a mile long. The only way I could make them was to go up a couple, rest, then go up a couple more. The outside door was open so I didn't bother ringing until I was at the apartment door, then I punched the bell and held it, leaning against the jamb.

Inside, I heard her heels click on the floor, hurried, then break into a run. Her fingers fumbled with the bolt, got it open and yanked the door back.

I guess I didn't look so hot. She said, 'Oh, Mike!' and her fingers went out to my face tenderly, holding my cheeks, then she took my hand and led me inside.

'I almost stood you up.' It wasn't easy to grin at her.

Lola looked at me and shook her head. 'Some day . . . will you come to see me when you're not a . . . a hospital case?'

Very slowly I turned her around. She was lovely, this woman. Tonight she had dressed up for me, hoping I'd do more than call. She stood almost as tall as me, her body outlined under an iridescent green dress that sent waves of light shimmering down her legs whenever she moved. I held her at arm's length doing nothing but looking at her, smelling the fragrance of a heady cologne. Her hair was a dark frame, soft and feathery, then rolled to her shoulders and made you want to close your eyes and pull it over you like a blanket. Somewhere she had found a new beauty, or perhaps it was there all along, but it was a beauty that was always hers now.

My hand found her waist and I drew her in close, waiting until her eyes half closed and her lips parted, eager to be kissed. Her mouth was a soft bed of fire, her tongue a searching thing asking questions I had to answer greedily. When I pushed her away she stood there a long moment breathing heavily before she opened her eyes and smiled. She didn't have to tell me that she was mine whenever I wanted it. I knew that.

Her eyes were watching me. 'Mike. . . .'

I ran my fingers through her hair like I had wanted to. 'What, honey?'

'I love you, Mike. No . . . don't love me back. Don't even try. Just let me love you.'

I pulled her face to mine and kissed her eyes closed. 'That isn't easy. It's hard not to do things.'

'You have to do this, Mike. I have a long way to go yet.'

'No, you don't, kid. You can forget everything that has ever happened. I don't give a damn what went on this year or last. Who the hell am I to talk, anyway? If there's any shame to attach to the way you run your life, then maybe I ought to be ashamed. I've done the same things you've done, but a man gets away with it. It's not what you do but the way you think. Hell, I've met bums in a saloon who would do more for you than half the churchgoers.'

'But I want it to be different with me, Mike. I'm trying so hard to be . . . nice.'

'You were always nice, Lola. I haven't known you long, but I bet you were always nice.'

She squeezed my hand and smiled. 'Thank you, Mr Hammer. You can make it awfully easy for me. That's why I love you so much.' Her finger went to my mouth so I couldn't answer. 'But it still works my way. I still have a long way to go. I want to be worth a love that's returned.'

I aimed a kiss at her nose, but it was too quick and I winced. Lola didn't need an explanation. Worry lines grew in the corner of her eyes and she pointed to a chair.

After I had let myself into it she said, 'Again, Mike?'

'Again.'

'Bad?'

'It could have been. A slug that was aimed at my chest ruined my gun. I'll never leave Betsy home after that. The same party must've clubbed me across the neck with a sledge hammer. Like to ripped my damn head off.'

'Who . . . who did it?'

'Beats me. It was dark, I was in a hurry, and I never had a chance to be introduced.'

She loosened my tie and shirt, sat on the arm of the chair and rubbed my neck and head. Her fingers were long and cool, probing into the hurt and wiping it away. I leaned my head back and closed my eyes, liking the touch of her hand, loving the nearness of her. She hummed a song in a rich, throaty voice, softly, until I was completely relaxed.

I said, 'They got Nancy's ring, Lola.'

'They did.' It wasn't a question; more a statement that meant she was ready to listen when I was ready to talk.

'I found Murray's place and went in there, His two boys were going through his wall library looking for something. He must have told where it was, but didn't have time to give them full details.'

'Did they find it?'

'No. I found it.'

Her hands were rubbing my shoulders, kneading the muscles. 'What was it?'

'A book. A book that was inside another book.' Without opening my eyes I reached around and slipped it out of my pocket. She took it from me with one hand and I heard her flip the cover back.

141

She stared at it for a while, then ruffled through the pages. 'It's gibberish.'

'That's what I expected.' I took her hand away from my neck and kissed it and she handed me the book, her face a puzzled frown.

It was no bigger than a small notepad, bound in black leather, a size that fitted nicely in an inside jacket pocket, easy to conceal almost anywhere. The writing was small and precise, in a book-keeper's hand, flowing straight across the page as if underruled by invisible lines.

Letters, numbers. Meaningless symbols. Capital letters, small letters. Some letters backward, deliberately so. Yet there was an order about it all that couldn't be mistaken. I went through the pages rapidly, coming to the end about three-quarters of the way. The rest of the pages were blank.

Lola had been watching over my shoulder. 'What is it, Mike?'

'Code.'

'Can you read it?'

'No, but there are people who can. Maybe you can. See if there's anything familiar to you in here.' I held the book out and began at the beginning again.

She scanned the pages with me, holding her lower lip between her teeth, carefully following my finger as I paced the lines with her. She shook her head at the end of each page and I turned to the next.

But it was always the same. She knew no more about it than I did. I would have closed it right there, except that I felt her hand tighten on my arm and I saw her teeth dig into her lip. She started to say something, then stopped.

'What is it?' I prompted.

'No, it can't be.' She was frowning again.

'Tell me, kid.'

Her finger was shaking as she pointed to a symbol that looked like a complex word in a steno's notebook. 'A . . . long time ago . . . I was in Murray's office when a man phoned him. Murray talked a while, then put down something on a pad. I think . . . I think it was that. He saw me watching and covered it up. Later he told me I had an appointment.'

'Who was it?'

'Do . . . I have to?' She was pleading with me not to make her remember.

'Just this once, baby.'

'I don't remember his name.' She said it fast. 'He was from out of town. He was fat and slimy and I hated him, Mike. Oh, please . . . no more, no more.'

'O.K., it's enough.' I closed the book and laid it on the end table. The ball had started to roll. The heads would follow. I reached for the phone.

Pat was in bed, but he wasn't sleeping. His voice was wide-awake, tense. 'I knew you'd get around to calling about this time,' he told me. 'What's going on?'

'That's what I'd like to know. Maybe you'd like to tell *me*.'

'Sure, I'll tell you. After all, you're the one who started this mess and, brother, I mean mess.'

'Trouble, Pat?'

'Plenty. We picked up Murray for questioning. Naturally, he didn't know a thing. According to his story Ann Minor was moody, brooding constantly, and a general pain in the neck. He considered firing her a while ago and thinks she got wind of it and got worse than ever. He took it calmly when we told him she was a suicide.'

'He would.'

'That's not all. He knew there was more to it than that, but he had a good lawyer. We couldn't hold him at all. About thirty minutes after we let him go hell started popping. Something's happening and I'm on the receiving end. Until tonight I didn't think the politics in this town were as dirty as they are. You started something, kid.'

'I'm going to finish it, too. What about the apartment . . . Ann's. Any prints?'

'None that mattered. The tub was clean as a whistle. On the far side were a few smudges that turned out to be hers, but

143

the rest had been wiped off. We took samples of the water and tested them. It worked. Some traces of the same soap.'

'Did you ask around about that suicide note?'

'Hell, I haven't had time. Two of the men on the case started to question some of the employees in the Zero Zero Club, but before they got very far they were called to a phone. A voice told them to lay off if they knew what was good for them.'

'What did they do?'

Pat's voice had a snarl in it. 'They didn't scare. They tried to have the call traced only to find it came from a subway phone booth – a pay station. They called me for instructions and I gave them to them. I told them to knock some heads together if they have to.'

I chuckled at that. 'Getting smart; huh?'

'I'm getting mad, damn it! The people pay for protection. What the hell do they take the police for, a bunch of private servants.'

'Some do,' I remarked sourly. 'Look, Pat, I have something for you. I know it's late and all that, but it's important. Get over here as fast as you can, will you?'

He didn't ask questions. I heard him slide out of bed and snap a light on. I gave him Lola's address and he said O.K., then hung up.

Lola rose and went into the kitchen, coming back with a tray and some beer. She opened the bottle and poured it out, giving me the big one. When she settled herself in a chair opposite me she said, 'What happens now?'

'We're going to scare the blazes out of some people, I think.'

'Murray?'

'He's one.'

We sipped the beer, finished it, had another. This time Lola curled up on the end of the couch, her legs crossed, one arm stretched out across the back. 'Will you come over here, or do I go over there?' she grinned impishly.

'I'll go over there,' I said.

She made room for me on the same cushion, putting a head on the beer. 'That's to keep one hand out of trouble.'

144

'What about the other hand?'

'Let it get in trouble.'

I laughed at her and hugged her to me so she could nuzzle against my shoulder. 'Mike . . . I think the college kids have something. It's nice to neck.'

I couldn't disagree with that. When the beer was gone she brought in another bottle and came back into my arm again. I should have been thinking of Nancy or doing something else maybe, but it was nice just sitting there with her, laughing at foolish things. She was the kind of a girl who could give you back something you thought you had lost to the years.

Pat came in too soon. He rang from downstairs and Lola pushed the buzzer to let him in. He must have run up the stairs because he was knocking on the door a few seconds later.

Lola let him in with a smile and I called out, 'Lola, meet Pat Chambers, the finest of the finest.'

Pat said, 'Hullo, Lola,' then came over to me and threw his hand on the back of the couch. He didn't waste any time.

'Gimme. What did you get?'

Lola brought the book over from the end table and I handed it to him. 'Part of Murray's collection, Pat. Code. Think you can break it?'

I scanned his face and saw his lips set in a line. He talked to himself. 'Memory code. Damn it to hell!'

'What?'

'It's a memory code, I'll bet a fin. He's got a symbol or a structure for everything and he's the only one who knows it.'

I set the glass down and inched forward on the couch. 'The Washington boys broke the Jap Imperial code, didn't they?'

'Yeah, but that was different.' He shook his head helplessly. 'Let me give you an example. Suppose you say a word to me, or several of them for that matter. You know what they mean, but I don't. How could I break that? If you strung out sentences long enough there would be repetition, but if you allowed nothing to repeat itself, using a different symbol or letter grouping that you committed to memory, there would be nothing to start with.'

145

'That takes a good memory, doesn't it?' I cut in.

'For some things. But there isn't too much to remember in this.' He tapped the book. 'Probably anyone could do it if he puts his mind to it.'

I reached for the glass and filled it, emptying the bottle. 'Lola recognized one of the symbols, she thinks. Murray used it to identify one of his "customers". That little gadget is Murray's account book with a listing of his clients and his fleshly assets.'

Pat jumped to his feet, a light blazing in his eyes. 'Son of a bitch, if it is we can rip him apart! We can split this racket right down the middle!'

His language was getting contaminated from hanging around private detectives. 'Only temporarily,' I reminded him.

'It's better than not at all. It'll pay for people getting killed. Where did you get it, Mike?'

'Your boy Candid has himself a party den in the Village. While you were popping the questions he sent his lads up to get that book, taking no chances. I surprised them at it. The damn thing was worth their trying to knock me off. I just missed having my head handed to me.'

'You can identify them, then?'

'Nope. I didn't see their faces. But one will have a cut on his hand and a beauty across his forehead. The other guy is his pal. Ask around the club. I think they were Murray's personal body-guards. We put the squeeze on so fast Murray didn't have time to pull that book himself. He probably figured nobody would question Ann's death except for routine questioning at his joint.'

'You might be right. I'll get this thing photostated and hand it around to the experts. I'll let you know what comes of it.'

'Good!'

'Where will I get in touch with you?'

'You won't. I'll get in touch with you.'

'I don't get it, Mike. Won't you be . . .?'

He stopped when he saw the expression on my face. 'I'm supposed to be dead.'

'Good Lord!'

'There were three guys at Murray's place. One wasn't in on it. All he wanted was the redhead's ring. He gave it to me square in the chest. So he's gonna drop his load when he sees me again.'

Pat caught the implications at once. 'He tailed you. The same guy killed the blonde, tailed you home, searched your place and stayed right, behind you until he had a clear shot at you.'

'Uh-huh. In a dark hallway.'

'And he just wanted the ring?'

'That's right. I had that book on me, and he never looked for it.'

'That makes two parties. Both after you for a different reason.'

'Could be the same reason, but they don't know it.'

A grin spread over his face. 'They'll be waiting for your body to show. They'll have their ears to the ground and their eyes open. They'll want to know what happened to your body.'

I nodded. 'Let 'em wonder,' I said slowly. 'They'll think the cops are keeping it quiet purposely. They'll think you have more than you're giving out. Let's see what happens, Pat.'

'Ummm.' That was all he said. He went to the door, looking satisfied, his mind pounding out the angles. He turned around once, grinned, waved goodbye and was gone.

Lola picked up the empty bottle and looked at me sideways.

'If you're really dead it's going to be a wonderful wake.'

I faked a kick at her and she ducked out for a refill. When she came back she was serious and I knew it. Her eyes questioned me before she asked, 'Could you tell me . . . about your place being searched, I mean? If I have to worry about you I want to know what I'm worrying about.'

I told her then, skipping some details, just a general outline of what had occurred. She let me bring it up to date, absorbing every word, trying to follow with her mind. When I was through I let her mull it over.

Finally she said, 'The baby clothes, Mike . . . it fits.'

'How?'

'Nancy had stretch marks on her abdomen. Purplish streaks that come with pregnancy. I never questioned her about it.'

'We discovered that. It was a stillbirth.'

'The father . . .?'

'No trace.'

She was thinking of something else and chewed on her fingernail. 'Those pictures that were stolen . . .'

'Only snapshots of her when she was younger.'

'That isn't it.'

'What then?'

'This person who was so careless . . . you said he just took the ring . . . didn't look for the book you had. . . .'

'He didn't know I had it.'

'No, I don't mean that. Maybe he just took the pictures. He didn't look at them, he just *took* them. He would have taken any pictures.'

I was beginning to get the point, but I wanted to make sure, 'What are you getting at, Lola?'

'Nancy had a camera, I told you that. Maybe it was pictures she took that were wanted. Maybe the others were taken by mistake.'

It made sense. I gave her neck a little squeeze and grinned through my teeth. 'Now you're the smart one,' I told her. 'You said Nancy wouldn't go in for blackmail.'

'I said I *thought* she wouldn't. I still don't think she would, but who can tell?'

'You know, we're throwing this right in Feeney Last's lap. If he's the bastard behind this he's going to get it right!'

Lola laid her hand over mine, reaching for my fingers.

'Mike, don't get excited too fast. You have to think about it first. If he's not the type. . . .'

'Hell, he's the type, all right. Could be that I didn't give him credit for being that smart. You can't tell what goes on behind their heads, Lola. Their faces might be blank as an empty coconut, but up here there's a lot of brain power. Damn! Just follow Feeney with me: he approached Red in the hash house; he had her scared and a lot of other people scared. He was tough and dirty, and decent people are usually scared of that kind. He could carry a gun to push a scare through, even if that wasn't the purpose of the gun. What a nice set-up he had!

'So Nancy had his blackmail stuff . . . he said it was pictures of somebody in a hotel room with a babe. Who was the somebody and who was the babe? Maybe it was Nancy herself. If she had a good camera she could take shots automatically with a time arrangement on the camera. Maybe Feeney knew she had it and wanted it – maybe it was the other way around and he had it and she got it. Hell, maybe they were in it together.

'One thing we know: Feeney searched her room. He's a snotty little bastard who'd take a chance on anything. There's only one trouble. Feeney has an alibi. He was with Berin-Grotin when Nancy was killed, and unless he was able to sneak off without the old boy knowing it he had to have somebody else to do the job.'

She reviewed it with an expression that reminded me of Pat, making me eat my own words. 'But you said Mr Berin was positive in his statement . . . and the police were just as positive that the boy ran down Nancy accidentally. How can you get around that?'

My chest started hurting again and I slumped back; 'Ah, I don't know. Nothing makes sense. If Nancy was an accident, who took her ring off and why – and why the trouble to get it back? The ring's the thing. If I could find what it meant I'd have it.'

I pulled out the cigarettes, stuck two in my mouth and lit them. Lola took hers from between my lips and dragged on it deeply. When I closed my eyes she said, 'That's not the point I'm trying to make, Mike. Nancy had pictures of some sort that were important. Her place was searched for them – must have been because then they already had the ring. You say they didn't find them. Then they searched your place and took pictures that apparently had no meaning. All right, suppose they *didn't* have any meaning . . . where are the ones that have?'

Good Lord, how could I be so incredibly stupid! I took the cigarette and squashed it out in my hand and never felt it burn me. The pictures, the pictures! Nancy must have used herself to work up the prettiest blackmail scheme that ever was. She had pictures of everything and everybody and was getting ready to use them when Feeney Last in his visits to her room saw the damn things and wanted them himself.

Of course, how could it be any other way? A cheap gunman with big ideas who saw a way to cash in. But before he could do the job himself Nancy stepped out in front of a car and got herself killed. Maybe Feeney even had a guy trailing her to keep track of things, a guy who knew enough to take the ring off and stall identification. And why? Because when she was identified somebody else might get to the stuff first. The ring was an accident.

And Nancy was just a blackmailer at heart.

Nuts! I still didn't care what she was. For a little while she was my friend. Maybe Feeney didn't kill her, but he had it in mind, which was the same thing to me, and he was going to pay for it. I had liked the blonde, too.

I blew a ring at the ceiling and Lola stuck her finger through it. She was waiting again, giving me time to think. Aloud, I said, 'The camera, Lola, where could it be?'

She answered me with a question. 'Didn't Nancy imply to you that she was up against it for some reason?'

The redhead had, at that. 'Uh-huh. Business was bad, she said. Feeney might have conceivably been driving her customers away purposely. He tried it with me that first night. She needed dough. She hocked the camera.'

Each thought brought a newer one. The puzzle that had been scattered all over the place was being drawn in on the table by an invisible vacuum cleaner. Ghostly fingers were picking up the pieces and putting them in place, hesitating now and then to let me make a move. It was a game. First, he'd put in one, then I'd put in one. Then he let me put in two, three, urging me to finish the puzzle myself. But some of the pieces would fit two places, and you'd have to hold them out until you were sure.

The old biddy at Nancy's rooming house said she showed up with a couple of bucks and nothing else. She was broke. Where did she come from? Was she trying to get away from Feeney Last . . . only to have him catch up with her anyway? Like Cobbie Bennett said, the grapevine had a loud voice. It could certainly keep track of a redheaded prostitute. So she moved around trying to get away from him and couldn't. Some place behind her she had left the wealth of pictures he was after, and they were still there. Still there waiting to be found, and right now somebody was looking for them and taking his time because he thought I was dead. Feeney Last was in for a big surprise.

Lola slipped her arm around me. 'Is it finished?'

'Almost.' I relaxed in peaceful anticipation.

'When?'

'Tomorrow. The next day. It'll be soon. Tomorrow we'll pick up the trail. First, I'll have to get a new gun. Pat'll fix me up. Then we'll begin.'

'Who's we?'

'Me and you, sugarpuss. I'm supposed to be dead, remember. A corpse can't go roaming around the streets. Tomorrow you're going to run your poor legs to the bone, checking every hock shop in town, until we find that camera. There will be an address on the ticket, if it's still around, and that's what we want.'

Lola showed her teeth in a grin and poked her legs out in front of her. Very temptingly she inched her dress up, letting me see the lush fullness of the calves, bringing it higher over her knees until the smooth white flesh showed over her stocking tops.

Her eyebrows were lifted in a tantalizing way and she whispered, 'Won't that take a lot of walking?'

It would take a hell of a lot of walking.

I reached over and pulled her dress down, which wasn't like me at all, but it was worth it because she threw her head back and laughed, and I kissed her before she could close her mouth, and felt her arms tighten around my neck until it hurt again.

I pushed her away roughly, still holding her close, and she said, 'I love you, Mike, I love you, I love you, I love you.'

151

I wanted to tell her the same thing, but she knew it was coming, and stopped me with her mouth again. She stood up then, holding out her hands so she could pull me to my feet. While I watched, she transformed the sofa into a bed and brought out a pillow from her bedroom. I kicked off my shoes and tossed my coat and tie on a chair. 'You go to bed,' I said, 'we'll hold the wake some other night.'

'Good night, Mike.' She blew a kiss. I shook my head, and she came back for a real one. I lay down on the sheets trying to figure out whether I was a jerk, just plain reformed, too tired, or in love.

I guessed it was because I was too tired, and I fell asleep grinning.

CHAPTER ELEVEN

It was the sound of coffee bubbling and the smell of bacon and eggs sizzling in a pan that awakened me. I yawned, stretched and came alive as Lola walked in. She was just as lovely in the morning as she had been last night. She crooked her finger at me. 'Breakfast is served, my lord.'

As soon as she went back to the kitchen I climbed into my clothes and followed. Over the table she told me that she had already called and told her boss that she was sick and was ordered to take the day off. Several, if she needed them.

'You're in solid, I guess.'

She wrinkled her nose at me. 'They're just being nice to a good worker. They like my modelling technique.'

When we finished she went into the bedroom and changed into a suit, tucking her hair up under her hat. She deliberately left off most of the make-up, but it didn't spoil her looks any. 'I'm trying to look like I can afford only to do my shopping in hock shops,' she explained.

'They'll never believe it, honey.'

'Stop being nice to me.' She paused in front of the mirror and surveyed the effect, making last-minute adjustments here and there. 'Now, what do I do and say, Mike?'

I leaned back in the chair, hooking my feet over the rungs. 'Take the phone book . . . the classified section. Make a list of all the joints and start walking. You know the camera . . . it may be in the window, it may be inside. Tell the guy what you want and look them over. If you see it, buy it. Remember, what you want is the address on the ticket. You can make up your own story as you go along . . . just make it good, and don't appear over-anxious.'

I dragged out my wallet and fingered off some bills. 'Here!

You'll need taxi fare and grub money, plus what the guy will ask. That is, if you find it.'

She tucked the bills in her pocket-book. 'Frankly, what do you think of the chances, Mike?'

'Not too good. Still, it's the only out I know of. It won't be easy to run down, but it's the only lead I have right now.'

'Will you be here while I'm gone?'

'I may be, I don't know.' I wrote down my home and office addresses, then added Pat's number as an afterthought. 'In case you find anything, call me here or at these numbers. If you're in a jam and I'm not around, call Pat. Now, have you got everything straight?'

She nodded. 'I think so. Does the faithful wife off to work get a farewell kiss from her lazy spouse?'

I grabbed her arm and hauled her down to me, bruising her lips with mine, and felt the fire start all over again. I had to push her away.

'I don't want to go,' she said.

'Scram!' She wrinkled her nose again and waved to me from the doorway.

As soon as she left I went over to the phone and dialled the office. Velda started with, 'I'm sorry, but Mr Hammer isn't here at the moment.'

'Where is he?'

'I'm not at liberty to say. He should . . . Mike! Where the devil are you now? Why don't you stop in and take care of your business? I never . . .'

'Off my back, chick. I'm tied up. Look, have I had any calls?'

'I'll say you have. So far I haven't had time to answer the mail!'

'Who called?'

'First off there was a man who wouldn't give his name. Said it was confidential and he'd call back later. Then two prospective clients called, but I told them you were engaged. Both of them thought their business was so urgent you'd drop what you were doing and go with them.'

'Get their names?'

'Yes. Both were named Johnson. Mark and Joseph Johnson, neither related.'

I grunted. Johnson was about the third or fourth most popular name in the phone directory. 'Who else?'

'There was a guy named Cobbie Bennett, I had a hard time getting his name because he was almost hysterical. He said he had to see you right away but wouldn't say why. I told him you'd call back soon as you came in. He wouldn't leave a number. He's called three times since.'

'Cobbie! What could he want? He said nothing at all, Velda?'

'Not a thing.'

'O.K., continue.'

'Your client, Mr Berin-Grotin, called. He wanted to know if his cheque got to the bank in time. I didn't know about it so I said you'd check with him. He said not to bother if everything was all right.'

'Well, everything's not all right, but it's too late to bother about now. You hold down the phone, kiddo. Give out the same answers to whoever calls. Keep one thing in mind . . . you *don't* know where I am and you *haven't* heard from me since yesterday. Got it?'

'Yes, but . . .'

'No buts. The only one you can feel free to speak to is Pat or a girl called Lola. Take their messages. If they have anything for me try to get me at home or here.' I rattled off Lola's number and waited while she wrote it down.

'Mike . . . what is it? Why can't you . . .'

I was tired of repeating it. 'I'm supposed to be dead, Velda. The killer thinks he nailed me.'

'Mike!'

'Oh, quit worrying. I'm not even scratched. The bullet hit my gun. Which reminds me . . . I got to get a new one. 'Bye baby. See you soon.'

I stuck the phone back and sat on the edge of the chair, running my hand across my face. Cobbie Bennett. He was hysterical and he wanted to see me. He wouldn't say why. I wondered which of the Johnson boys was the killer trying to make certain I was gone from the land of the living. And who was the caller with the confidential info? At least I knew who Cobbie was.

I hoped I knew where I could find him.

My coat was wrinkled from lying across the chair, and without a rod under my arm the thing bagged like a zoot suit. The holster helped fill it out, but not enough. I closed the door behind me and walked downstairs, trying to appear like just another resident, maybe a little on the seedy side. In that neighbourhood nobody gave me a tumble.

At Ninth Avenue I grabbed a cab and had him drive me over to a gunsmith on the East Side. The guy who ran the shop plight have made Daniel Boone's rifle for him, he was so old. At one time guns had been his mainstay, but since the coming of law and order he specialized in locks, even if the sign over the door didn't say so.

He didn't ask questions except to see my licence, and when he had gone over it to the extent of comparing the picture with my face, he nodded and asked me what I liked. There were some new Army .45's mounted in a rack on the wall and I pointed them out. He took them down and let me try the action. When I found one that satisfied me I peeled off a bill from my roll, signed the book and took my receipt and a warning to check with the police on the change in gun numbers on my ticket.

I felt a lot better when I walked out of the place.

If the sun had been tucked in bed I would have been able to locate Cobbie in a matter of minutes. At high noon it was going to be a problem. In a cigar store on the corner I cashed in a buck for a handful of nickels and started working the phone book, calling the gin mills where he usually hung out. I got the same answer every time. Cobbie had dropped out of sight. Two wanted to know who I was, so I said a friend and hung up.

Sometimes the city is worse than the jungle. You can get lost in it with a million people within arm's length. I was glad of it now. A guy could roam the streets for a week without being recognized if he were careful not to do anything to attract attention. A cab went by and I whistled it, waited while it braked to a stop and backed up, then got in. After I told the driver where to go, I settled back against the cushions and did exercises to loosen up my neck.

I missed the redhead's ring. I was doing good while I had it. Nancy, a mother . . . a blackmailer? A girl down on her luck. A good kid. I could never forget the way she looked at me when I gave her the dough. I'd never forget it, because I told her that kind of stuff was murder.

I didn't know how right I was.

She must have had fun shopping for those clothes, being waited on, seeing herself in the mirror as a lady again. What had happened to her attitude, her personal philosophy after that? She was happy, I knew that. Her letter was bubbling over with happiness. What was it that meant so much to her? . . . and did I help change her mind about it?

Nancy with the grace of a lady, the veneer of a tramp. A girl who should have been soft and warm, staying home nights to cook supper for some guy, was being terrorized by a gun-slinging punk. A lousy greaseball. A girl who had no defence except running, forced to sell herself to keep alive. I did her a favour and her eyes lit up like candles at an altar. We were buddies, damn good buddies for a little while.

The driver said, 'Here you are, mister.'

I passed a bill through the window and got out, my eyes looking up and down the street until I spotted a familiar blue uniform. I was going to have to do it the quickest way possible. The cop was walking towards me and I stared into a drugstore window until he went by, and when he had a half-block lead I followed him at a leisurely pace.

A lot of people like to run down the cops. They begin to think of them as human traffic lights, or two faces in a patrol car cruising down the street hoping some citizen will start some trouble. They forget that a cop has eyes and ears and can think. They forget that sometimes a cop on a beat likes it that way. The street is his. He knows everyone on it. He knows who and what they are and where they spend their time. He doesn't want to get pulled off it even for a promotion, because then he loses his friends and becomes chained to a desk or an impersonal case. The cop I was following looked like that kind. He was big from the ground up, and almost as big around. There was a purpose in his stride and pride in his carriage, and several times I saw him nod to women sitting in doorways and fake a pass at fresh brats that yelled out something nasty about coppers. Some day those same kids would be screaming for him to hurry up and get to where the trouble was.

When the cop called in at a police phone I picked up on him. He turned into a lunch-room, climbed on a stool and I was right beside him. He took off his coat and hat, ordered corn beef and cabbage and I took the same. The plates came and we both ate silently. Half-way through, the two guys next to me paid up and left, which was the chance I waited for.

One had left a tabloid on the stool and I propped it up in front of me, using it as a shield while I took my badge and identification card from my pocket. I only had to nudge the cop once and he looked over, saw the stuff I palmed and frowned.

'Mike Hammer, private cop.' I kept my voice low, chewing as I spoke. 'Don't watch me.'

The cop frowned again and went back to his lunch. 'Pat Chambers will vouch for me. I'm working with him on a case.' This time the frown deepened and lines of disbelief touched his cheeks.

'I have to find Cobbie Bennett,' I said. 'Right away. Do you know where he is?'

He took another mouthful of corn beef and threw a dime on the counter. The chef came over and he asked for change. When he had two nickels he got up, still chewing, and walked over to a phone booth up front and shut the door.

About a minute later he was back and working on the corn beef again. He shoved the plate away, drew his coffee to him and seemed to notice me for the first time.

'Done with the paper, feller?'

'Yeah.' I handed it to him. He took a pair of horn-rimmed glasses from his pocket and worked them on, holding the paper open to the baseball scores. His lips worked as if he were reading, only he said, 'I think Cobbie's hiding out in a rooming-house one block west. Brownstone affair with a new stoop. He looks scared.'

The counterman came over and took the plates away. I ordered pie and more coffee, ate it slowly, then paid up and left. The cop was still there reading the paper; he never glanced up once and he probably wouldn't for another ten minutes.

I found the stoop first, then the house. Cobbie Bennett found me. He peered out of a second-storey window just as I turned up the stairs and for a split second I had a look at a pale, white face that had terror etched deep into the skin.

The door was open and I walked into the hallway. Cobbie called to me from the head of the stairs. 'Here, up here, Mike.' This time I watched where I was going. There were too many nice places for a guy to hide with a baseball bat in those damn hallways. Before I reached the landing Cobbie had me by the lapels of my coat and was dragging me into a room.

'Christ, Mike, how'd ya find me? I never told nobody where I was! Who said I was here?'

I shoved him away. 'You're not hard to find, Cobbie. Nobody is when they're wanted badly enough.'

'Don't say that, Mike, will ya? Christ, it's bad enough having you find me. Suppose . . .'

'Stop jabbering like an idiot. You wanted me, so I'm here.'

He shoved a bolt in the door and paced across the room, running his fingers through his hair and down his face. He couldn't stand still and the fact that I parked myself in the only chair in the place and seemed completely at ease made him jumpier still.

'They're after me, Mike. I just got away in time.'

'Who's they?'

'Look, ya gotta help me out. Jeez, you got me inta this, now ya gotta help me out. They're after me, see? I can't stick around.

159

I gotta get outa town.' He stuck a cigarette in his mouth and tried to light it. He made it with the fourth match.

'Who's they?' I asked again.

Cobbie licked his lips. His shoulder had a nervous twitch and he kept turning his head towards the door as if he were listening for something. 'Mike, somebody saw you with me that night. They passed the word and the heat's on. I – I gotta blow.'

I just sat there and watched him. He took a drag on the cigarette before he threw it on the worn-out carpet and ground it in with his heel. 'Damn it, Mike, don't just sit there. Say something!'

'Who's they?'

For the first time it sank in. He got white around the corners of his mouth. 'I dunno. I dunno. It's somebody big. Something's popping in this town and I don't know what it is. All I know is the heat's on me because I got seen messing around with you. What'll I do, Mike? I can't stay here. You don't know them guys. When they're out to get ya they don't miss!'

I stood up and stretched, trying to look bored. 'I can't tell you a damn thing, Cobbie, not unless you sound off first. If you don't want to speak, then the hell with you. Let 'em get you.'

He grabbed my sleeve and hung on for dear life. 'No, Mike, don't . . . I'd tell you what I know only I don't know nothing. I just got the sign, then I heard some things. It was about that redhead. Because of you I'm getting the works. I saw some big boys down the street last night. They wasn't locals. They was here before when there was some trouble, and a couple guys disappeared. I know why they're there . . . they're after me . . . and you maybe.'

He was doing better now. 'Go on, Cobbie.'

'Th' racket's organized, see? We pay for protection and we pay plenty. I don't know where it goes, but as long as we pay there's no trouble. As long as we make like clams there's still no trouble. But, damn it, you came around and somebody saw me shooting my mouth off, now there's plenty of trouble again and it's all for me.'

'How do they know what you said?'

His face grew livid. 'Who cares? Think they worry about what I said? Some guys is poison and you're one, because you was on that redhead! Why didn't she drop dead sooner!'

I reached out and grabbed his arm and brought him up to my face. 'Shut up,' I said through my teeth.

'Aw, Mike, I didn't mean nothin', honest. I'm just trying to tell ya.'

I let him go and he backed off a step, wiping his forehead with a sleeve. The light glistened on a tear that rolled down his cheek. 'I don't know what it's about, Mike. I don't wanna get knocked off. Can't you do something?'

'Maybe.'

Cobbie looked up, hopefully. His tongue passed over his parched lips. 'Yeah?'

'Think, Cobbie. Think of the boys you saw. Who were they?'

The lines in his face grew deeper. 'Hard boys. They were carrying rods. I think they came outa Detroit.'

'Who do they work for?'

'The same guy what gets the pay-off jack, I guess.'

'Names, Cobbie?'

He shook his head, the hope gone. 'I'm only a little guy, Mike. How would I know? Every week I give a quarter of my take to a guy who passes it along in a chain until it reaches the top. I don't even want to know. I'm . . . I'm scared, Mike, scared silly. You're the only one I knew to call. Nobody'll look at me now because they know the heat's on, that's why I wanted to see you.'

'Anybody know you're here?'

'No. Just you.'

'What about the landlady?'

'She don't know me. She don't care, neither. How'd you find me, Mike?'

'A way your pals won't try. Don't worry about it. Here's what I want you to do. Sit tight, don't leave this room, not even to go downstairs. Keep away from the window and be sure your door is locked.'

161

His eyes widened and his hands went to my arms. 'You got an out figgered? You think maybe I can get outa town?'

'Could be. We'll have to do this carefully. You got anything to eat in the place?'

'Some canned stuff and two bottles of beer.'

'It'll hold you. Now remember this. Tomorrow night at exactly nine-thirty I want you to walk out of this place. Go down the street, turn right one block, then head west again. Keep walking as if you didn't know a thing was up. Take a turn around your neighbourhood and say hullo to anyone you want to. Only keep walking. Got that?'

Little beads of sweat were standing out on his forehead. 'Christ, ya want me to get killed? I can't leave here and . . .'

'Maybe you'd sooner get bumped off here . . . if you don't starve to death first.'

'No, Mike. I don't even mean that! But, jeez, walking out like that! . . .'

'Are you going to do it or not? I haven't got time to waste, Cobbie.'

He sank into the chair and covered his face with his hands. Crying came easy for Cobbie. 'Y-yeah. I'll go. Nine-thirty.' His head jerked up, tears streaking his face. 'What're ya thinking of? Can't you tell me?'

'No, I can't. You just do what I told you. If it works, you'll be able to leave town in one piece. But I want you to remember something.'

'What?'

'Don't – ever – come – back.'

I left him with his face white and sick-looking. When the door closed I heard him sobbing again.

Outside, a premature dusk was settling over the city as the grey haze of rain clouds blew in from the south-east. I crossed the street and walked north to a subway kiosk. Before I reached it the rain had started again. A train had just pulled out of the station, giving me five minutes to wait, so I found a phone and called Lola's apartment. Nobody answered. No news was good news, or so they say. I tried the office and Velda told me it had been a fairly quiet afternoon. I hung up before she could ask questions. Besides, my train was just rattling past the platform.

At Fifty-ninth I got off, grabbed another cab and had the driver haul me over to where my car was parked. I thought I saw a guy I knew walk past and I went into a knee bend fumbling for my shoelace. It was getting to be a pain in the butt playing corpse.

When I finally got the chance I hopped in and shot away from there as fast as I could. Some chances I couldn't afford, one was being spotted near Lola's place. She was one person I wanted to myself, all nice and safe.

The wind picked up and began throwing the rain around. The few pedestrians left on the sidewalks were huddled under marquees or bellowing for cabs that didn't stop. Every time I stopped for a red light I could see the pale blur of faces behind the glass store-fronts, the water running down making them waver eerily. All with that same blank look of the trapped when nothing can be done to help.

I was wondering if Lola was having any trouble. The rain was going to slow her up plenty at a time when speed was essential. That damn camera! Why did Red ever mess with it in the first place?

Lola had said a job, didn't she? A place called Quick Pix or something. It had slipped my mind until now. I spotted a parking place ahead and turned into it, ready to make a dash into a candy store the moment the rain slackened. There was a lull between gusts that gave me a chance to run across the pavement and work my way through the small crowd that had gathered in the doorway out of the wet.

Inside I pulled out the directory and thumbed through it, trying each borough, but nothing like Quick Pix showed up. Not even a variation. I bought a pack of butts and asked the clerk if he had an old directory around and he shook his head, paused, then told me to wait a minute. He went into the back

163

room and came up with a dog-eared Manhattan phone book, covered with dust.

'They usually take 'em back, but this was an extra they forgot,' he explained. 'Saw it the other day at the back of the shelf.'

I thanked him and ran through it. The hunch paid off. Quick Pix had a phone number and an address off Seventh Avenue. When I dialled the number there was a series of clicks and the operator asked me who I was calling. I gave her the number and she said it had been discontinued some time ago.

That was that. Or not quite. Maybe they still had an office, but no phone.

One of the boys asked me if I was going uptown and I nodded for him to come along. For ten blocks he kept up an incessant line of chatter that I didn't hear until he poked me to let him out at a subway station. I pulled over, he opened the door and thanked me and ran down the stairs.

Behind me a line of horns blasted an angry barrage in my direction, and over it a cop's whistle shrilled a warning. I came back to the present with a dirty word and my mind in a spin, because on the news-stand by the subway was a pile of the late evening papers and each one screamed to the world that the police were conducting a city-wide clean-up campaign of vice.

Somebody had talked.

I stopped for another red light, yelling to a newsy to bring one over and I gave him a buck for his trouble. It was there, all right, heads, captions, and sub-captions. The police were in possession of information that was going to lead to the biggest round-up of this, that, and the next thing the city ever saw.

Which was fine, great. Just what we wanted in the pig's neck. Pat must be raving mad. The papers were doing a beautiful civic job of chasing the rats out of town. Damn them, why couldn't they keep quiet!

The light changed and I saw my street coming up. I had to circle the block because it was a one-way, then squeeze in between a decrepit delivery truck and a battered sedan. The number I wanted was a weather-beaten loft building with an upholstery shop fronting on the street. On one side was a narrow entrance with a service elevator in the rear and a sign announcing the available vacancies hanging on the door.

I rang the bell and heard the elevator rattle its way downwards and come to a stop. The door opened and a guy with a week's growth of beard looked at me with rheumy eyes and waited for me to say something.

'Where can I find the super of this building?'

'Whatcha want him fer?' He spat a stream of tobacco juice between the grill of the elevator.

I palmed my badge in one hand and a fin in the other and let him see both. 'Private cop.'

'I'm the super,' he said.

He reached for the fin and tucked it in his shirt pocket. 'I'm listening.'

I said, 'I'm looking for an outfit called Quick Pix. They were listed as being here.'

'That was a long time ago, buster. They pulled out in a hurry 'most a year ago.'

'Anybody there now?'

'Naw. This place's a dive. Who the hell would want to rent here? Maybe another outfit like Q.P. They was a fly-by-night bunch, I think.'

'How about a look at the place?'

'Sure, come on.'

I stepped aboard and we crept up to the fourth floor and stopped. He left the elevator there and turned the lights on, pointing to the end of the hall. 'Room 209.'

The door wasn't locked. Where an ordinary house night-latch should be was a round hole like an eye in a skull. The super did some trick with a switch box in a closet and the lights went on in the room.

It was a mess, all right. Somebody had packed out of there like the devil was on his tail. Finished, proofs and negatives littered the floor, covered with spider webs and long tendrils of dust. The two windows had no shades and didn't need them, that's how thick the dirt was. Hypo had blown or was knocked from a box, covering one end with once white powder. Even now a few heel prints were visible in the stuff.

I gathered up a handful of snaps and looked them over. They were all two-by-three prints taken on the streets of couples walking arm-in-arm, sitting on park benches, coming out of Broadway theatres grinning at each other. On the backs were numbers in pencil and scrawled notations of the photogs.

A large packing-box served as a filing cabinet, spilling out blank tickets with a slit built for a quarter. The back half of the box contained other tickets that had been sent in with the mailer's name and address written in the right spot. They were tied in groups of about a hundred, and, all in all, there was a couple thousand dollars represented in cash right there. Quick Pix had done all right for itself.

To one side was a shelf running around the wall lined with shoe boxes and inscribed with names. One said 'N. Sanford' and my interest picked up. In it were cards numbered to correspond with the film in the camera, which looked like a three- or four-day supply. A pencilled note was a reminder to order more film. Neat, precise handwriting. Very feminine: It was Nancy's without a doubt. I plucked it out and tucked it in my pocket.

The guy had been standing near the door watching me silently. I heard him grunt a few times, then: 'You know something? This place wasn't like this when they moved out.'

I stopped what I was doing. 'How's that?'

'I came in to see if they left the walls here and all this junk on the floor was stacked in one corner. Looks like somebody kicked it around.'

'Yeah?'

He spat on the floor. 'Yeah.'

'Who ran the business?'

'Forgot his name.' He shrugged. 'Some character on his uppers. Guess he did pretty good after a while. One day he packs in here with a new convertible, tells me he's moving out and scrams. Never gimme a dime.'

'What about the people that worked for him?'

'Hell, they was all out. They came in here that night and raised a stink. What was I supposed to do, pay their wages? I was lucky I tagged the guy, so I got the rent. Never said nothing to nobody, he didn't.'

I stuck a match in my mouth and chewed the end off it. When I gave one last quick glance I walked out. 'That does it.' He shut the door and played with the switch box again, then stepped into the elevator after me and we started down.

'Get what you come for?' he asked.

'I didn't come for anything special. I'm, er, checking on the owner. He owed some money and I have to collect – for films.'

'You don't say! Come to think of it, there's some stuff down in the cellar yet. One of the kids what worked there asked me if she could park it there. I let her when she slipped me a buck.'

'She?'

'Yeah, a redhead. Nice kid.'

He spat through the grill again and it splattered against the wall. 'Do you ever read the papers?' I asked him.

'Funnies sometimes. Just the pictures. Broke my glasses four years ago and never got new ones. Why what's going on?'

'Nothing. Let's see that stuff downstairs.'

Before he could suggest it I came across with another five and it went in the pocket with the other. His grin showed teeth that were brown as mud. We passed the main floor and jolted to a stop at the basement. The air was damp and musty, almost like the morgue, but here was the smell of dirt and decay and the constant whirr of rat feet running along the pipes and timbers. There weren't any lights, but the guy had a flashlight stashed in a joint and he threw the beams around the walls. Little beady eyes looked back at me and ran off, to reappear again farther down. I got the creeps.

He didn't seem to mind it at all.

'Down back, I think.' He pointed the flash at the floor and we stepped over crates, broken furniture and the kind of trash that accumulates over a span of years. We stopped by a bin

167

and he poked around with a broom handle, scaring up some rats but nothing else. Beyond that was a row of shelves piled to capacity and he knocked the dust off some of the papers with a crack of the stick. Most of them were old bills and receipts, a few dusty ledgers and a wealth of old paper that had been saved up carefully. I opened a couple of boxes to help out. One was full of pencil stubs; the other some hasty sketches of nudes. They weren't very good.

The light got away from me before I could shove them back and the super said, 'Think this is it.' I held the light while he dragged out a corrugated cardboard box tied with twine. A big SAVE was written across the front in red crayon. He nodded and pursed his mouth, looking for a rat to spit tobacco juice at. He saw one on a pipe and let loose. I heard the rat squeaking all the way to the end, where he fell off and kicked around in some papers. The stuff he chewed must have been poison.

I pulled the twine off and opened the top. Inside was another box tied with lighter cord that broke easily enough. My hand was shaking a little as I bent back the cover and I pulled the light closer.

There were pictures in this one, all neatly sorted in two rows and protected by layers of tissue paper. Both sides of the box were lined with blotters to absorb any moisture, and between each group of shots was an index card bearing the date they were taken.

Perhaps I expected too much. Perhaps it was the thought of the other pictures that were stolen from me, perhaps it was just knowing that pictures fitted in somewhere, but I held my breath expectantly as I lifted them out.

Then I went into all the curse words I knew. All I had was another batch of street photos with smiling couples waving into the camera or doing something foolish. I was so damn mad I would have left them there if I hadn't remembered that they cost me five bucks and I might as well get something for my dough. I tucked the box under my arm and went back to the elevator.

When we got to the street floor the super wanted to know if I felt like signing the after-hours book and I scratched J. Johnson in it and left.

At eight-fifteen I called Pat's home. He still hadn't come in, so I tried the office. The switchboard located him and the minute I heard his voice I knew there was trouble. He said, 'Mike? where are you?'

'Not far from your place. Anything new?'

'Yes.' His words were clipped. 'I want to speak to you. Can you meet me in the Roundtown Grill in ten minutes?'

'I'll be there. What's up?'

'Tell you then. Ten minutes.' Someone called to him and he hung up. Ten minutes to the second I reached the Roundtown and threaded my way to the back and found Pat sitting in the last booth. There were lines of worry across his forehead that hadn't been there before, giving him an older look. He forced a grin when he saw me, and waved me to sit down.

Beside him he had a copy of the evening paper and he spread it out on the table. He tapped the headline. 'Did you have anything to do with this?'

I shoved a butt in my mouth and fired it. 'You know better than that, Pat.'

He rolled the paper up into a ball and threw it aside, his mouth twisting into a snarl. 'I didn't think so. I had to be sure. It got out some way and loused things up nice.'

'How?'

A waiter set two beers down in front of us and Pat polished his off before the guy left and ordered another, quick. 'I'm getting squeezed, pal. I'm getting squeezed nice. Do you know how many rotten little jerks there are in this world? There must be millions. Nine-tenths of them live in the city with us. Each rotten little jerk controls a block of votes. Each rotten little jerk wants something done or not done. They make a phone call to somebody who's pretty important and tell him what they want. Pretty soon that person gets a lot of the same kind of phone calls and decides that maybe he'd better do something about it, and the squeeze starts. Word starts drifting up the line to lay off or go slow, and it's the kind of a word that's blocked up with a threat that can be made good.

'Pretty, isn't it? You get hold of something that should be done and you have to lay off.' The second beer followed the first and another was on its way. I had never seen Pat so mad before.

'I tried to be a decent cop,' he ranted. 'I try to stick to the letter of the law and do my duty. I figure the taxpayers have a say in things, but now I begin to wonder. It's coming from all directions – phone calls, hints that travelled too far to trace back, sly reminders that I'm just a cop and nothing but a captain, which doesn't carry too much weight if certain parties feel like doing something about it.'

'Get down to cases, Pat.'

'The D.A. called Ann Minor's death murder. He's above a fix and well in the public eye, so there's no pressure on him. The murder can be investigated if necessary, but get off the angles. That's the story. Word got out about the book, but not the fact that it's in code.'

I tapped the ashes in the tray and squinted at him. 'You mean there are a lot of boys mixed up with call-girls and the prostitution racket who don't want their names to get out, don't you.'

'Yes.'

'And what are you going to do about it?'

No, Pat wasn't a bit happy. He said. 'Either I go ahead with it, dig up the stuff and then get nicely pushed into a resignation, or I lay off and keep my job, sacrificing this case to give the public their money's worth in future cases.'

I shook my head pathetically. 'That's what you get for being honest. What'll it be?'

'I don't know, Mike.'

'You'll have to make up your mind soon.'

'I know. For the first time I wish I were wearing your badge instead of mine. You aren't so dumb.'

'Neither are you, kid. The answer's plain, isn't it?' I was sneering myself now. He looked up and met my eyes and nodded. A nasty grin split his lips apart and his teeth were together, tight.

'Call it, Mike.'

'You take care of your end. I'll brace the boys who give you trouble. If I have to I'll ram their teeth down their throats and I hope I have to. There's more to it than that. I don't have to tell you how big this racket is. The girls in the flashy clothes and the high-price tags are only one side of it. The same group with its hand on them reaches down to the smaller places, too. It's all tied in together. The only trouble is that when you untie one knot the whole thing can come apart.

'They're scared now. They're acting fast. We have that book, but you can bet it isn't much. There are other books, too, nicely ducked out of sight where it'll take a lot of looking to dig up. They'll come. We'll get hold of somebody who will sing, and to save their own necks the others will sing, too. Then the proof will pop up.'

I slammed my hand against the table and curled my fingers into a tight knot until the flesh was white around the knuckles. 'We don't need proof, Pat. All we have to do is *look* for proof. The kind of boys behind the curtain won't take that. They'll make a move and we'll be ready for them.'

'Yeah, but when?'

'Tomorrow night. The big boys are hiring their work done. One of their stoolies is on the list because he sounded off to me. Tomorrow night at exactly nine-thirty, a pimp called Cobbie Bennett is going to walk out of his rooming-house and down the street. Some time that night he's going to be spotted and a play will be made. That's all we need. Beat them to the jump and we'll make the first score. It will scare the hell out of them again. Let them know that politics are going to pot. We can get the politicians later if we have to.'

'Does this Bennett know about this?'

'He knows he's going to be a clay pigeon of some sort. It's his only chance of staying alive. Maybe he will and maybe he won't. He has to take it. You have your men spotted around

171

ready to wade in when the trouble starts. After it's finished, let Cobbie beat it. He's no good any more. He won't be back.'

I wrote the address of the rooming-house on the back of an envelope, diagraming the route Cobbie would take, and passed it over. Pat glanced at it and stuck it in his pocket. 'This can mean my job, kid.'

'It might mean your neck, too,' I reminded him, 'If it works you won't have any more sly hints and phone calls, and those rotten little jerks with the bloc of votes will be taking the next train out of town. We're not going to stop anything because the game is as old as Eve. What we will do is slow it up long enough to keep a few people alive who wouldn't be alive, and maybe knock off some who would be better off dead.'

'And all because of one redheaded girl,' Pat said slowly.

'That's right. All because of Nancy. All because she was murdered.'

'We don't know that.'

'I'm supposing it. I've uncovered a few other things. If it was an accident, she wasn't expected to die that way. Nancy was slated to be killed. Here's something else, Pat. This *looks* like one thing, the part you can't see is tied in with that same redhead. I can't understand it, but I'm kicking a few ideas around that look pretty good.'

'The insurance company is satisfied it was an accident. They're ready to pay off if her inheritors can be found.'

'Ah, that's the rub, as the bard once said. That, my chum, is the big step.'

My watch was creeping up on itself. I stood up and finished the beer that had turned flat while we talked. 'I'll call you early tomorrow, Pat. I want to be in on the show. Let me know what comes out of the little black book.'

He still wore his sneer. Back of his eyes a fire was burning bright enough to put somebody in hell.

'Something came out of it already. We paid a call on Murray Candid. Among his belongings we found a few doodles and some notes. The symbols compare with some of those in his book. He's going to have to do some tall explaining when we find him.'

My mouth fell open at that. 'What do you mean . . . find him?'

'Murray Candid has disappeared. He wasn't seen by anybody after he left us,' he said.

CHAPTER TWELVE

As I got into my car I thought over what Pat had said. Murray was gone. Why? That damned, ever-present why! Did he duck out to escape what would follow, or was he taken away because he knew too much? A guy like Murray was a slicker. If he knew too much he knew he knew it, and knew what it could cost him, so he'd have to play it smart and have insurance. Murray would let it be known that anybody who tried to plough him under would be cutting their own throats. He'd have a fat, juicy report in a lawyer's hands, ready to be mailed to the police as soon as he was dead. That's double indemnity . . . the bigger boys would have to keep him alive to keep their own noses clean.

No, Murray wasn't dead. The city was big enough to hide even him. He'd show sooner or later. Pat would have covered that angle, and right now there'd be a cop watching every bus terminal, every train station. I bet they'd see more rats than Murray trying to desert the sinking ship.

The rain had turned into a steady drizzle that left a slick on the pavement and deadened the evening crowd. I turned north with the windshield wipers clicking a monotonous tune, and stopped a block away from Lola's apartment. A grocery store was still open and the stack of cold cuts in the window looked too inviting to pass up. When I had loaded my arms with more than I could eat for a month, I used the package to shield my face and walked up to her place.

I kicked the door with my foot and she yelled to come in. I had to peek around the bundle to see her stretched out on the couch with her shoes off and a wet towel across her forehead.

'It's me, honey.'

'Do tell. I thought it was a horse coming up the stairs.'

I propped the package in a chair and sat down on the edge of the couch, reaching for the towel. She came out from under it grinning. 'Oh, Mike! It's so good to see you!'

She threw her arms around my neck and I leaned over and kissed her. She was nice to look at. I could sit there all day and watch her. She closed her eyes and rubbed her hair in my face.

'Rough day, kid?'

'Awful,' she said. 'I'm tired, I'm wet and I'm hungry. And I didn't find the camera.'

'I can take care of the hungry part. There's eats over there. Nothing you have to cook either.'

'You're a wonderful guy, Mike. I wish . . .'

'What?'

'Nothing. Let's eat.'

I slid my arms under her and lifted her off the couch. Her eyes had a hungry sparkle that could mean many things. 'You're a big girl,' I said.

'I have to be . . . for you. To the kitchen, James.' She scooped up the bag as I passed the chair and went through the doorway.

Lola put the coffee on while I set the table. We used the wrappings for plates and one knife between us, sitting close enough so our knees touched. 'Tell me about today, Lola.'

'There isn't much to tell. I started at the top of the list and reached about fifteen hock shops. None of them had it, and after a few discreet questions I learned that they never had had it. A few of the clerks were so persuasive that they almost made me buy one anyway.'

'How many more to go?'

'Days and days worth, Mike. It will take a long time, I'm afraid.'

'We have to try it.'

'Uh-huh. Don't worry, I'll keep at it. Incidentally, in three of the places that happened to be located fairly close to each other, someone else had been looking for a camera.'

My cup stopped half-way to my mouth. 'Who?'

'A man. I pretended that it might have been a friend of mine who was shopping for me and got one clerk to remember that the fellow had wanted a commercial camera for taking street pictures. Apparently the kind I was after. He didn't look any over; just asked, then left.'

It was a hell of a thought, me letting Lola run head on into something like that. 'It may be a coincidence. He may have shopped just those three places. I don't like it.'

'I'm not afraid, Mike. He . . .'

'If it wasn't a coincidence he might shop the other places and find that you were ahead of him. If he guessed what you were doing he could wait up for you. I still don't like it.'

She became grim then, letting a shadow of her former hardness cloud her face for an instant. 'Like you said, Mike, I'm a big girl. I've been around long enough to stand any guy off if he pulls something on the street. A knee can do a guy a lot of damage in the right places, and if that doesn't work, well . . . one scream will bring a lot of heroes around to take care of any one guy no matter how tough he is.'

I had to laugh at that. 'O.K., O.K., you'll get by. After that speech I'll even be afraid to kiss you good night.'

'Mike, with you I'm as powerless as a kitten and as speechless as a giraffe. Please kiss me good night, huh?'

'I'll think about it. First, we have work to do.'

'What kind, I hope . . .?'

'Look at pictures. I have a batch of pics Nancy had tucked away. They're pictures and I paid for them, so I'll look at them.'

We cleared the mess off the table and I went in for the box. I took them out of the box and piled half in front of Lola and half in front of me. When we took our seats I said, 'Give every one a going-over. They may mean something, they may not. They weren't where they should have been, that's why I'm thinking there might be something special in the lot.'

Lola nodded and picked a snapshot from the top of her pile. I did the same. At first I took in every detail, looking for things out of the ordinary, but the pictures followed such a set pattern that my inspection grew casual and hurried. Faces and more faces. Smiles, startled expressions, deliberate poses. One entire group taken from the same spot on Broadway, always the same background.

In two of them the man in the picture tried to shield his face. The camera was fast enough to stop the motion, but the finger on the shutter trigger was too slow to prevent him getting his hand in the way. I went to put one back on the discard pile, looking at it again carefully and put it aside instead. The portion of the face that showed looked familiar.

Lola said, 'Mike . . .'

She had her lip between her teeth and was fingering a snap. She turned it around and showed it to me, a lovely young girl smiling at a middle-aged man who was frowning at the camera. My eyes asked the question. 'She was . . . one of the girls, Mike. We . . . went on dates together.'

'The guy?'

'I don't know.'

I took the snap and laid it face down with the other. Five minutes later Lola found another. The girl was a zoetic creature, about thirty, with the statuesque lines of a mannequin. The guy she was with could have been a stand-in for a blimp. He was short and fat, in clothes that tried to make him look tall and thin and only made him look shorter and fatter.

'She's another one, Lola?'

'Yes. She didn't last long in New York. She played it smart and married one of the suckers. I remember that man, too. He runs a gambling joint uptown. Some sort of a small-time politician, too. He used to call for her in an official car.'

It was coming now. Little reasons that *explained* the *why*. Little things that would be big things before long. My pile was growing nicely. Maybe every picture on the table had a meaning I couldn't see. Maybe most were just camouflage to discourage hasty searchers.

I turned the snap over, and lightly pencilled on the back near the bottom was 'See S-5.' There was more to it than the picture, evidently.

Could it be nothing more than an office memo . . . or did Nancy have a private file of her own?

My breath started coming in quick, hot gasps. It was like seeing a half-finished picture and recognizing what it would be like when it was finished. If this was an indication . . . I pulled the remaining photos closer and went to work on them.

The next one came out of my deal. I got it because I was lucky and I was hating some people so damn hard that their faces drew an automatic response. The picture was that of a young couple, no more than twenty. They smiled into the camera with a smile that was youth with the world in its pocket and a life to be led. But they weren't important.

It was the background that was important. The faces in the background. One was that of my client, his hand on the knob of a door, a cane swinging jauntily over his arm. Behind him was Feeney Last in a chauffeur's uniform, closing the door of the car. It wasn't just Feeney, it was the expression on his face. It was a leer of hateful triumph, a leer of expectancy as he eyed a guy in a sports outfit that had been about to step past him.

The guy was pop-eyed with fear, his jaw hanging slack, and even at that moment he had started to draw back as he saw Feeney.

He should have been scared. The guy's name was Russ Bowen and he was found shot full of holes not long after the picture was taken.

I could feel the skin pulling tight around my temples and my lips drew back from my teeth. Lola said something, but I didn't hear her. She grabbed my hand, made me look at her, 'What is it. What is it, Mike? Please . . . don't look that way!'

I shoved the picture in front of her and pointed to the little scene in the background. 'This guy's dead, Lola. The other guy is Feeney Last.'

Her eyes came up slowly, unbelievingly. She shook her head. 'Not Feeney . . . it can't be, Mike.'

'Don't tell me, kid. That's Feeney Last. It was taken when he worked for Mr Berin. I couldn't miss that greaseball in a million years.'

She stared at me hard. Her eyes drifted back to the picture and she shook her head again. 'His name is Miller. Paul Miller. He – he's one of the men who supplies girls to . . . the houses.'

'What?'

'That's right. One of the kids pointed him out to me some time ago. He used to work the West Coast, picking them up there and sending them East to the syndicate. I'm positive that's him!'

Nice going, Feeney, I thought, very nice going. Keep a respectable job as a cover-up for the other things. Good heavens if Berin-Grotin in all his insufferable pride ever knew that, he would have had Feeney hanging by the thumbs! I looked at the snap again, saw my client unaware of the little scene behind him, completely the man-about-town bent on an afternoon of mild pleasure. It was a good shot, this one. I could see the lettering on the door there. BAR ENTRANCE, ALBINO CLUB, it read. Apparently Mr Berin's favourite haunt. He'd have his cup of good cheer while five feet away a murder was in progress.

'Do you know the other guy?'

'Yes. He ran some houses. They – found him shot, didn't they?'

'That's right. Murdered. This thing goes back a long way.'

Lola closed her eyes and dropped her head forward. Her face was relaxed in sadness. She took a deep breath and opened her eyes. 'There's something on the back, Mike.'

It was another symbol. This one said, 'See T-9-20.' If that dash stood for 'to', it meant eleven pages of something was connected with this. The details of the Russ Bowen murder maybe? Could there be a possibility that the redhead had come up with something covering that murder? Ye gods, if that were true, no wonder Feeney was on her neck. How many angles could there be to this thing?

I could not find anything else; I went through my pile twice and nothing showed for me, so I swapped with Lola and started all over again. I didn't find any more, either, but Lola did. When she was through she had half a dozen shots beside her and called my attention to the women. They were her former associates. She knew some of the men by sight, too, and they weren't just pick-ups. They dipped dough in the cut of their clothes and the sparkle of diamonds on their fingers.

180

And always there was that notation on the back referring to some other file. There was an envelope on the dish closet and I tucked the prints in it, stowing them in my pocket. The rest I threw back in the box and pushed aside. Lola followed me into the living-room, watched me pace up and down the room. When she held out a cigarette I took it, had one deep drag and snuffed it out in a dish.

Feeney Last. Paul Miller. He came from the Coast. He saw a way to get back East without arousing suspicion. He was connected with the racket but good, and he could operate under the cover of old boys' respectability. Feeney was after Nancy and for good reason. If it was blackmail, the plot went pretty deep. She wasn't content to stick to strangers with herself as the catch . . . she used the tie-up with girls already in the racket.

I stopped in the middle of the floor, fought to let an idea battle its way into my consciousness, felt it blocked by a dozen other thoughts. I shook my head and began pacing again.

'I need a drink,' I said.

'There's nothing in the house,' Lola told me.

I reached for my hat. 'Get your coat. We're going out.'

'Aren't you supposed to be dead?'

'Not that dead. Come on.'

She pulled a raincoat from the closet, stepped into frilly boots that did things for her legs. 'All set, Mike. Where are we going?'

'I'll tell you better when we get there.'

All the way downtown I put my mind to it. Lola had snuggled up against me and I could feel the warmth of her body soaking through her coat to mine. She knew I was trying to think and kept quiet, occasionally looking up at me with interest. She laid her head on my shoulder and squeezed my arm. It didn't help me think any.

The rain had laid a pall over the city, keeping the spectators indoors. Only the tigers were roaming the streets this night. The taxis were empty hearses going back and forth, the drivers alert for what few fares there were, jamming to a stop at the wave of a hand or a shrill whistle.

We went past the Zero Zero Club and Lola sat up to look. There wasn't much to see. The sign was out and the place in darkness. Somebody had tacked a 'Closed' sign on the door. Pat was going whole hog on this thing. I pulled into a half-empty parking lot and we found a small bar with the windows steamed up. Lola had a Martini and I had a beer there, but the place had a rank odour to it and we left. The next bar was three stores down and we turned into it and climbed on the stools at the end.

Four guys at the other end with nothing much to talk about until we came in suddenly found a topic of conversation and eight eyes started looking Lola up and down. One guy told the bartender to buy the lady a drink and she got another Martini and I got nothing.

She was hesitant about taking it at first and I was too deep in thought to argue the point. The redhead's face floated in front of me. She was sipping her coffee again, the ring on her finger half-turned to look like a wedding band: Then the vision would fade and I'd see her hands again, this time folded across her chest and the ring was gone, leaving only a reddish bruise that went unnoticed among the other bruises. The greaseball would laugh at me. I could hear his voice sneering, daring, challenging me to get the answer.

I ordered another beer. Lola had two Martinis in front of her now and one empty pushed aside. The guys were laughing, talking just loud enough to be heard. The guy on the end shrugged as he threw his leg off the stool, said something dirty and came over to Lola with a cocky strut.

He had an arm around her waist and was pulling out the stool next to her when I rolled the cigarette down between my fingers and flipped it. The lit end caught him right in the eye and his sweet talk changed into a yelp of pain that dwindled off to a stream of curses.

The rest of the platoon came off the stools in a well-timed manœuvre that was a second later than mine. I walked around and kicked the wise guy right in the belly, so hard that he was puking his guts out before he hit the floor doubled up like a pretzel. The platoon got back on their stools again without bothering to send a first-aid party out.

I bought Lola the next Martini myself.

The guy on the floor groaned, vomited again, and Lola said, 'Let's leave, Mike. I'm shaking so hard I can't lift the glass.'

I shoved my change towards the bartender who was watching me with a grin on his face. The guy retched again and we left.

'When are you going to talk to me?' Lola asked. 'My honour has been upheld and you haven't even bestowed the smile of victory on me.'

I turned a smile on her, a real one. 'Better?'

'You're so ugly you're beautiful, Mike. Some day I want you to tell me about those scars over your eyes . . . and the one on your chin.'

'I'll only tell you part of the story.'

'The woman in your life, huh?'

When I nodded happily she poked me in the ribs and pretended to be hurt.

One side of the street was fairly well deserted. We waited for a few cars to pass and cut over, our collars turned up against the drizzle. The rain in Lola's hair reflected a thousand lights, each one shimmering separately on its deep-toned background. We swung along with a free stride, holding hands, our shoulders nearly touching, laughing at nothing. It struck me that we were the faces in those pictures, the kind of people the redhead snapped, a sure thing to buy a print to remember the moment.

I wondered what her cut of the quarter was. Maybe she got five cents for every two bits sent in. A lousy nickel. It wasn't fair. Guys like Murray Candid rolling in dough, monkeys with enough capital to finance a weekend with a high-class prostitute. Greaseballs like Feeney Last being paid off to talk a girl into selling her body and soul for peanuts. Even Cobbie Bennett got his. Hell, I shouldn't squawk, I had mine . . . and now I had five hundred bucks too much. Ann Minor certainly didn't have time to cash that cheque. It should still be in her apartment, nobody else could cash it, not with the newspapers carrying all the tripe about the investigation and her death.

'Where are we going?' Lola had to step up her pace to keep abreast of me.

'The Albino Club. Ever been there?'

'Once. Why there? I thought you didn't want to be seen.'

'I've never been there either. I owe my client five bills and there's a chance he might be there. He may want an explanation.'

'Oh!'

The club wasn't far off. Ten minutes' walking brought us to the front entrance and a uniformed doorman obviously glad to see a customer for a change. It was a medium-sized place, stepped down from the sidewalk a few feet, lacking the gaudy atmosphere of the Zero Zero. Instead of chrome and gilt, the wall lights reflected the sheen of highly polished oak and brought out the colour of the murals around the room. There was an orchestra rather than a band – one that played, soft and low, compositions to instil a mood and never detract from the business of eating and drinking.

As we stepped into the ante-room we both had a chance to look at the place over the partitions. A few tables were occupied by late diners. Clustered in a corner were half a dozen men still in business suits deep in discussion with occasional references to pictures sketched on the tablecloth. The bar ran the length of the room and behind it four bartenders fiddled with glasses or did something to while away the time. The fifth was pouring whisky into the glasses of the only two patrons.

Lola went rigid and she breathed my name. I saw what she meant. One of the guys at the bar was Feeney Last. I wasn't interested in him right then. The other was the guy I had beat the hell out of in the parking lot. The one I thought *might* have been looking for his car keys. My conscience felt much better when I looked at the wreck of his nose. The bastard was after the ring.

Lola read my mind again. 'Are . . . you going in . . . after him?'

I wanted to. God, how I wanted to! I couldn't think of anything I'd sooner do. Feeney Last, right here where I could get to him. Man, oh man, the guy sure felt secure. After all, what did the cops have on him? Not a damn thing . . . and if anything hung over his head he was the only one that had an idea where it could be found. Except me.

And I was supposed to be dead.

We didn't go in the Albino Club after all. I snatched my hat back from the rack and pushed Lola outside. The doorman was cut to the quick yet able to nod good night politely.

On the corner of Broadway a glorified dog-wagon was doing a land-office business in late snacks. When I saw the blue-and-white phone disc on the front I steered Lola, in, told her to order us some coffee, then went down the back to the phone booth.

Pat was home. He must have just gotten in because he was breathing hard from the stairs. I said, 'This is Mike kid. I just saw Feeney Last in the Albino Club with a guy I tangled with not long ago. Can you put a man on him? I have things to do or I'd tail him myself.'

'You bet!' Pat exploded. 'I've had him on the wires for over two hours. Every police car in the city is looking for him.'

It puzzled me. 'What . . .?'

'I had a teletype from the Coast. It's Feeney they want out there for that murder. He answers the description in every respect.'

Something prompted me to ask, 'What kind of a kill was it, Pat?'

'He broke the guy's neck in a brawl. He started off with a knife, lost it in the scuffle, then broke his neck.'

A chill crept up my back and I was in that hallway again, feeling the cut of a smashing blow under my ear. There wasn't any doubt about it now, not the slightest. Feeney had more than one technique. He could kill with a rod or a knife, and with his hands if he had to.

'The Albino Club, Pat. You know where it is. He's there. I'm going to race the patrol car and if I win you'll need the dead wagon.'

I slammed the phone back and shoved my way through the crowd at the counter. Lola was looking for me and she didn't have to be told that something had happened. When I went past her as though she wasn't there she called after me and spun off her stool, but by that time I was on the street and running, running as fast as I could go and the few people on the sidewalk got out of the way to stare after me with their mouths dropping open.

My gun was in my hand when I took the corner. My chest was a ball of fire that ejected the air in quick, hot gasps and all I could think of was smashing the butt end of the rod in Feeney's face. From far off I heard the wail of a siren, a low moaning that put speed in my feet and craving desire to get there first.

We both lost. In the yellow light of the street I saw a car pull away from the kerb and when I got outside the Albino Club Feeney Last and his friend had left.

I found out why in a minute. There was a radio at the bar and Feeney had persuaded the bartender to keep it on police-calls just for laughs. He had the laugh, all right. He was probably howling his goddamn head off.

CHAPTER THIRTEEN

Pat arrived seven minutes after the patrol car. By that time Lola had caught up to me and stood to one side catching her breath. As usual, the curious had formed a tight ring around us and the cops were busy trying to disperse them. Pat said, 'It's a hell of a note. You didn't get the make of the car?'

I shook my head. 'Only that it was a dark one. The doorman didn't notice either. Goddamn, that makes me mad!'

A reporter pushed his way through the cordon ready to take notes. Pat told him tersely, 'The police will issue an official statement later.' The guy wouldn't take it for an answer and tried to quiz the cops, but they didn't know any more than the police-call told them, to close in on the Albino Club and hold anyone from leaving.

I stepped back into the crowd and Pat followed. I couldn't press my luck too far. I was still dead and I might as well stay that way for a while if I could. I leaned up against the fender of a car and Pat stayed close. Lola came over and held my hand.

'How's it going, Pat?'

'Not good. I'm catching hell. It's coming at me from all directions now and I don't know which way to turn. Somebody has one devil of a lot of pull in this town. They're talking, too, enough to put the papers wise. The reporters are swarming around headquarters looking for leads. I can't give them anything and they jump me for it. The publicity is going to cause a lot of eye-lifting tomorrow.'

There was a determined set to his jaw anyway. Pat could dish it out, too. His time was coming. 'What are you doing about it?'

His grin wasn't pleasant. 'We staged a couple of raids tonight. Remember what you said about the police knowing things . . . and still having to let them go on?' I nodded. 'I used hand-picked men. They raided two fancy houses uptown and came up with a haul that would make your eyes pop out. We have names now, and charges to go with them. Some of the men we netted in the raid tried to bribe my officers and are going to pay through the nose for it?'

'Brother!'

'They're scared, Mike. They don't know what we have or what we haven't and they can't take chances. Between now and tomorrow the lid will be off City Hall unless I miss my guess. They're scared and worried.'

'They should be.'

Pat waited, his tongue licking at the corner of his mouth.

'Nancy had been working at a scheme. Oh, it was a pretty little scheme that I thought involved petty blackmail. I think it went further than that.'

'How much further?'

I looked at Lola. 'In a day or two . . . maybe we can tell you then.'

'My legs have a long way to go yet,' she said.

'What are you getting at?' Pat asked.

'You'll find out. By the way, have you got things set up for tomorrow night?'

Pat lit a cigarette and flipped the burnt match into the gutter. 'You know, I'm beginning to wonder who's running my department. I'm sure as hell not.'

But he was smiling when he said it.

'Yeah, we're ready. The men are picked, but they haven't been told their assignments. I don't want any more leaks.'

'Good! They'll pull their strings and when they find that doesn't work they'll pull their guns. We beat them at that and they're up the tree, ready for the net. Meanwhile we have to be careful. It's rough, Pat, isn't it?'

'Too rough. The city can be damn dirty if you look in the right places.'

I ground out my butt under my heel. 'They talk about the Romans. They only threw human beings into a pit with lions. At

188

least, then, the lions had a wall around them so they couldn't get out. Here they hang out in bars and on the street corners looking for a meal.'

The crowd had thinned out and the cops were back in the car trying to brush off the reporter. Another car with a press tag on the window swerved to a stop and two stepped out. I didn't want to wait around. Too many knew me by sight. I told Pat so-long and took off up the street with Lola trotting alongside me.

I drove her to the apartment and she insisted I come up for the coffee I didn't have before. It was quiet up here, the absolute early-morning quiet that comes when the city has gone to bed and the earliest risers haven't gotten up yet. The street had quieted down, too. Even an occasional horn made an incongruous sound in that unnatural stillness.

From the river the low cry of dark shapes and winking lights that were ships echoed and re-echoed through the canyons of the avenues. Lola turned the radio on low, bringing in a selection of classical piano pieces, and I sat there with my eyes closed, listening, thinking, picturing my redhead as a blackmailer. In a near sleep I thought it was Red at the piano fingering the keys while I watched approvingly, my mind filled with thoughts. She read my mind and her face grew sad, sadder than anything I had ever seen, and she turned her eyes on me and I could see clear through them into the goodness of her soul, and I knew she wasn't a blackmailer and my first impression had been right. She was a girl who had come face to face with fate and had lost, but in losing hadn't lost all, for there was the light of holiness in her face that time when I was her friend, when I thought that a look like that belonged only in a church when you were praying or getting married or something – a light that was there now for me to see while she played a song that told me I was her friend and she was mine, a friendship that was more than that, it was a trust and I believed it . . . knew it and wanted it, for here was a devotion more than I expected or deserved and I wanted to be worthy of it. But, before I could

189

tell her so, Feeney Last's face swirled up from the mist beside the keyboard, smirking, silently mouthing smutty remarks and leering threats that took the holiness away from the scene and smashed it underfoot, assailing her with words that replaced the hardness and terror that had been ingrown before we met, and I couldn't do a thing about it because my feet were powerless to move and my hands were glued to my sides by some invisible force that Feeney controlled and wouldn't release until he had killed her and was gone with his laugh ringing in the air and the smirk still on his face, daring me to follow when I couldn't answer him. All I could do was stand there and look at my redhead's lifeless body until I focussed on her hands to see where he had scratched her when he took off her ring.

Lola said, 'The coffee's ready, Mike.'

I came awake with a start, my feet and hands free again and I half-expected to see Feeney disappearing around the corner. The radio played on, an inanimate thing in the corner with a voice of deep notes that was the only sound in the night.

'Thinking, honey?'

'Dreaming.' I lifted the cup from the tray and she added the sugar and milk. 'Sometimes it's good to dream.'

She made a wry mouth. 'Sometimes it isn't.' She kissed me with her eyes then. 'My dreams have changed lately, Mike. They're nicer than they used to be.'

'They become you, Lola.'

'I love you, Mike. I can be impersonal because I can't do a thing about it. It isn't a love like that first time. It's a cold fact. Is it that I'm in love with you or do I just love you?'

She sipped her coffee and I didn't answer her. She wouldn't have wanted me to.

'You're big, Mike. You can be called ugly if you take your face apart piece by piece and look at it separately. You have a brutish quality about you that makes men hate you, but maybe a woman wants a brute. Perhaps she wants a man she knows can hate and kill yet still retain a sense of kindness. How long have I known you: a few days? Long enough to look at you

190

and say I love you, and if things had been different I would want you to love me back. But because it can't be that way I'm almost impersonal about it. I just want you to know it.'

She sat there quietly, her eyes half-closed, and I saw the perfection in this woman. A mind and body cleansed of any impurities that were, needing only a freedom of her soul. I had never seen her like this, relaxed, happy in her knowledge of unhappiness. Her face had a radiant glow of unusual beauty; her hair tumbled to her shoulders, alive with the dampness of the rain.

I laid my cup on the end table, unable to turn my head away. 'It's almost like being married,' she said, 'sitting here enjoying each other even though there's a whole room between us.'

It was no trouble to walk across the room. She stretched out her hands for me to pull her to her feet and I folded her into my arms, my mouth searching for hers, finding it without trouble, enjoying the honey of her lips that she gave freely, her tongue a warm little dagger that stabbed deeper and deeper.

I didn't want her to leave me so soon when she sidled out of my hands. She kissed me lightly on the cheek, took a cigarette from the table and made me take it, then held up a light. The flame of the match was no more intense than that in her eyes. It told me to wait, but not for long. She blew out the match, kissed me again on the cheek and walked into the bedroom, proud, lovely.

The cigarette had burned down to a stub when she called me. Just one word.

'Mike! . . .'

I dropped it, still burning, in the tray. I followed her voice.

Lola was standing in the centre of the room, the one light on the dresser throwing her in the shadow. Her back was towards me and she faced the open window, looking into the night beyond. She might have been a statue carved by the hands of a master sculptor so still and beautiful was her pose. A gentle breeze wafted in and the sheer gown of silk she wore folded back against her body, accentuating every line, every curve.

191

I stood there in the doorway hardly daring to breathe for fear she would move and spoil the vision. Her voice was barely audible. 'A thousand years ago I made this to be the gown I would wear on my wedding night, Mike. A thousand years ago I cried my heart out and put it away under everything else and I had forgotten about it until I met you.'

She swung around in a little graceful movement, taking a step nearer me. 'I never had a night I wanted to remember. I want to have this one for my memories.' Her eyes were leaping, dancing coals of passion.

'Come here, Mike!' It was a demand that wasn't necessary.

I grabbed her shoulders and my fingers bit into her flesh.

'I want you to love me Mike, just for tonight,' she said. 'I want a love that's as strong as mine and just as fierce because there may be no tomorrow for either one of us, and if there is it will never be the same. Say it, Mike. Tell me.'

'I love you, Lola. I could have told you that before, but you wouldn't let me. You're easy to love, even for me. Once I said I'd never love again, but I have.'

'Just for tonight.'

'You're wrong. Not just for tonight. I'll love you as long as I please. If there's any stopping to be done I'll do it. You're brand new, Lola . . . you're made for a brand-new guy, somebody more than me. I'm trouble for everything I touch.'

Her hand closed over my mouth. My whole body was aching for her until my head felt dizzy. When she took her hand away she put it over one of mine that squeezed her shoulders and moved it to the neckline of the gown.

'I made this gown to be worn only once. There's only one way to get it off.'

A devil was making love to me.

My fingers closed over the silk and ripped it away with a hissing, tearing sound and she was standing in front of me, naked and inviting.

Her voice had angels in it, though. 'I love you, Mike,' she said again.

She was my kind of woman, one that you didn't have to speak to, for words weren't that necessary. She was honest and strong in her honesty, capable of loving a man with all her heart had to give, and she was giving it to me.

Her mouth was cool, but her body was hot with an inner fire that could only be smothered out.

It was a night she thought she'd never have.

It was a night I'd never forget.

I was alone when I woke up. The tinkling of a miniature alarm-clock on the dresser was a persistent reminder that a new day was here. Pinned to the pillow next to mine was a note from Lola and signed with a lipstick kiss. It read, 'It ended too soon, Mike. Now I have to finish the job you gave me. Breakfast is all ready – just warm everything up.'

Breakfast, hell! It was after twelve. I ate while I was getting dressed, anxious to get into things. The coffee was too hot to touch and while it cooled I snapped the radio on. For the first time in his life the news commentator seemed genuinely excited. He gave out with a spiel at a fast clip, only pausing to take a breath at the end of each paragraph. The police had staged two more raids after I left Pat, and the dragnet was pulling in every shady character suspected of having dealings with the gigantic vice ring that controlled the city.

The iron fist had made a wide sweep. It closed in on places and persons I never thought of. A grin crossed my face and I ran my hand over the stubble of beard on my chin. I was seeing Pat again, acknowledging the knowledge of the existence of such a ring, yet readily agreeing that there was little that could be done about it. He was eating his own words and liking it.

One thing about a drive like that, it can't be stopped. The papers take up the crusade and the hue and cry is on. The public goes on a fox-hunt in righteous indignation, ready to smash something they had unconcernedly supported with indifference only the day before. To them it was fun to see a public name grovelling in the mud, a thrill to know they were part of the pack.

But the big scenes weren't written yet. They'd come later in a court-room after postponements, stalls, anything to gain time to let the affair cool down. Then maybe a fine would be handed out, maybe a light jail sentence here and there, maybe a dismissal for lack of evidence.

Evidence – the kind that could stick. The police would do their share, but if the evidence didn't stick there would be people walking out of that court with the memory of what had happened and a vow never to let it happen again. They'd be people with power, of course, filthy, rotten squibs who liked the feeling of power and money, determined to let nothing interfere with their course of life. They'd undermine the workings of the law. A little at a time, like the waves lapping at the sand around a piling, uncovering it until it was ready to topple of its own accord. Then they could get in their own kind . . . people who would look the other way and interpret the law to their own advantage.

I got into my coat and went downstairs for a paper, hurrying back to the apartment to read it. The story was there complete with pictures, but it was the columnists that went further than fact. They hinted that more than one prominent personage had been hurriedly called away from town on the eve of the investigation and, if the revelations continued, the number in the Blue Book was going to diminish by many pages. One of the more sensational writers inferred that the police were getting able assistance outside their own circle, a subtle implication that they couldn't handle the situation unless they were prodded into action.

The police themselves had little or nothing to say. There was no statement from higher headquarters as yet, but a few of the lesser politicos had issued fiery blasts that the law was taking too much on its shoulders and was more concerned with smear tactics than law enforcement. I had to laugh at that. I was willing to bet those boys were trying to cover up by making more noise than the police.

I picked up the phone and dialled Pat. He was dog tired and glad to hear from me. 'Read the papers yet?' he asked.

'Yeah, and listened to the radio. The exodus has begun.'

'You can say that again. We're picking them up left and right trying to beat it. Some of them talked enough to lead us into other things, but all we have are the mechanics, the working group of the outfit – and the customers.'

'They're the ones who support the racket.'

'They're going to pay more than they expected to. It's getting rougher. A lot of dirty noses are looking for someone to wipe them on.'

'And you're the boy?'

'I'm the boy, Mike.'

'Who's going bail for all the big names?'

It's coming in from all over. I've been called more dirty names than any one guy in the city. . . .'

'Except me.'

'Yeah, except you, But nobody wants your job like they want mine. I've been cajoled, threatened, enticed and what not. It makes me feel ashamed to know that I live within a hundred miles of some people.'

He yawned into the phone and muttered, 'I have news, friend. Murray Candid has been seen in the city, hopping from one place to another. He's accompanied by an alderman in a downtown district.'

'He isn't trying to make a break for it, then?'

'Evidently not. He's keeping out of sight until something happens. I think he wants to see how far we're going to go. He'll be pretty surprised.'

'You have a murder warrant out on him?'

'Couldn't make it, Mike. He had an alibi for that. He's ducking out on this investigation. Here's something else that might interest you, but keep it under your hat. There's been an influx of tough guys who are walking around the city just being seen by the right persons. One look and you couldn't make them talk for love or money.'

'How do you like that!'

'I don't. They have records, most of them, but they're clean now and we can't touch them. We started holding them for

195

questioning. It didn't work. Every one of them is loaded with dough and sense enough to have a lawyer pull them out fast. None of them was armed or talked back to a cop, so there wasn't a thing we could stick them with.'

My hands got sticky with sweat. 'That's big money talking again, Pat. The combine is still in business, using its retrenching dough to scare off the talkers. Those babies can do it, too. They aren't just kidding. What the hell is happening . . . are we going back to the Wild West again? Damn it, if they keep that up, you'll have a jugful of claims on your hands and I don't blame them! It's not nice to know that sooner or later you'll get bumped because a guy has already been paid to do the job and he's a conscientious worker.'

'Our hands are tied. That's the way it is and we're stuck with it. They know where to go, besides. It seems like they've contacted right parties before we got to them.'

Damn! I smacked my fist against the back of the chair. All right, let them play tough. Let them import a gang with smart, knowing faces and minds that weren't afraid of taking a chance. They were just mugs who couldn't think for themselves, but they could feel, and they had emotions, and they could scare just as easily as any one else, and when they saw the blood run in the streets they wouldn't be quite so cocky or eager to reach for a rod. They'd run like hell and keep on running until their feet gave out.

'You still there, Mike?'

'I'm still here, I was thinking.'

Well, I'm going home and get some sleep. You'll be there tonight?'

'I wouldn't miss it for anything.'

'Right! Keep out of sight. The D.A. is getting ideas about me and if he finds out that you have a hand in this I'll be on the carpet.'

'Don't worry, I'll stay dead until I need resurrection. I told Lola to get in touch with you if it's necessary. Do me a favour and don't ask questions, just do what she asks. It's important.'

'She's working on it, too?'

'Lola's handling the most important end of this case right now. If she finds what I think she might find, you cinch your case without kickbacks. See you tonight. I'll be there, but you won't see me.'

I said so-long and hung up. The end was near, or at least it was in sight. The showdown was too close to risk spoiling it by getting myself involved. All I wanted was Feeney. I wanted to get his neck in my hands and squeeze. But where the hell would Feeney be now? The city was too big, too peppered with fox holes and caves to start a one-man search. Fenney had to be forced out into the open, made to run so we could get a crack at him.

The catch was, the little guys did the running. The big boys stayed out of sight after they buried their gold, ready to dig it up again when the enemy was gone. Feeney wasn't big. He was the kind that would watch and wait, too, ready to jump out and claim part of the loot. It could be that he wanted more than his share and was ready to take all if he had the chance. Murray Candid, another one content to stay at home, still trusting the devices they had set up to protect themselves. Cobbie Bennett waiting to die. How many more would there be?

I grabbed the phone again and asked for long-distance, waited while the operator took my number and put it into Mr Berin's address. I asked for my client and the butler told me he had left for the city only a short while before, intending to register at the Sunic House. Yes, he had reservations. He asked who was calling, please, and wanted to take a message, but there wasn't anything I could tell him, so I grumbled goodbye and put the phone back.

Velda must have been out for lunch. I let the phone ring for a good five minutes and nobody picked it up. Hell, I couldn't just sit there while things were happening outside. I wanted to do some hunting of my own, too. I pushed out of the chair and slung my coat on. Something jingled in the pocket and I pulled out a duplicate set of door keys Lola had left for me and each one had lipstick kisses on the shanks, with a little heart dangling from the chain that held them together. I opened the heart and saw Lola smiling up at me.

I smiled back and told her picture all the things she wouldn't let me tell her last night.

There was still a threat of rain in the air. Overhead the clouds were grey and ruffled, a thick, damp blanket that cut the tops off the bigger buildings and promised to squat down on the smaller ones. From the river a chill wind drove in a wave of mist that covered everything with tiny wet globules. Umbrellas were furled, ready to be opened any instant; passengers waiting for buses or standing along the kerb whistling at taxis carried raincoats or else eyed the weather apprehensively.

Twice a radio car screamed its way south, the siren opening a swath down the centre of the avenue. I passed a paper stand and saw a later edition and an extra, both with banner headlines. A front-page picture showed the alderman and a socially prominent manufacturer in a police court. The manufacturer looked indignant. A sub-caption made mention of some highly important confidential information the police had and wouldn't disclose at the moment. That would be Murray's code book. I wondered how Pat was getting on with it.

At the bar on the corner I found a spot in the rear and ordered a beer. There was only one topic of discussion going on in the place and it was being pushed around from pillar to post. A ratty little guy with a nose that monopolized his face said he didn't like it. The police were out of order. A girl told him to shut up. Every fifteen minutes a special bulletin would come out with the latest developments, making capital of the big names involved, but unable to give information of any special nature.

For a little over two hours I sat there, having one beer after another, hearing a cross-sectional viewpoint of the city. Vice was losing ground fast to the publicity of the clean-up.

When I had enough I crawled into the phone booth and dialled the Sunic House. The desk clerk said Mr Berin had arrived a few minutes before. I thanked him and hung up, Later I'd go up and refund his dough. I went out where the mist had laid a slick on the streets and found another bar that was a little more cheerful and searched my mind for that other piece to the puzzle.

My stomach made growling noises and I checked my watch. Six-thirty. I threw a buck on the counter for the bartender and walked out and stood in the doorway.

It had started to rain again.

When I finished eating and climbed behind the wheel of the car it was almost eight. The evening shadows had dissolved into night, glossy and wet, the splatter of the rain on the steel roof an impatient drumming that lulled thoughts away. I switched on the radio to a news programme, changed my mind and found some music instead.

Some forty-five minutes later I decided I had had enough aimless driving and pulled to the kerb between two sheer walls of apartment buildings that had long ago given up any attempt at pretentiousness. I looked out and saw that there were no lights showing in Cobbie Bennett's room and I settled down to wait.

I might have been alone in that wilderness of brick and concrete. No one bothered to look at me huddled there, my coat collar turned up to merge with the brim of my hat. A few cars were scattered at odd intervals along the street, some old heaps, a couple more respectable by a matter of a few years. A man came out of a building across the way holding a newspaper over his head and hurried to the corner where he turned out of sight.

Off in the distance a fire engine screamed, demanding room, behind it another with a harsh, brassy gong backing up the order. I was listening to the fading clamour when the door of Cobbie's house opened and the little pimp stepped out. He was five minutes early. He had a cigarette in his mouth and was trying to light it with a hand that shook so hard the flame went out and, disgusted, he threw the unlit butt to the pavement and came down the steps.

He didn't walk fast, even in the rain, nor a straight course. His choppy stride carried him through a weaving pattern, avoiding the street lights, blacking him out in the shadows. When he came to a store front I saw his head turn to look into the angle of the window to see if he was being followed.

I let him turn the corner before I started the car. If the police were there, they weren't in sight. Nothing was moving this night. I knew the route Cobbie would take, and rather than follow him, decided to go ahead and wait, taking a wide sweep around the one-way street and coming up in the direction he was walking.

There were stores here, some still open. A pair of gin mills operated at a short stagger apart, smelling the block up with the rank odour of flat beer. Upstairs in an apartment a fight was going on. Somebody threw a coffee-pot that smashed through the window and clattered down the basement well. Cobbie was part of the night until it hit, then he made a short dash to the safety of a stairway and crouched there determining the origin of the racket before continuing his walk. He stopped once to light a cigarette and made it this time.

He was almost opposite me when a car pulled up the street and stopped in front of the gin mill. Cobbie went rigid with fear, one hand half-way to his mouth. When the driver hopped out and went into the dive he finished dragging on the cigarette.

I had to leave the car where it was, using Cobbie's tactics of hugging the shadows to pass him on the opposite side of the street without being seen. Following did no good. I had to anticipate his moves and try to stay ahead of him. The rain came in handy; it let me walk under awnings, stop in doorways for a breather before starting off again.

A cop went by, whistling under his slicker, his night club slapping his leg in rhythm to his step. It was ten minutes after ten then. I didn't see Pat or his men. Just Cobbie and me. We were in his own bailiwick now, the street moving with people impervious to the rain and the tension. Beside a vacant store I stopped and watched Cobbie hesitate on the corner, making his decision and shuffling off into a cross street.

I didn't know where I expected it to come from, certainly not from the black mouth of an apartment. Cobbie's weave had been discarded for an ambling gait of resignation. Tension can be borne only so long, then the body and mind reverts to normal. His back suddenly stiffened and I heard a yelp that was plain fear. His head was swivelled around to the building and his hands came up protectively.

If the guy had shot from the doorway he would have had him, but he wanted to do it close up and came down the steps with a rod in his fist. He hadn't reached the third step when Cobbie screamed at the top of his lungs, trying to shrink back against the inevitable. The gun levelled with Cobbie's chest but never went off because a dark blur shot out of the same doorway and crashed into the guy's back with such force that they landed at Cobbie's feet together.

My own rod was in my hand as I ran. I heard the muted curses mingled with Cobbie's screaming as a heavy fist slammed into flesh. I was still fifty yards away when the two separated, one scrambling to his feet immediately. Cobbie had fallen into a crouch and the guy fired, flame lacing towards his head.

The other guy didn't bother to rise. He propped his gun arm on the sidewalk, took deliberate aim and pulled the trigger. The bullet must have gone right through his head because his hat flew off faster than he was running and was still in the air when the man was nothing but a lump of lifeless flesh.

A gun went off farther up the street. Somebody shouted and shot again. I was on top of the guy with the rod and it didn't worry me at all seeing it pointed at my middle. It was a police positive and the guy had big, flat feet.

Just the same, I raised my hands, my .45 up and said, 'Mike Hammer, private op. Ticket's in my pocket, want to see it?'

The cop stood up and shook his head. 'I know you, feller.'

A prowl car made the corner on two wheels and passed it, the side door already open with a uniformed patrolman leaning out, his gun cocked. The cop and I followed it together, crossing the street diagonally where the commotion was.

Windows were being thrown open, heads shouted down asking what went on and were told to get back in and stay there. A voice yelled, 'He's on the roof!' There was another shot, muffled by the walls this time. A woman screamed and ran, slamming a door in her passage.

Almost magically the searchlights opened up, stretching long arms up the building fronts to the parapets, silhouetting half a dozen men racing across the roof in pursuit of someone.

The reflection of the lights created an artificial dawn in the tight group, dancing from the riot guns and blued steel of service revolvers. The street was lousy with cops, and Pat was holding one of the lights.

We saw each other at the same time and Pat handed the light over to a plain-clothes man. I said, 'Where the hell did you come from? There wasn't a soul on the street a minute ago.'

Pat grimaced at me. 'We didn't come, Mike . . . we were there. The hard boys weren't too smart. We had men tailing them all day and they never knew it. Hell, we couldn't lay a trap without having everybody and his brother get wise, so the men stuck close and stayed on their backs. Cobbie was spotted before he got off his block. The punks kept in touch with each other over the phone. When they saw Cobbie turn down here one cut behind the buildings and got in front of him. There was another one up the block to cut him off if he bolted.'

'Good deal! How many were there?'

'We have nine so far. Seven of them just folded up their tents and came along quietly. We let them pass the word first so there would be no warning. What came of that guy down the block?'

'He's dead.'

From the roof there was a volley of shots that smashed into stone and ricochetted across the sky. Some didn't ricochet. A shrill scream testified to that. One of the cops stepped into the light and called down. 'He's dead. Better get a stretcher ready, we have a wounded officer up here.'

Pat snapped, 'Damn! Get those lights in the hallway so they can see what they're doing!' A portable stretcher came out of a car and was carried upstairs. Pat was directing operations in a clear voice, emphasized by vigorous arm movements.

There wasn't anything I could do right then. I edged back through the crowd and went up the street. There was another gang around the body on the sidewalk, with two kids trying to break away from their parents for a closer look.

Cobbie Bennett was nowhere in sight.

CHAPTER FOURTEEN

Seeing a job well done can bring a feeling of elation whether you did it yourself or not. There was a sense of pride in me when I climbed behind the wheel of my heap, satisfaction extraordinary because the bastards were being beaten at their own game. I switched on the radio a few minutes later in time to catch the interruption of a programme and a news flash of the latest coup. I went from station to station, but it was always the same. The noses for news were right in there following every move. Scattered around town would be other tough boys hearing the same thing. Money wouldn't mean a damn thing now, not if the cops were going to play it their way. It's one thing to jump the law, but when the law is right behind you, ready to jump back even harder, it's enough to make even the most stupid, hopped-up killer think twice.

Ha! They wouldn't be wearing their metallic smiles tonight. The ball was piling up force as it rolled along. The half-ways were jumping on the wagon, eager to be on the winning side. Political injustice and string-pulling were taking one hell of a beating. I *knew* where I stood and I felt good about it.

My route uptown was taking me within a few blocks of the Sunic House, and late as it was I wanted to stop off and see my client. This the old boy would like. He was paying for it. At least he was getting his money's worth. The name of Berin-Grotin would be remembered in places long after the marble tomb was eaten away by the sands of time, and that's what he wanted . . . someone to remember him.

There was a driveway beside the old brownstone structure that curved into a parking space in back. I pulled half-way in and handed the keys over to a bell-boy old enough to be my father. As I walked to the door I heard him grind it into gear, then jerk out of sight. I waited to hear him hit something else, but apparently he made it.

The Sunic House was a well-kept relic of yesteryear, reserved for gentlemen guests only. The hushed atmosphere wasn't due to the late hour: it probably was that way all day. The lobby was done in plush, gilt and leather. From the ceiling ancient gas fixtures had been converted to electric whose yellow bulbs did little to brighten the mortuary effect of the mahogany-panelled walls. The pictures spotted around the place showed the city of long ago when it was at peace with itself, and the Sunic House was a name to hold honour among the best.

I asked the desk-clerk if Mr Berin was in.

He nodded slowly and knit his eyebrows. 'I'm certain Mr Berin does not care to be disturbed, sir. He has been coming here these many years and I know his preferences well.'

'This is a very unusual circumstance, pop. Give him a call, will you?'

'I'm afraid that . . . really, now, sir. I don't think it proper to . . .'

'If I suddenly stuck my fingers between my teeth and whistled like hell, then ran up and down the room yelling at the top of my lungs, what would you do?'

His eyebrows ran up to where his hairline used to be. He craned his head to the wall where an old guy was nodding in a chair. 'I'd be forced to call the house detective, sir!'

I gave him a great big grin and stuck my fingers between my teeth. With, the other hand I pointed to the phone and waited. The clerk got pale, flushed, went white again as he tried to cope with the situation. Evidently, he figured one upset customer would be better than a dozen and picked up the house phone.

He tugged the call bell while watching me nervously, jiggled it again and again until a voice barked hard enough in his ear to make him squirm. 'I beg your pardon, sir, but a man insists he should see you. He . . . he said it was very urgent.'

The phone barked again and the clerk swallowed hard. 'Tell him it's Mike Hammer,' I said.

It wasn't so easy to get it in over the tirade my client was handing out. At last he said bleakly, 'It's a Mr Hammer, sir . . . a Mr Hammer. Yes, sir, Mike Hammer. Yes, he's right here, sir. Very well, sir. I'll send him right up.'

With a handkerchief the clerk wiped his face and gave me his look reserved for the most inferior of persons. 'Room 406,' he said. I waved my thanks and climbed the stairs, ignoring the elevator that stood in the middle of the room, working through a well in the overhead.

Mr Berin had the door open waiting for me. I pushed it in and closed it behind me, expecting to find myself in just another room. I was wrong, dead wrong. Whatever the Sunic House looked like on the outside, its appearance was deceiving. Here was a complete suite of rooms, and as far as I could see executed with the finest taste possible.

A moment later my client appeared, dressed in a silken smoking jacket, his hair brushed into a snow-white mane, looking for all the world like a man who had planned to receive a guest rather than be awakened out of a sound sleep by an obnoxious employee.

His hand met mine in a firm clasp. 'It's good to see you, Mike, very good. Come inside where we can talk.'

'Thanks.' He led me past the living-room, that centred around a grand piano, into a small study that faced on the street, a room banked with shelves of books, mounted heads of animals and fish, and rows of framed pictures showing himself in his younger days. 'Some place you have here, Mr Berin.'

'Yes, I've used it for years as you can see. It's my city residence with all the benefits of a hotel. Here, sit down.' He offered me an overstuffed leather chair and I sank into it, feeling the outlines of another person who had made his impression through constant use.

'Cigar?'

'No, thanks.' I took out my deck of Luckies and flipped one into my mouth. 'Sorry I had to drag you out of bed like this.'

'Not at, all, Mike. I must admit that I was rather surprised: That all comes of having fixed habits for so many years, I presume. I gathered you had a good reason for wanting to see me.'

I breathed out a cloud of smoke. 'Nope, I just wanted to talk to somebody. I have five hundred bucks of yours and that's my excuse for picking you as that somebody.'

'Five hundred . . .' he began, 'you mean that money I sent to your bank to cover that, ah, expense?'

'That's right. I don't need it now.'

'But you thought it would be worth spending to secure the information. Did you change your mind?'

'No, the girl didn't live to cash it, that's all.' His face showed bewilderment, then amazement. 'I was tailed. Like a jerk I didn't think of it and was tailed. Whoever was behind me killed the girl and fixed it to look like suicide. It didn't work. While I was out the same party went through my room and copped some of the stuff.'

'You know . . .? his voice choked off.

'Feeney Last. Your ex-hired hand, Mr Berin.'

'Good Lord, no!'

'Yes.'

His fingers were entwined in his lap and they tightened until the knuckles went white. 'What have I done, what have I done?' He sat there with his eyes closed, looking old and shrunken for the first time.

'You didn't do a thing. It would have happened, anyway. What you did do was stop the same thing from happening again.'

'Thank you, Mike.'

I stood up and laid my hand on his shoulder. 'Look come off it. You don't have anything to feel bad about. If you feel anything, feel good. You know what's been going on in town all day and night?'

'Yes, I – I've heard.'

'That's what your money bought, a sense of decency to this place. It's what the town has needed for a long time. You hired me to find a name for the redhead. We found a package of dirt instead, all because a girl lies in the morgue unidentified.

I didn't want her buried without a name, neither did you. Neither of us expected what would come, and it isn't over yet by a long shot. One day the sun is going to shine again and when it does it will be over a city that can hold its head up.'

'But the red-headed girl still doesn't have a name, does she?' He glanced at me wryly, his eyes weary.

'No. Maybe she will have soon. Mind if I use your phone?'

'Not at all. It's outside in the living-room. I'll mix a drink in the meantime. I believe I can use one. I'm not used to distressing news, Mike.'

There was sadness in his carriage that I hated to see. The old boy was going to take a lot of cheering up. I found the phone and dialled Velda's number at home. She took a long time answering and was mad as hell. 'It's me, Velda. Anything doing at the office?'

'Gee whiz, Mike, you call at the most awful hours. I waited in the office all evening for you to call. That girl, Lola, was it? . . . sent up an envelope by special messenger. There was a pawn ticket in it and nothing else.'

'A pawn ticket?' My voice hit a high note. 'She's found it then, Velda! Hot damn, she's found it! What did you do with it?'

'I left it there,' she said, 'on top of my desk.'

'Damn, that's wonderful. Look, kid, I left my office keys home. Meet me there in an hour . . . make it an hour and a half. I want a drink first to celebrate the occasion. I'll call Pat from there and we can go on together. This is it, Velda, see you in a jiffy!'

I slapped my hand over the bar, holding it a moment before I spun out Lola's number on the dial. Her voice came on before the phone finished ringing. She was breathless with excitement. 'Mike, baby! . . . Oh, Mike, where are you? Did you get my envelope?'

'I just called Velda, and she has it at the office. I'm going up to get it in a little while. Where did you find it?'

'In a little place just off the Bowery. It was hanging in the window like you said it might be.'

209

'Great! Where's the camera now?'

'I have it.'

'Then why the rigmarole with the pawn ticket?'

A new note crept into her voice. 'Someone else was looking for it, too, Mike. For a while they were right ahead of me. Five different clerks told me that I was the second party after a camera like that.'

The chill went up my back this time. 'What happened?'

'I figured that whoever he was had been using the same method . . . going right from the phone book. I started at the bottom and worked backwards.'

Mr Berin came in and silently offered me a highball. I picked it off the tray with a nod of thanks and took a quick swallow. 'Go on.'

'I found it then, but I was afraid to keep the ticket on me. I addressed an envelope to your office and sent the ticket up with a boy.'

'Smart girl! I love you to pieces, little chum. You'll never know how much.'

'Please, Mike.'

'I laughed at her, happy, bubbling over with joy I hadn't known in a long time. 'You stow it this time, Lola. When this is done you and I will have the world in our hands and a lifetime to enjoy it. Tell me, Lola. Say it loud and often.'

'Mike, I love you, I love you!' She sobbed and said it again.

My voice went soft. 'Remember it, sugar . . . I love you, too. I'll be along in just a little while. Wait up for me?'

'Of course, darling. Please hurry. I want to see you so much it hurts.'

When I put the phone back I finished the drink in one long pull and went into the den. I wished I could give some of my happiness to Mr Berin. He needed it badly.

'It's finished,' I said.

There was no response save a slow turn of his head, 'Will there be more . . . killing, Mike?'

'Maybe. Might be the law will take its course.'

His hand lifted the glass to his lips. 'I should be elated, I suppose. However, I can't reconcile myself to death. Not when my actions are partly responsible for it.' He shuddered and put the glass down. 'Care for another? I'm going to have one.'

'Yeah, I have time.'

He took my glass on the tray, and on the way out opened the lid of a combination radio-phonograph. A sheaf of records was already in the metal grippers, and he lowered the needle to the first one. I leaned back and listened to the pounding beat of a Wagnerian opera, watching the smoke curl upwards from the red tip of my cigarette.

This time Mr Berin brought the bottle, the mixer and a bowl of ice with him. When he handed me the drink he sat on the edge of his chair and said, 'Tell me about it, Mike, not the details, just the high points, and the reasons for these things happening. Perhaps if I knew I could put my mind at rest.'

'The details are what count, I can't leave them out. What I want you to realize is that these things had to be, and it was good to get rid of them. We chased a name and found crime. We chased the crime and we found bigger names. The police dragnet isn't partial to anyone now. The cops are taking a long chance and making it stick. Every minute we sit here the vice and rot that had the city by the tail gets drawn closer to the wringer . . .'

'You should feel proud, Mr Berin. I do. I feel damn proud. I lost Nancy but I found Lola . . . and I found some of myself, too.'

'If only we could have done something for that girl . . .'

'Nancy?'

'Yes. She died so completely alone. But it was all her own doing. If it was true, as you said, that she had an illegitimate child and went downwards into a life of sin, who can be blamed? Certainly the girl herself.' He shook his head, his eyes crinkling in puzzled wonder. 'If only they had some pride . . . even the slightest essence of pride, these things would never happen. And not only this girl Nancy . . . how many others are like her? No doubt this investigation will uncover the number.

'Mike, there were times when I believed my own intense pride to be a childish vanity, one I could afford to indulge in, but I am glad now to have that pride. It *can* mean something, this pride of name, of ownership. I can look over my fine estate and say, "This is my own, arrived at through my own efforts." I can make plans for the future when I will be nothing but a name and take pride that it will be remembered.'

'Well, it's the old case of the double standard, Mr Berin. You can't blame these kids for the mistakes they make. I think nearly everyone makes them, it's just a few that get caught in the web. It's rough then, rough as hell.'

Half the bottle was gone before I looked at my watch and came to my feet. I reached for my hat, remembered the cheque in time and wrote it out. 'I'm late already. Velda will chew me out.'

'It has been nice talking to you, Mike. Will you stop back tomorrow? I want to know what happens. You will be careful, won't you?'

'I'll be careful,' I said. We shook hands at the door and I heard it shut as I reached the stairway. By the time I reached the main floor the desk-clerk was there, his finger to his lips urging me to be quiet. Hell, I couldn't help whistling. I recovered my car from the lot and roared out to the street. Just a little while longer, I thought.

Velda had nearly given me up. I saw her pacing the street in front of the Hackard Building, swinging her umbrella like a club. I pulled over and honked at her. 'I thought you said an hour and a half.'

'Sorry, honey, I got tied up.'

'You're always getting tied up.' She was pretty when she was mad.

We signed the night book in the lobby and the lone operator rode us up to our floor. Velda kept watching me out of the corner of her eye, curiosity getting the better of her. Finally she couldn't hold it any longer. 'Usually I know what's going on, Mike.'

I told her as briefly as I could. 'It was the redhead. She used her camera to take pictures.'

'Naturally.'

'These weren't ordinary pictures. They could be used for blackmail. She must have had plenty . . . it's causing all the uproar. Pat went ahead on the theory we were right in our thinking. We'll need that stuff for evidence.'

'Uh-huh.'

She didn't get it, but she made believe she did. Later I'd have to sit down and give her a detailed account. Later, not now.

We reached the office and Velda opened the door with her key and switched on the light. It had been so long since I had been in, that the place was almost strange to me. I walked over to the desk while Velda straightened her hair in front of the mirror.

'Where is it, kid?'

'On the blotter.'

'I don't see it.'

'Oh, for pity sakes. Here . . .' Her eyes went from the desk to mine, slowly, widening a little. 'It's gone, Mike.'

'Gone! Hell, it can't be!'

'It is. I put it right here before I left. I remember it distinctly, I put my desk in order . . .' she stopped.

'What is it?' I was afraid to talk.

Her hand was around the memo pad, looking at the blank sheet on top. Every bit of colour had drained from her face.

'Damn it, speak up!'

'A page is torn off . . . the one I had Lola's phone number and address on.'

'My God!'

I grabbed the front door and swung it open, holding it in the light. Around the key slot in the lock were a dozen light scratches made by a pick. I must have let out a yell, because the noise of it reverberated in my ears as I ran down the hall. Velda shouted after me, but I paid no attention. For once the elevator was where I wanted it, standing with the door back and the operator waiting to take us back down.

He recognized the urgency in my face, slammed the door shut and threw the handle over. 'Who was up here tonight?' I demanded.

213

'Why, nobody I know of, sir.'

'Could anyone get up the stairs without being seen?'

'Yes, I guess they could. That is, if the attendant or myself happened to be busy.'

'Were you?'

'Yes, sir. We've been swabbing down the floors ever since we came on.'

I had to keep my teeth shut to keep the curses in. I wanted to scream at the guy to hurry. Get me down. It took an eternity to reach the bottom floor and by then Velda had her hand on the button and wouldn't take it off. I squeezed out before the door was all the way open and bolted for my car.

'Oh, God!' I kept saying over and over to myself. 'Oh, God! . . .'

My foot had the accelerator on the floor, pushing the needle on the speedometer up and around. The tyres shrieked at the turns protestingly, then took hold once again until another turn was reached! I was thankful for the rain and the hour again; no cars blocked the way, no pedestrians were at the crossings. Had there been I never would have made it, for I was seeing only straight ahead and my hands wouldn't have wrenched the wheel over for anything.

I didn't check my time, but it seemed like hours before I crowded in between cars parked for the night outside the apartment. My feet thundered up the stairs, picking their way knowingly through the semi-darkness. I reached the door and threw it open and I tried to scream but it crammed in my throat like a hard lump and stayed there.

Lola was lying on the floor, her arms sprawled out. The top of her dress was soaked with blood.

I ran to her, fell on my knees at her side, my arms going to her face. The hole in her chest bubbled blood and she was still breathing. 'Lola . . .'

Her eyelids fluttered, opened. She saw me and her lips, once so lusciously ripe with the redness of life, parted in a pale smile. 'God, Lola! . . .'

214

I tried to help her, but her eyes told me it was too late. Too late! Her hand moved, touched me, then went out in an arc, the effort racking her with pain. The motion was so deliberate I had to follow it. Somehow she managed to extend her forefinger, point towards the phone table, then swing her hand to the door.

She made no sound, but her lips moved and said for the last time, 'I love you, Mike.' I knew what she wanted me to do. I bent forward and kissed her mouth gently, and tasted the salt of tears. 'Dear God, why did it have to happen to her? Why?'

Her eyes were closed. The smile was still on her face. But Lola was dead. You'll always know one thing. I love you. No matter where you are or when, you will know that wherever I am I'll be loving you. Just you.

The joy was gone. I was empty inside. I had no feeling, no emotion. What could I feel . . . how was I supposed to act? It happened so fast, this loving and having it snatched away at the moment of triumph. I closed my eyes and said a prayer that came hard, but started with, 'Oh, God! . . .'

When I opened my eyes again she was still pointing at the door, even now, in death, trying to tell me something.

Trying to tell me that her killer was outside there and I had come up too fast for him to get away. By all that was holy he'd never get away! My legs acted independently of my mind in racing for the door. I stopped in the hall, my ears tuned for the slightest sound . . . and I heard it. The soft tread of feet walking carefully, step by step, trying to be quiet. Feet that expected me to do the natural thing and call for the doctor first, then the police, and let just enough seconds go by for the killer to make his escape.

Like hell!

I didn't try to be quiet. I hit the stairs, took them two at a time, swinging around the banister at the landing. Below me the killer made no pretence at secrecy any longer and fled headlong into the street. I heard the roar of an engine as I came out the door, saw a car nose out of the line as I was climbing into mine and rip out into the street.

CHAPTER FIFTEEN

Whoever drove that car was stark mad with terror, a crazy madness that sent him rocketing down the avenue without the slightest regard for life. Maybe he heard my wild laugh as I closed the distance between us. It could be that his mind pictured my face, eyes bright with the kill, my teeth clamped together and lips drawn back, making me lose all resemblance to a human being.

I was just one tight knot of muscle, bunched together by a rage that wanted to rip and tear. I couldn't breathe; I could only take a breath, hold it as long as I could, and let it out with a flat hissing sound. A police car picked up our trail, tried to follow and was lost in the side streets.

Every second saw the distance shorten, every second heaped more coal on the fire that was eating at my guts and blurring my vision until all that was left was a narrow tunnel of sight with that car in front on the other end. We were almost bumper to bumper as we turned across town, and I felt my car start to go over, fighting the speed of the swerve. It was fear that led me out of it and back on four wheels again, fear that I would lose him. The tyres slammed back to the pavement, pulled to the side, and when I was straight again, the car in front of me had a half-block lead.

The sharp jolts of trolley tracks almost snatched the wheel from my hands, then it was gone and we were going west towards the river and the distance between us closed to yards, then feet. I knew where he was heading . . . knew he wanted to make the West Side Highway where he could make a run for it without traffic hazard, thinking he might lose me with speed.

He couldn't lose me now or ever. I was the guy with the cowl and the scythe. I had a hundred and forty black horses

217

under me and an hour-glass in my hand, laughing like crazy until the tears rolled down my cheeks. The highway was ahead all of a sudden and he tried to run into it, brakes slamming the car into a skid.

If the steep pillar hadn't been there he would have done it. I was on my own brakes as I heard the crash of metal against metal and saw glass fly in all directions. The car rolled over once and came to a stop on its wheels. I had to pull out and around it, brakes and tyres adding a new note to that unearthly symphony of destruction.

I saw the door of the other car get kicked open. I saw Feeney Last jump out, stagger, then turn his gun at me. I was diving for the ground when the shot blasted over my head, rolling back of the pillar clawing for my gun when Feeney made his break for it.

Run, Feeney, run. Run until your heart is ready to split open and you fall in a heap unable to move but able to see how you are going to die. Run and run and run. Hear the feet behind you running just a little bit faster. Stop for one second and you'll be as dead as hell.

He turned and fired a wild one and I didn't bother to answer him. There was panic in his stride, wild, unreasoning panic as he ran head down to the shadows of the pier, heading for the black throat of the shed there. The darkness was a solid wall that shut him out, then enveloped me because I was right behind him, pitch-black darkness that threw a velvet cloth over your eyes so that you might as well be blind.

I hit a packing case with my hands, stopped, and heard a body trip and fall, curse once and crawl. I wanted to keep my eyes closed because they felt so bright he couldn't miss them in the dark. Things took shape slowly, towering squares of boxes heaped to the ceiling with black corridors between them. I bent down and untied my shoes, kicked them off and eased into a walk without sound.

From the other side of the room came the rasp of hoarse breathing being restrained, Feeney Last, waiting for me to close the interval, step between himself and the gaping doorway where I would be outlined against the blue night of the city.

Hurry, I thought, before he gets wise. He'll know in a minute. He'll understand that rage lasts only so long before giving way to reason. Then he'll figure it. I stepped around the boxes, getting behind him, trusting to luck to bring myself through that maze to the end. I found an alley that led straight to the door, but Feeney wasn't standing there where he should have been. My foot sent a board clattering across the concrete and automatically I pulled back into the protection of the crates.

And I was lucky because Feeney was stretched out on the floor under an over-hang of the boxes and the shot he threw back over his shoulder missed me by inches.

But I had him spotted. I fired a snap shot around the corner and heard him scramble farther under the crate. Maybe he thought he was safe because neither one of us could take the chance of making the first break.

My fingers searched for handholds, found them, and I pulled myself up, climbing slowly and silently over the rough frames of the crates. Splinters worked into my flesh and nails tugged at my clothes until I disengaged them. A cat couldn't have been more quiet.

The tops formed a platform and I crept across it, inch by inch, my brain measuring distances. When I looked over the edge I saw Feeney's arm protruding from the shadow, a gun in his hand, slowly sweeping up and down the narrow lane, his finger tensed on the trigger ready to squeeze off a shot.

I leaned over and put a bullet right through his goddamn hand and jumped just as he made a convulsive jerk of pain and writhed out from under the box. My feet hit him in the shoulders and cut off his scream and we were one kicking, gouging mass rolling in the dust.

I didn't want my gun . . . just my hands. My fists were slashing into the pale oval of his face, reaching for his throat. He brought his knees up and I turned just in time and took it on my leg. He only had one hand he could use, and he chopped with it,

219

trying to bring the side of his palm against my neck. He kicked me away, pushed with the warm bloody mess that used to be fingers, and swung again, getting me in the ear.

Feeney tried to say 'No!' but my hands had his throat, squeezing . . . slamming his head to the concrete floor until he went completely limp. I rolled on top of him and took that head like a sodden rag and smashed and smashed and smashed and there was no satisfying, solid thump, but a sickening squashing sound that splashed all over me.

Only then did I let go and look at Feeney, or what was left of him, before I got sick to my stomach.

I heard the police whistles, the sirens and the shouting around the wreck of the car outside. Dimly I heard voices calling that we were in the shed. I sat on the floor trying to catch my breath, reaching in Feeney's pockets until my fingers closed about an oblong of cardboard with a rough edge where the stub had been torn off and I knew I had the ticket that had cost Lola's life.

They took me outside into the glare of the spotlights and listened to what I said. The radio car made contact with head-quarters, who called Pat, and after that I wasn't a gun-mad killer any more, but a licensed private cop on a legitimate mission. A double check led to Lola, and the clincher was in Feeney's hip pocket, a bloodstained knife.

Oh, they were very nice about it. In fact, I was some sort of hero. They didn't even bother to take me in for questioning. They had my statement and Pat did the rest. I rode home in a patrol wagon while a cop followed in my car. Tomorrow, they said, would be time enough. Tonight I would rest. In a few hours the dawn would come and the light would chase the insanity of the night away. My phone was ringing as I reached the apartment. I answered it absently, hearing Pat tell me to stay put, he'd be right over. I hung up without saying a word, my eyes searching for a bottle and not finding it.

Pat was forgotten, everything was forgotten. I stumbled out again and down the stairs, over a block to the back of Mast's joint where he had his own private party bar and banged on the door to be let in.

After a minute a light went on and Joe Mast opened the door in his pyjamas. Men can see things in other men and know enough to keep quiet. Joe waited until I was in, closed the door and pulled down the shades. Without a word he went behind the tiny bar and pulled a bottle down from the shelf, pouring me a double hooker while I forced myself on to a stool.

I didn't taste it; I didn't feel it go down.

I had another and didn't taste that one either.

Joe said, 'Slow, Mike. Have all you want, but do it slow.'

A voice started speaking, and I knew it was mine. It came of its own accord, a harsh, foreign voice that had no tone to it. 'I loved her, Joe. She was wonderful and she loved me, too. She died tonight and the last thing she told me was that she loved me. It would have been nice. She loved me most, and I had just started to love her. I knew that it wouldn't be long before I loved her just as much. He killed her, the bastard. He killed her and I made a mess of his head. Even the devil won't recognize him now.'

I reached in my pocket for a butt and felt the pawn ticket. I laid it on the bar next to the glass and the cigarettes. The name said Nancy Sanford and the address was the Seaside Hotel in Coney Island. 'He deserved to die. He had a murder planned for my redhead and it didn't come off, but it worked out just as well. He was a big guy in the vice racket with sharp ideas and he killed to keep them sharp. He killed a blonde and he killed Lola. He wanted to kill me once but he got talked out of it. It was too soon to kill me then. Murder unplanned is too easily traced.'

My mind went back to the parking lot, then before it, when I had walked into Murray Candid's office and seen the door closing and heard the cough. That was Feeney. He had spotted me in the club and put Murray wise. No wonder they wanted to warn me. Feeney was the smart one, he wanted me dead. He knew I wasn't going to be scared out of it. Too bad for him he got talked out of it. He was there that night. Did he have the ring? Damn it, why did that ring present a problem. Where the hell *did* it tie in? The whole thing started because of it . . . would it end without it?

Vacantly, I stared at the back bar, lost in thought. The ring with the battered fleur-de-lis design. Nancy's ring. Where was it now? Why was it there? The beating of my heart picked up until it was a hammer slamming my ribs. My eyes were centred on the bottles arranged so nicely in a long row.

Yeah! YEAH! I knew where the ring was!

How could I have been so incredibly stupid as to have missed it!

And Lola, who sent me after Feeney, had tried to tell me something else too . . . and I didn't get it until now!

Joe tried to stop me, but I was out the door before he could yell. I found my car and crawled in, fumbling for the ignition switch. I didn't have to hurry because I knew I had time. Not much, but enough time to get to the Seaside Hotel in Coney Island and do what I had to do.

I knew what I'd find. Nancy had left it there with her baggage. She was broke, she had to hock her camera. And being broke she had to get out of the Seaside Hotel without her baggage. But she knew it would be safe. Impounded but safe, redeemable when she had the money.

I found the Seaside Hotel tucked away on a street flanked by empty concession stands. Maybe from the roof it had a view of the sea. There wasn't any from where I stood. I parked a block away and walked up to it, seeing the peeling walls, the shuttered windows, the sign that read CLOSED FOR THE SEASON. Beneath it was another sign that told the public the building was protected by some obscure detective agency.

I took another drag on the cigarette and flipped it into the sand that had piled up in the gutter.

One look at the heavy timbers across the door and the steel bars on the ground-floor windows told me it was no use trying to get in that way. I scaled a fence beside the concession booth and walked around to the back. While I stood there looking at

222

the white sand underneath the darker layer of wet stuff my feet had lacked up, the rain began again, and I smiled to myself. Nice rain. Wonderful, beautiful rain. In five minutes the tracks would be wet, too, and blend in with the other.

The roof of the shack slanted down towards the back. I had to jump to reach it, preferring to chin myself up rather, than use any of the empty soda boxes piled there. I left part of my coat on a nail and took the time to unsnag it. The slightest trace would be too much to leave behind.

I was able to reach a window, then; tried it and found it locked. A recession in the wall farther down had stair steps of bricks making an interlocking joint and I ran my hand over it. I saw I had about ten feet to go to the roof, a vertical climb with scarcely a thing to hang on to.

I didn't wait.

My toes gripped the edges of the brick, holding while I reached up for another grasp, then my hands performed the same duty. It was a tortuous climb, and twice I slipped, scrambling back into position to climb again. When I reached the top I lay there breathing hard a minute before going on.

In the centre of the roof was a reinforced glass skylight, next to it the raised outlines of a trap door. The skylight didn't give, but the trap door did. I yanked at it with my hands and felt screws pull out of weather-rotted wood, and I was looking down a black hole that led into the Seaside Hotel.

I hung down in the darkness, swinging my feet to find something to stand on, and finding none, dropped into a welter of rubbish that clattered to the floor around me. I had a pencil flash in my pocket and threw the beam around. I was in a closet of some sort. On the side shelves were piled with used paint cans and hard, cracked cakes of soap. Brooms lay scattered on the floor where I had knocked them. There was a door on one side, criss-crossed with spider webs, heavy with dust. I picked them off with the flash and turned the knob.

Under any other conditions the Seaside Hotel would have been a flophouse. Because it had sand around the foundations

223

and sometimes you could smell the ocean over the hot dogs and body odours, they called it a summer hotel. The corridors were cramped and warped, the carpet on the floor worn through in spots. Doors to the rooms hung from tired hinges, eager for the final siege of dry rot, when they could fall and lie there. I went down the hallway, keeping against the wall, the flash spotting the way. To one side a flight of stairs snaked down, the dust tracked with the imprints of countless rat feet.

The front of the building was one storey higher, and a sign pointed to the stairs at the other end. As I passed each room I threw the light into it, seeing only the empty bed and springs, the lone dresser and chair.

I found what I was looking for on the next floor. It was a room marked STORAGE, with an oversized padlock slung through the hasps. I held the flashlight in my teeth and reached for the set of picks I always carried in the car. The lock was big, but it was old. The third pick I inserted sent it clicking open in my hand. I laid it on the floor and opened the door.

It had been a bedroom once, but now it was a morgue of boxed sheets, mattresses, glassware and dirty utensils. A few broken chairs were still in clamps where an attempt had been made to repair them. Against the wall in the back an assortment of luggage had been stacked; overnight bags, foot lockers, an expensive Gladstone, cheap paper carriers. Each one had a tag tied to the handle with a big price marked in red.

The runner of carpet that ran the length of the room had been laid down without tacks and I turned it over to keep from putting tracks in the dust. I found what I was looking for. It was a small trunk that had Nancy Sandford stencilled on it and it opened on the first try.

With near reverence I spread the folders apart and saw what was in them. I wasn't ashamed of Nancy now, I was ashamed of myself for thinking she was after blackmail. There in the trunk was her reason for living, a complete expose of the whole racket, substantiated with pictures, documents, notes that had no meaning at the moment but would when they were studied.

There were names and familiar faces. More than just aldermen. More than just manufacturers. Lots more. The lid was coming off City Hall. Park Avenue would feel the impact. But what was more important was the mechanics of the thing, neatly placed in a separate folder, enlarged pictures of books the police and the revenue men would want, definite proof of to whom those books belonged. The entire pretty set-up.

My ears picked up the sound, a faint metallic snapping. I closed the lid, locked it, then walked back my original path, taking time to fold the carpet over and study it, and satisfied that I had left no trace, closed the door and snapped the padlock in place. From the baseboard around the wall I scooped a handful of dust and blew it at the lock, restoring to it the age my hands had wiped off.

A yellow flood of light wandered up the hall, centred on the stairs and held. I stepped back into a bedroom, stuffing my watch in my pocket so the luminous face would be out of sight.

The light was poking into the rooms just as I had done. Feet sounded on the stairs, trying to be careful. Whoever stood behind that light was taking no chances, for it went down on the carpet, scanning it for tracks.

Back there in the room I grinned to myself.

The light came up the stairs throwing the whole corridor into flickering shadows, giving off a hissing noise that meant he carried a naphtha lantern. It came on to the door of the storage-room. There was a sigh. He sat the lantern on the floor, directing the beam towards the lock, and I heard him working over it with a pick.

He took longer than I did. But he got it open.

When I heard him enter the room I reached for my rod and stood with it in my hand. The racket he made dragging the trunk into the light covered the sound of my feet carrying me to the door. He was too excited to use a pick in the lock; instead he smashed it open and a low chuckle came out of his throat as he pawed through the contents.

I said, 'Hullo, Mr Berin-Grotin.'

I should have shot the bastard in the back and kept quiet. He whipped around with unbelievable speed, smashing at the light and shooting at the same time. Before I could pull the trigger a slug hit my chest and spun me out of the doorway. Then another tore into my leg.

'Damn you anyway!' he screamed.

I rolled to one side, the shock of the bullet's impact numbing me all over. I lay on my face and pulled the trigger again and again, firing into the darkness.

A shot licked back at me and hit the wall over my head, but that brief spurt of flame had death in it. The lantern had overturned, spilling the naphtha over the floor, and it rose in a fierce blaze right in Berin's face. I saw his eyes, mad eyes, crazy eyes. He was on his hands and knees shoving himself back, momentarily blinded by the light.

I had to fight to get a grip on the gun, bring it back in line. When I pulled the trigger it bucked in my hand and skittered across the floor. But it was enough. The .45 caught him in the hip and knocked him over backwards.

Everything was ablaze now, the flames licking to the bedding, running up the walls to the ceilings. A paint can and something in a bottle went up with a dull roar. It was getting hard to feel anything, even the heat. Over in the corner Berin groaned and pushed himself erect. He saw me then, lying helpless on the floor, and his hand reached out for his gun.

He was going to kill me if it was the last thing he did. He would have if the wall hadn't blossomed out into a shower of sparks and given way. One of the timbers that had lost the support of rusted nails wavered, and like a falling giant pine tree, crashed into the room and nailed the goddamn killer to the floor under it.

I laughed like a fiend, laughed and laughed even though I knew I was going to die anyway.

'You lost, Berin, you lost! You could have gotten away, but you lost!'

He fought the heavy timber, throwing his hands against the flame of the wood to push it away and I smelt the acrid odour of burning flesh. 'Get it off me, Mike! Get it off . . . please. You can have anything you want! Get it off me!'

'I can't . . . I can't even move. Maybe I would if I could, but I can't even move!'

'Mike! . . .'

'No good, you filthy louse. I'll die with you. I don't give a damn any more. I'll die, but you'll go, too. You never thought it would happen, did you? You had the ring and you thought you'd have time. You didn't know I killed Feeney and got the ticket from him.

'There was Lola waiting for me. You heard me tell her that on the phone. While you got the drinks you called Feeney and covered up by playing the phonograph for me. He must have walked right in on her. She was expecting me and she got a killer. Sure, you stalled me while Feeney went to my office and broke in. He did a good job of it, too. But he had to go back and kill Lola because she knew the address on the ticket, and the camera could have been traced.

'Feeney called you right after he sank his knife in her, but she wasn't dead and saw him do it. You told Feeney to get out of there and wait for you somewhere. Sure, you wouldn't want Feeney to get his hands on that stuff. He got out . . . just as I came in and Lola put the finger on him. She put the finger on you, too, when she pointed to the phone. Feeney got out, but I was coming in and he stepped back to let me pass and I didn't see him. I caught him, though. Yeah, you played it cautious right to the end. You took your time about getting here, careful not to attract attention in any way. Did you sneak out of your hotel or just pretend you were up early as usual?'

'Mike, I'm burning!'

His hair smoked, puffed up in a ball of flame and he screamed again. He looked like a killer, being bald like that. The other wall was a sheet of fire now.

'I didn't get the connection until tonight. It was the ring after all. The ring was very important. I sat there looking at a bottle of whisky. The label had three feathers spread across the front just like the fancy plaque on your private morgue. I happened to think that the spread of feathers looked just like a fleur-de-lis pattern, then I got it. The design on the ring *was* three feathers, battered out enough to make it hard to recognize.'

He fought the timber now, his face contorted in agony. I watched him a second and laughed again.

'The three feathers were part of your family crest, weren't they? An imitation of royalty. You and your damn pride, you bastard! Nancy Sanford was your own grand-daughter. She was going to have a baby and you kicked her out. What did you think of *her* pride? So she turned from one job to another, working under an assumed name. She became a prostitute on the side. She got to know guys like Russ Bowen and his connexion with Feeney. Then one day she saw you two together.'

'I can imagine what she thought when she realized you were one of them, living your vain life of wealth on money that came from the bodies of the girls, hiding behind the front of respectability. You had it set up nice until she came along. She only had one thing in mind and that was to break the whole racket to pieces.

'Only she had to leave her baggage behind her until she had money to redeem it. Then you got the breaks. Feeney ran across her looking for a piece on the side and saw something. What was it, more pictures? Enough to make you get wise? Did he see the ring and know what it meant?'

Berin rolled from side to side. The timber, out of the flame, wasn't burning. It lay across his chest smoking. His eyes were on the ceiling watching the plaster crack and fall. The fire had spread, eating at everything it touched. Only on the floor was there an escape from the intense heat. But not for long. Soon the flames would come up from the floor, and that would be it. I tried to move, drag myself, but the effort was too great, and all I could do was stare at the man under the timber and be glad to know that I wouldn't die alone.

I laughed and Berin turned his head. A hot spark lit on his cheek and he didn't feel it. 'Nancy was murdered, wasn't she?'

I said. 'It wasn't planned to work out so nice, but who could tell that a girl who had been clubbed so hard by an expert that her neck was broken, would get up from where she was thrown out of a car and stagger down the street and out into the path of another car.

'*You* were Feeney's alibi the night she was killed. You tailed her, forced her into the car, went into your act and heaved her out – and it all very nicely worked into your normal routine!

'Feeney didn't usually miss those shots, but he missed on Nancy and he missed on me. I should have known that sooner, too, when Lola told me Nancy had no vices. No, she didn't drink, but people swore she staggered and assumed she was drunk. I bet you had a big laugh over that.

'Pride! Pride did it to you. In the beginning you were a playboy and spent all your dough, but your pride wouldn't let you become a pauper. The smart operators got hold of you and then you fronted for them until you squeezed them out and had the racket all to yourself. You could work the filthiest racket in the world, but your pride wouldn't let you take back your grand-daughter after she made a mistake. Then your pride kept you from letting her interfere with your affairs.'

I could hardly talk over the roar of the flames now. Outside the engines were clanging up the streets and far-away voices mingled with crashing walls. Only because the fire had to eat its way down had we stayed alive as long as this.

'But it's all there in that box, mister. You'll die and your fancy hyphenated name will be lost in the mud and slime that'll come out of it.'

'It won't, goddamn you! It won't!' Even in pain his eyes grew crafty. 'The box will burn and even if it doesn't they'll think I was here with you, Mike. Yes, you're my alibi, and my name *won't* be lost. Nobody will trace that girl now and the world will never know!'

He was right, too. He was so right that the anger welling up in me drove the numbness out of my leg and the pain from my chest and I pulled myself across the room. I reached the trunk, shoved it, shoved it again, my hands brushing aside the hot embers that fell from the ceiling. Berin saw what I was doing and screamed for me to stop. I grinned at him. He was bald and ugly. He was a killer in hell before he died.

Somehow I got the box on edge and heaved, the effort throwing me back to the floor. But it smashed the window out and fell to the ground and I heard an excited shout and a voice yell, 'Somebody is in the room up there!'

The sudden opening of the window created a draught that sucked the flames right out of the wall, sent them blasting into my face. I smelled hair burning and saw the legs of Berin's pants smoulder. His gun was lying under my hand.

He should never have spoken to me that way, but he did and it gave me strength to go it all the way. I reached for the gun, a .38, and fitted the butt into my hand.

'Look at your employee, Berin. See what I'm going to do? Now, listen carefully to what I tell you and think about it hard, because you only have a few minutes left. That tomb of yours won't be empty. No, the redhead will live there. The girl your pride kicked out. She'll be in that tomb. And do you know where you'll be? In potter's field next to Feeney Last, or what's left of you. I'll tell the police what happened. It won't be the truth, but it'll fit. I'll tell them the body up here is that of one of your boys you sent to get me. They'll never find you even though they'll never give up looking, and whenever your name is mentioned it will be with a sneer and a dirty memory. The only clean thing will be the redhead. You'll died the kind of death you feared most . . . lost, completely lost. Animals walking over your grave. Not even a marker.'

The horror of it struck him and his mouth worked.

'But I won't deprive myself of the pleasure of killing you, mister rat. It will make up for the blonde and Lola. I'll kill you so I can live with myself again. I'll tell them we fought it out and I killed you. But you'll know the truth. It hurts, doesn't it?'

The pain in his eyes wasn't physical any longer.

'They'll be up here in a minute. I'll be waiting for them. I'll let them take me down and tell them there's no use going back in again. I'll let you burn until there isn't a thing left to identify you.'

A stream of water hit the side of the wall, centred on the window and turned the room into a steaming inferno.

'A ladder will be pushed up here in just a minute now. When it comes I'll pull the trigger. Think about it, think hard.'

A truck was being run into position. The shouts below grew louder. I crouched in the protection of the same timber that had him pinned down. The ceiling over the corridor outside fell in with a crash, dragging the front wall with it. I heard the crackling and looked up. Directly overhead the ceiling began to buckle, sagging in the middle with flame lancing through the cracks.

I looked at Berin and laughed. He turned his head and stared right into the muzzle of his own gun. Minutes – seconds – fractions of time. The ceiling was swaying now. The killer's face was a vile mask of hatred, praying for the ceiling to get us both. He was going to go first if it happened that way.

Something banged against the side of the window and slid over the sill: two prongs with a crossbar between them. A ladder bobbed as someone came up it, covered by the stream of water.

Berin had his mouth open, screaming with all the furies of the gods dethroned, but my laugh was even louder.

He was still screaming when I pulled the trigger.